"Mercedes M. Yardley's signature whimsi⟨
display in *Love is a Crematorium and Other Tales*—a beguiling collection
that explores suffering, longing, vengeance, resilience, and love. These stories
will delicately carve out your heart."

—ANGELA SYLVAINE, AUTHOR OF *CHOPPING SPREE* AND *THE DEAD SPOT.*

"Love is a Crematorium is packed with stories that burrow under your skin
from the first word and won't come out until you're finished. Maybe not
even then. "

—MATT BETTS, AUTHOR OF *GONE WHERE THE GOBLINS GO*

"*Love is a Crematorium* is Mercedes doing what she does best: she lulls you
in with sweet language and then wraps you in darkness both strange and
beautiful. She doesn't let go until you've been reduced to ashes. It's a fantastic
assemblage of tales that are raw wounds to lick, lament, and dream about."

—JOHN BODEN, AUTHOR OF *THE ETIQUETTE OF BOOBY TRAPS*

"Quite simply, Mercedes M. Yardley is one of the most powerful writers in
horror today. This collection fuses magic, wonder, and hope with terror, darkness, and dread—every story a gem, every story a curse come home to roost."

—RICHARD THOMAS, BRAM STOKER, SHIRLEY JACKSON,
AND THRILLER AWARD FINALIST

"In *Love is a Crematorium*, Mercedes M. Yardley masterfully blends the super-
natural with the profoundly human. Each well-crafted story delves into dark,
haunting themes of love, loss, and transformation, showcasing the delicate
strength of the human spirit. With her signature ability to explore the maca-
bre and the poignant, readers will rejoice in Yardley's masterful storytelling."

—MARTIN LASTRAPES, AUTHOR OF *GROVER WILCOX GOES
TO THE CIRCUS* AND *INSIDE THE OUTSIDE*

LOVE is a
CREMATORIUM
and Other Tales

LOVE is a CREMATORIUM
and Other Tales

Mercedes M. Yardley

CEMETERY DANCE PUBLICATIONS

Baltimore
2024

Cemetery Dance Publications
132B Industry Lane, Unit #7
Forest Hill, MD 21050
www.cemeterydance.com

The characters and events in this book are fictitious.
Any similarity to real persons, living or dead,
is coincidental and not intended by the authors.

Trade Paperback Edition

ISBN:
978-1-58767-994-0

Cover Artwork and Design © 2024 by Kealan Patrick Burke
Interior Design © 2024 by Desert Isle Design, LLC

To all those who burn alive with desire, rage, and passion.
Keep that fire.

Trigger Warnings:

Sexual Assault, Violence, Childbirth,
Suicidal Ideation, Self-Harm,
Drug Use, Death

Table of Contents

Introduction by Gabino Iglesias — **11**

Loving You Darkly — **15**

The Making of Asylum Ophelia — **29**

Clocks — **39**

Night's Ivy — **49**

A Love Not Meant to Outlast the Butterflies — **59**

A Threadbare Shirt — **73**

Just Beyond Her Dreaming — **77**

Mean Girls — **95**

Heart of Fire, Body of Stone — **109**

The Bone-Shaker's Daughter — **115**

This Broken Love Story — **137**

Water Thy Bones — **139**

Unpretty Monster — **147**

Salt — **155**

Stanley Tutelage's Two-Year-Shiny-Life Plan — **159**

Urban Moon — **169**

Love is a Crematorium — **179**

Notes From the Crematorium — **229**

Thou Shalt be Devoured from the Inside Out

An introduction by Gabino Iglesias

"Silva's lover was built of bones she scavenged from the Killing Fields."

Boom. There it is. A line that's a vibe, one that captures the essence of *Love is a Crematorium and Other Tales* by Mercedes M. Yardley.

Yeah, the collection you're about to read.

This, dear reader, is what I call a smart choice. You're in for a treat; sometimes sweet and sometimes sour, but always a treat.

Listen, this isn't a normal collection, so I won't write a normal intro. You see, for many years, no one asked me to write introductions for them, but I always wrote reviews. After a while, some authors started asking for intros, and I always jumped at the opportunity to write them. Not many venues allow you to review every book exactly the way you want to, with wild changes in format or voice that match the spirit, tone, or aesthetic of the book. Luckily, intros are different. In an intro, you can do whatever you want. For this collection, I was tempted—before

I read it, obviously—to go with a traditional approach. Two stories in, I knew I was going to come up with something different, something that was a better fit for this collection. Then the idea came to me: a list. Why? Well, because readers love lists. Also, because as much as I'd love to talk here about the shining sun with a precious crooked grin and great hair that shines its light on Mercedes every day or about the way I connected with Nikilie because we're both island folk or about what I think the appearance of bones

11

means in each of the stories that features bones (I really want a bone flute now!), the truth is this collection—unique, lyrical, gruesome, sad, feminine/feminist to the core, brilliant, touching—deserves better.

So yeah, here is a list of things this book is like and things you can expect and things I want you to pay attention to. It's also a list of reasons why picking this up was, as I told you above, a great idea. Every line below is extremely accurate, and both of my violent sides (sounds better than saying you're entirely violent) won't tolerate discussions about this. Here you go:

— This collection is like the sweet, warm kiss of a lover who slowly slides a knife into your chest as they kiss you. The pain is there, sure, but you're smiling. It hurts so good. With your last whisper, you spill one last wish into the cava of your lover's mouth: "More."

— You know what? Let's stay with knives for a second! Every story here is a small cut in your soul, especially the ones where flesh is sliced open, sometimes by someone else, sometimes by someone looking for something beneath their own skin. Ah, and every cut is a statement, a sharp truth, a lesson, a scream: *"The women know what pain is, and fear, and how it feels to shriek for help."*

— "Clocks" is one of the most beautiful short stories about neurodivergence I've ever read. *"You taught me what it was to truly love"* Read it twice and let it fuck you up. Then drop Mercedes a line somewhere—social media, email, whatever—and respectfully thank her for bleeding on the page and sharing it with us.

— Mercedes M. Yardley is a force of nature. She writes lines that look like butterflies but hit harder than a peacock mantis shrimp.

— This book is what happens when a talented author wants to hurt you in the best ways possible. Every hit will feel awfully good. Every story will make a space for itself under your skin, quietly becoming, even if only for a brief moment, part of you.

THOU SHALT BE DEVOURED FROM THE INSIDE OUT

— "Threadbare Shirt" is a promise of more beautiful, heart-wrenching non-fiction to come.

— There is a group of "men" who think women shouldn't write horror. They're the same as the men who used to call smart women witches just so they could burn them at the stake. This smart, witchy book is their worst nightmare, and that is truly a beautiful thing.

— This collection is an education in love. It teaches us that love is often dark, that love is also grief. It teaches us that love is a sickness, an abomination. Love is pain, a thing that can eat you from the inside out. Love is a magical thing full of promises that travels inside kisses that feel like *the beginning of everything.* Love can be a constant end, a perpetual wound, a space where only one thing matters and the rest of the world fades away.

— You will soon turn the page and start reading. I advise you to proceed carefully. You will be entertained and surprised, touched and unsettled, loved and wounded. These stories will enter your bloodstream and thou shalt be devoured from the inside out. As it happens, just remember one thing: everything is always all about love.

A lot of things come back to their beginning when they reach the end, and this intro is one of them. *"That one has fire."* That's another line from the opening story. It says a lot, and while poetic, its meaning is clear. When I tell you a woman has fire, you know what I mean. Well,

Mercedes M. Yardley doesn't have fire; she is fire, and so is this collection. Enjoy.

—Gabino Iglesias
In Austin, August of 2024, watching
the world burn with a heart full of hope

Loving You Darkly
By Mercedes M. Yardley

Loving You
Darkly

Silva's lover was built of bones she scavenged from the Killing Fields. A shard of gleaming femur here, a handful of vertebrae there. She held him together with wire and glue and the most charming of ribbons. When she put his jawbone into place, he opened and shut it a few times to make sure it was working correctly. It fit nicely, and he grinned, as skeletons are wont to do. His hollow sockets glowed with something deeper than dark magic. They glowed with love.

"Thank you," he said, and the clicking of his teeth reminded Silva of wooden puppets dancing around a stage with a fine red curtain. "I feel ever so much better."

"You're welcome," she said, and her voice nearly sounded like bones themselves. "I was afraid that perhaps you didn't want to be collected. Maybe you were happier at rest where you were."

He shook his head. "There was no rest. Only staring at the sky and being eaten by worms. Memories of a thousand lives lived by those who left me. Men and women, but now it's mostly me." He held out his hand, and Silva took it. "I do enjoy being simply me."

He made himself at home in the hidden burrow where Silva lived. It was deep and dark and sheltered, and his dead eyes saw perfectly in the blackness. When Silva came back the next morning, the skeleton showed her a new dress he was making from scraps and fur.

"Is that for me?" Silva asked, her eyes shining.

"It wouldn't do me much good, now, would it?" he asked, glancing down at his mismatched ribs and pelvis. "But a living girl? Ah, loved one, you need

15

something to cover your sack of skin. You look so cold when you return. I would keep you warm in other ways if only I could."

Silva smiled, but her lips quivered, and she dashed at her cheeks with the backs of her hands. The skeleton nearly remembered the purpose of water leaking from the eyes, but it was soon lost with the rest of his memories. He moved on instinct alone, taking a thin bone from his foot and sharpening it into a needle. He took sinew and made a staunch thread, and then he sewed, sewed, sewed, his needle darting as songs of the Old Ways fell from his mouth.

"Which part of you knows those songs?" Silva asked, and the skeleton cocked his head, thinking. "I think it is my left scapula," he answered. "It remembers songs and stories and a bit about playing music. The fellow who left these bones was a lucky man indeed. He loved to dance. Do you love to dance, small one?"

Silva smiled. "I did dance, once. Before the Breeders came. We lived in a home with a great hall, and my father would invite people to the finest balls. I would dance and dance until I was sent to bed, and then I would sneak out onto the staircase in my nightgown and watch the lords and ladies. It was a wonderful thing."

"Why don't you dance now?" The skeleton asked, and Silva looked away sharply.

"Dance here? In the burrow? It is but an animal's burrow, and I carved it bigger day by day until a human could fit. There is barely room to sit, let alone dance. How silly."

He watched her with his missing eyes. He could wait. He could listen.

She drew her hands through the packed earth of the burrow. "There was a time when I would give anything to dance. The sound of a flute silvered through my soul in a way I can't even describe to you. I dreamed in pirouettes."

"It sounds lovely," he said. "I can imagine you twirling your way to breakfast in the morning."

Her lips fluttered into a smile that quickly disappeared. "There was room, then. And joy. This place is so small. It's nothing but roots and refuse." She kicked, and an angry shower of earth fell upon her.

He wanted to ask her why she didn't dance when she was outside under the moon. She only scavenged at night and in the early morning when the Breeders slept. Why didn't she dance then, in her too-short, tattered gray dress?

"It was white once," she mentioned when he asked. "Beautiful and white, and it fit me perfectly. I was to meet the man I should marry, and I wore my best dress."

"And then what happened?"

Silva's eyes were lovely. "I was in this dress, and my father was beside me. We were walking to the carriage. My shoes were made of linen and silver, and my father wore such a wonderful jacket. He had met my husband-to-be and approved. I was afraid, but he told me I would soon fall in love with his kindness and his humor. He told me it would be okay." A frown pulled at her mouth. "But it wasn't okay, never again."

Part of the skeleton's radius, which had belonged to a gentle, wise woman, told him to put his bony arm around Silva. He did so.

"There are different levels of okay," he said simply. "And now you are okay. You're even comfortable. You have a companion who loves you, and you have somebody to love. You are safe while you share your story."

Silva stilled her trembling mouth. "The ground shook. There was a sound like thunder. Noise that I couldn't comprehend. The Breeders played horns and bugles that confused us. They rode tall beasts that made our horses seem stunted by comparison. They set fire to everything they could find. My father..."

Her father had gone up like a wick, his hair flaming and his legs high-stepping in his fiery coat. His skin popped and ran, and he looked like a clown doing a foxtrot before he fell. She stared at him, watching his fine shoes char as he kicked and bucked. She remembered dancing with her handsome daddy as a little girl, standing on his shoes and holding his hands as they box-stepped and cha-chaed. He whirled her around, making her laugh, and she realized that he was laughing, too, deep and free and so utterly happy. "I hope you always dance, Little Bird," he had told her, and she had. Oh, she had. She would dance forever if it would make him laugh like that.

But now those fine shoes were burning, singeing away to reveal his vulnerable skin, the flesh curling to reveal the white bones beneath.

Silva stared at him in horror, unable to move, only able to scream along with the hunting horns. Around her, men were chopped down like trees. Children were trampled, and womenstolen and tied to the beasts.

"I was able to unhook one of the horses from the carriage. I climbed on and rode until the animal was in a lather. Still, it wouldn't stop, its eyes rolling in its head like madness itself, and quite honestly, I don't know if I would have let it stop if it tried. We did escape that day, and after a few days' walk, I found this burrow."

"And the horse?" He knew, seeing as not all his bones were human. A small fragment of something larger had been smoothed down to create one of his arms.

"I thanked that horse, but soon I ran out of food, and he was all I had."

"You hit him on the head with a rock if my bones are recalling correctly."

"Yes," Her voice was unflinching. "And then I skinned him with another sharp rock. I ate him, and you're making me a dress with some of his skin. I used his hair to tie things together, and his bones to make tools. His jaw helped me dig out some of this burrow. Never have I loved a horse or been so grateful as I was to this one."

The horse in the skeleton's soul was pleased, and he told her as much. Her eyes shone when she answered.

"Thank you. For everything."

The next night, he handed her the finished rawhide dress, and it fit well. She kissed him on his ravaged cheek, and if he had a heart, it would have beaten harder.

The skeleton began to worry when Silva stayed out later and later in the mornings. His bones whispered to him about the horrors of the Breeders, what she would endure if she didn't make it home before they awoke.

"You can't be reckless," he said. He had holes in the tips of his fingers where the needle poked and pricked. He was working on some scraps to cover Silva's feet better. "They won't kill you right off, but you will eventually die. It will be a horrible thing."

"Tell me," she said, and sat down, smoothing her soft dress over her thighs. "How much of you was killed by the Breeders?"

"I'd say nearly half, in one way or another," he said. He kept his voice matter-of-fact, but a strange light burned in the hollows of his eyes. "I was torn apart in so many different ways. Some fast, some slow. Always in terror, though. Always alone. Even if you're surrounded, death has a way of making you feel alone."

She thought of her father and wondered if his fine jacket buttons had burned into his skin as he had died.

"The women, though," he said, and his voice was haunted by bastions and leaves. "The women suffered the worst."

"Tell me," Silva said. She knew what he was going to say but needed to hear it. She would poke at this bruise and commit the pain to memory. It would keep her safe. It would keep her alive.

The skeleton took a breath. "The women know what pain is, and fear, and how it feels to shriek for help. They know what it is to be planted with a seed not of their own kind and to feel it squirm and grow inside of them." He shuddered and continued mournfully. "Monster children, sired by hate and desperation, who kill their mothers at birth with their horns and armored plates. Males only, and the only way to carry on their race is to spread the terror, spread the pain."

Silva's already pale face went carcass white.

"You feel that then?" She asked. "You feel all of that in your bones? Like it has happened to you?"

He nodded and pointed to one of his crushed ribs. "Here." He pointed to two vertebrae. "Here and here. This one took her own life before the monster could be born. She is at peace now, at long last. She has earned it. Her child. The Breeder's spawn. Its bones were in the Killing Fields as well, next to its mother's. It could very well have been a part of me." He turned his dead eyes upon her. "I'm afraid if you aren't careful, something like this could be part of you." Silva's stomach roiled, and she turned her face to the wall of soil.

"I will be no Breeder's sow," Silva vowed. "I'm smart and quick and want to be alive. I'm only so long in the Killing Fields because I have scavenged most of the area. I need to go farther to find something new, something to eat. Very soon, I'm afraid, the time must come to move on."

She left that evening, body shivering in the frost. The cold was more than she was prepared for, and she rubbed her thin arms for warmth. She peered at the ground, alight in the moonlight, and saw something shining dully. She dug with her fingers in the hard earth and found a piece of copper wire. Something that looked like a broken comb. A button from a soldier's uniform that had most likely gleamed once.

The buttons on her father's fine jacket had gleamed once.

She squirreled these treasures away, and then a sound made her flatten herself to the frozen ground.

It was a groan, muffled but clearly human. She crept closer, not daring to breathe.

She saw a crumpled figure that she had mistaken for the branches of a downed tree. That wasn't the case at all, for it was a man. He was poorly dressed, shivering, while sweat dotted his face like disease.

"You're sick," she whispered to the man, who merely moaned back.

"I have to get you out of here before the Breeders find you," she said. "Can you walk?"

He could walk, barely, and only by leaning heavily on her fragile shoulder. She dragged him over the ground, his feet hardly moving.

"We need to hurry," she urged. "One foot in front of the other. Come on."

The sun was starting to rise in the sky. Silva realized she was shaking, but it wasn't from the cold.

"Faster," she said. Her voice had a pleading quality now. "The Breeders will be getting up soon. They'll kill us if they find us!"

They'll kill us…they'll kill us…

She remembered stories her father told her, warnings couched in the form of fairytales. Good little girls stayed in bed at night and didn't wander the house. They did what their fathers told them. Good little girls obeyed and were safe from the monsters whose long, sharp teeth flashed in the dark. The Breeders were only tales then, harmless stories.

"Please speed up," she begged again, and the sunlight melting the frost and warming the earth was a terrible thing. There were no shadows to hide in, no place to escape. She thought she heard snorting over the horizon and nearly chittered with fear.

What if she dropped him? What if she let him fall to the earth, and she ran and ran and ran back to the burrow, scurrying inside its womb-like safety? Her muscles started, bunched, and the man nearly fell to the ground.

"No," he said roughly, as if he could sense her thoughts. Perhaps he could. Maybe her sweat stunk of terror and helplessness. Maybe he could read it as the old man at the end of the lane used to be able to read the weather. "Don't leave me here. We've come so far."

Yes, they had come far, but they had so much farther to go. Silva's breath came out in panicked gasps, and she tried calming herself. She turned her attention to the man, who was gritting his teeth to keep from crying out. Delirious, his head turning blindly to the left and right, he muttered to beings Silva couldn't see. But he still fought his way forward, his pinched face determined amid the pain. She studied it, the bones pressing sharp against his skin, the way his lips were tinged with unhealthy blue.

It had been so long since she had seen another living person, and here one was. He had scars on his face and welts on his hands. Sweat ran into his eyes, and he didn't bother to wipe it away. He was everything perfect and broken about being human. Even in her fear, she wanted to run her hands over his arms and legs to assure herself that he truly existed, that he was really alive. She imagined that once, he had been a little boy playing with sticks, and then he had been a teenager with a crush. Perhaps he had gone to dances like she had, possibly the very same ones, and they might have spun themselves dizzy under the same stars. Then that daydreaming teenager had become a man, and now he was very nearly a corpse. Her heart, usually knotted down with the grim rope of experience, lurched a bit as she wondered about this man's childhood. She had a childhood, too. She had chased butterflies and followed her father around the yard as he showed her beautiful things—like where to find bird nests and how to sit very still so a scared animal would learn to trust her. She always needed to be worthy of that trust.

Silva pictured her father's gentle face and knew what she had to do. If she left this man now, he would surely die. The Breeders would find him and rip him apart, his bones snapping like ruined sage. She would hear his screams from inside her burrow would listen as they went higher and higher until they were finally cut off. She'd hear the Breeders feasting on the last bits of his body, chunks of flesh hanging from their jaws, and the next time she dared to scavenge, she'd find pieces of him in the moonlight. Would she recognize his face then, she wondered? Would she squat over what was left of his body, picking over his remains to find something useful?

The thought sickened her.

"Okay," she agreed and shielded her eyes against the dawn. "I won't let you go. I couldn't anyway, even if I tried. It isn't who I am."

She was growing weaker, her strength taxed by his large frame. She heard wild bugles off in the distance.

"They're here!" She tried to run, pulling the man with her. They were close to the burrow, but she was afraid the long-legged beasts would arrive before she could. Her feet scrabbled against the earth, and her breath was coming harder. "Please, oh please, oh please!"

He was trying, bless him. A wound in his side had torn open, and he was bleeding heavily, but he was moving his exhausted muscles as fast as he could.

It wouldn't be enough.

Suddenly, the skeleton was at their side.

"You're cutting it close, Silva," he said, grabbing the stranger with his mismatched hands. "It's going to be a tight fit."

The skeleton was surprisingly strong, his body fueled by the people and parts that were his makeup. Silva nearly wept with relief as he helped her drag the stranger down into the burrow. They pulled pieces of wood atop them and then hid quietly.

"I can hear them," Silva said, and the skeleton put a bony finger to her lips.

"Sleep," he commanded, and she nodded, curling herself into the smallest ball she could. The skeleton wrapped his ribbons around her and consoled her as she wept in her sleep.

THE stranger's name was Amon, and he had been a horse trader. He had been married. He had been happy, once.

"The Breeders?" Silva asked.

"The Breeders," he agreed. "Took everything. My wife, my son. It's been nearly six months now, I would think. Back when the sun was hot, and the ground felt like fire."

"What are you doing in the Killing Fields?" The skeleton asked. He had already stitched up Amon's side and was now repairing Amon's clothes as best he could. He took a ribbon from his joints and threaded it through as a belt for Amon.

"I was at the Killing Fields to kill, of course. I'm hunting the Breeders."

Silva started, "Why would you do that? Hunt the Breeders? They cannot be killed!"

Amon stretched out his aching muscles. "They can, and they will, but only if somebody steps up. Somebody needs to fight back and show others it can be done.

"You can't!" Silva exclaimed. "It's suicide. It's madness!"

"Doesn't matter to me much," Amon said. "I'd rather go out fighting than curl up and wait for death. Wasting away isn't for me. Sorry, miss," he said, and tipped an invisible hat to Silva. "Not to imply that that's what you're doing."

"It is *not* what I'm doing," Silva told him. Her fists were clenched so tightly that her bones hurt. "I'm living. I'm surviving. And it takes strength to do it when it's bleak, I'll have you know. So much easier to give up and walk into your death, isn't it?"

Then she left, up and out of the burrow, her footsteps stomping the ground above.

Amon sighed. "That one has fire."

The skeleton shrugged, and his joints chimed together like bells. "She does. She'll make it, you know, if she's careful. If she doesn't lose her temper and forget how to be cautious."

Amon eyed him. "And you. What are you to her, exactly?"

The skeleton grinned a perfect hollow grin, and the lights in his eyes danced weirdly. "I'm all things to her. Everything she needs. She built me herself, you know. Picked up my parts and strung them together. I imagine it was time-consuming. She adorned me with feathers, and glass beads, and the tiny beauties that she finds in the fields. So much better than being found all in one piece, a chunk of meat, don't you think?"

Amon smiled at that, but it faded quickly. "I appreciate all you've done for me. I would have surely died out there if you hadn't let me stay with you these past few weeks. But my plan doesn't change. I need to slip into the Breeder's tents and destroy them. Take down as many as I can before they kill me."

"Rest up another day, then," the skeleton advised. He pulled a bone from his ankle and handed it to Amon. "Stick this in that pot of water. We'll build a fire. That's a bone from a pig, and there's still some good marrow in it. The bone broth will give you and Silva strength."

"While stealing it from you, I imagine?"

The skeleton shrugged. "It doesn't matter much, does it? If worse comes to worse, I can always be rebuilt. This is a land of death. There's no shortage of bones around."

Silva came back early before the sun even had a chance to blush the landscape. The skeleton sighed in relief. Silva smiled at him and adjusted one of his ribbons.

"Thank you," he said. "I hardly noticed that was getting a bit loose."

"I can't have you falling apart on me," she told him. "Then what would I do?"

She shifted her eyes to Amon and nervously straightened her skirts. The skeleton reached out and took her hand. She squeezed back.

"I'm sorry," she told Amon, dropping her eyes to the ground. Her cheeks were flushed, although she couldn't tell if it was from the outside air or from the apology. "I don't mean to tell you what to do with your life," she said. "I can imagine your anger at losing your family. I…think of my father every day." She went silent, shuffling her feet uncomfortably until the skeleton's touch encouraged her. Then she spoke quickly. "But do you have to go? We struggled so hard to survive, and you're tossing everything away. Can't you stay? Is it really so bad here, with us?"

Amon put his hand on her cheek. His skin was warm, flowing with blood, fairly singing with life, and Silva closed her eyes and leaned into it. This was the reason, right here. Skin touching skin, sharing breath, sharing space. This togetherness, this bit of humanity, was what she had clung to and fought for, and now it was being ripped away again.

The skeleton pulled his hand from Silva's and touched his own dead cheek. There was no song, no music of the living. His eyes hungrily ate up the life that Silva and Amon shared, and he pulled himself farther away so as not to intrude. He would be there to wrap his wired bones around her when she needed him later. The dead were always patient.

"I can't," Amon said, and Silva's tears were hot on his skin. This was what it was to be human, as well. Pain and feeling and tenderness. Disappointment and grief. His own eyes burned, and he leaned forward to touch his forehead against hers, as he used to do with his small son.

"Families are worth fighting for," he whispered, and she nodded. "We shouldn't be hiding and alone. We should be with those we love, free. I have to do something."

"I understand," she said, and tried to smile. Her tears betrayed her, running down her face like the disloyal things they were. She wiped them away. "I do. But oh," she said, and she leaned against him, letting her head rest on his shoulder, "I'm going to miss you."

He smiled his chipped grin. "And I, you. Both of you. Very much. It felt good to belong again."

They sat this way for a long time, not saying anything but listening to the sounds of their living bodies: breath, flesh, heartbeats. The skeleton moved quietly, ladling bone meal broth into chipped bowls. He watched them sip, and Amon sharpened his knife with a rock until its edge was cruel and delicious.

"Tell me about life in better times," the skeleton said. "Tell me how it will feel to fight, to dance, to die, to do all of the things that would finally make you free."

Silva looked at him. "Do you really believe we'll ever find freedom?"

"Death is its own kind of freedom," he said simply, and his mismatched bones rattled.

NIGHT came far too soon. Silva glanced at the moon and cursed its treachery.

Her friends stood beside her, otherworldly in the firelight's strange glow. It cast the most peculiar of shadows, elongating Amon and Silva's thin bodies while twisting the skeleton's outline. His bones left hollow stripes of death on Amon's face.

Silva shivered. Amon removed his worn coat and wrapped it around her.

"I won't need it," he said simply, and Silva shut her eyes briefly as she tried to breathe.

She tried to say "thank you" but could only manage to hold the coat to her gaunt body. "I need to go," Amon said. "I need to get to the Breeder's tents while they're still asleep. I'll cause more damage that way."

The night sky was full of stars, and Silva knew Amon's soul would join them soon.

"Do I just stand here and listen to you die, then?" She asked.

"I hope you will do something to remember me," Amon answered. He kissed her forehead and then held her close. Skin and bone and heart and blood. Silva felt their hearts beat together like a long-practiced dance. Amon pulled back, and Silva's heart beat alone.

Amon pulled a hide-wrapped object from his pocket and handed it to the skeleton. "This is for you to open later. Don't forget me," Amon said, and the skeleton grinned his unholy grin.

He turned and headed toward the Breeders' camp without looking back. Silva watched him until he disappeared, until she was squinting so hard to see him that her head ached. In case he had second thoughts. In case he turned back or decided that striding to his death was foolish, or realized that he should take her with him. Two can die just as gloriously as one.

"He's gone," the skeleton said softly. His voice was simply wind without his larynx. It was loss.

Silva stamped her feet in the cold.

"I'm going to scavenge for a while," she said, and disappeared into the mist.

She looked lackadaisical and found nothing. The earth yielded no treasures. She thought perhaps she'd never find anything of value ever again. She picked her way carefully through the Killing Fields, her tentative feet wrapped in hides. She remembered how heavy Amon had been as she had dragged him back to her burrow, how she had almost put him down then. It was so much more difficult to let him go now. Silva almost laughed at the thought. Her new coat smelled like him. It smelled alive. That's when she finally let her tears come.

But deep within the midnight hours, her ears picked up a resonance in the darkness. It was a rhythmic, steady sound, underscored by the panicked shrieking of beasts.

The Breeders' drums. Boom. Boom. Boom. Without thinking, she matched her pace to the rhythm, her feet coming down in slow, heavy steps. They had discovered Amon in the village. What was he doing now? She thought of him with his killing knife, so sharp that the blade would register as ice rather than pain. She took a step forward and feigned stabbing a beast. Perhaps Amon did the same thing.

The drums began playing with more urgency, faster and faster. Silva spun on one foot, kicking at the imaginary Breeder that Amon faced. She imagined how the shining knife would arc to its target, buried to the hilt in hide and fur and blood, and Silva followed suit. The drums pushed her, thrumming through her soul like the music of her childhood, and Silva matched it.

Her pace picked up. She threw a kick high in the air and felt the imaginary Breeder tumble to the ground. Her stoniness tumbled with him. The desperation to survive, the stress and hate and misery fell from her like armor. The hunting bugles broke out, a hysterical cry against the ambience of the drums, and she knew Amon was doing damage, living his revenge, hurting those who had hurt so many. She helped him. Silva swayed and danced and spun to the music, throwing her arms in the air and celebrating that instant. She had never danced so hard before, or felt the music deep in her bones like this.

She had never felt so free.

The bugles subsided, and the drums eventually stopped. Silva paused, her breast heaving and her cheeks colored with the healthy roses of sorrow and joy. This was life. This was exactly what living felt like.

She slid down into the burrow.

"It is done," she said, and her eyes were strangely tearless. She breathed in a lungful of air, and it felt good. "He is dead." She took off Amon's coat and folded it carefully. She couldn't quite put it down but held it in her lap, her fingers twisting in the fabric.

"Yes," the skeleton agreed. "He is dead, and he did this dark thing for love."

"Love is often a dark thing," she said, and reached for his bony hand. His fingers wrapped around hers in the familiar way that nearly made everything all right.

They sat together in silence, staring at the fire. The burrow now seemed far too large.

The skeleton spoke. "There is one thing I wanted to show you. He gave me this before he left."

"What is it?"

The skeleton unwrapped the package and showed Silva what was inside. She gasped, and her hands flew to her mouth. "Could it really be?" She breathed.

The skeleton grinned at her as only he could. "It is. He left us his finger. All that knife sharpening wasn't for the Breeders alone." Silva's eyes widened in horror and understanding. The skeleton patted her shoulder gently. "Let me just get it down to the bone, and I have the perfect place for it. I'd like it close to my heart. He will be with us, always."

Silva reached out and held the precious gift wrapped in skins. "Can you feel anything of him yet?" She asked. "Did you…you know. When he…"

The skeleton's grin widened.

"I felt his joy. That's what it was, Silva. Not rage, but a certain kind of happiness. He fought to the music of the drums, and in the back of his mind, he saw his wife, his child, his parents, and the girl who saved his life in the Killing Fields. He hoped he could return the favor and save her."

Silva thought of her dance under the moon. She had only saved his life, but Amon had saved the most beautiful and wild parts of her soul.

The firelight danced on the walls of the burrow. When the skeleton patted her hand in his gentle way, his bones were warmed through. She had pieced him together, bit by bit, from refuse and remains of the dead, but he had become so much more. "When this land is picked clean, and the Breeders are forced to abandon the Killing Fields, we, too, will leave for someplace better. Where you can dance every day, and not just for weddings and funerals. Does that sound good to you, my Silva?"

"Yes, it does," she answered, returning his wide smile. She pillowed Amon's coat under her head and watched the skeleton tend to the precious sliver of bone wrapped in hides. When she fell asleep, she had only the most beautiful of dreams.

The Making of Asylum Ophelia

Being mad wasn't enough. She also had to be beautiful. Thankfully, Brigitte, whose name meant "strong, firm, healthy woman," chose the perfect name for her baby girl.

She named her Ophelia.

What is in a name? So very much, Brigitte thought. The name Ophelia brings so many things to mind! Wonderful things. Emotive things. She knew her lovely daughter would wander around with a garland of flowers in her hair. How did she know this? Because she, Brigitte, with her sturdy hands, would make that garland herself. She would weave it through Ophelia's long, loose curls.

Ophelia's tresses would tumble, of course. She would grow her hair long and sit at her mother's knee while Brigitte cooed and sang and brushed Ophelia's wild locks.

She would sing songs of madness. She would sing songs of want. She would sing them in her husky voice until her winsome daughter sang them back to her, her voice clear like a bird's.

Ophelia wanted to wear Wonder Woman shirts and dinosaur pajamas like the other kids she saw from her window, but Brigitte, like her name, and her solid orthopedic shoes, stood firm.

"No, Ophelia," she said. She put her hands on her hips for emphasis, as her own mother had taught her. "Pretty little girls should only wear white nightgowns. They look lovely when you ghost down the halls. When you become a woman, they'll flutter behind you as you walk on the moors in the night. Can you see in your mind's eye how you will glow under the moon? An unearthly thing of beauty? The evening's chill will prick your arms and legs, but you won't even feel it. You'll dance in bare feet, humming and swaying gracefully to music that only you will be able to hear."

"What if I can't hear it?" Little Ophelia asked. She wanted to play with trucks. She wanted to watch movies on her mother's tablet. But Firm Brigitte took these things away and made sure she played with charmingly clumsy handstitched dolls and wooden figurines instead.

"You'll hear it," Brigitte said loosely. "We'll begin music lessons soon so you can always hear the music in your soul."

Ophelia didn't go to school like other little boys and girls. Her mother taught her at home. She had teachers come in to teach her ballet and embroidery and Shakespeare. Brigitte worked at the large store across the moors, the local Walmart, and she locked Ophelia inside the house while she was gone. Ophelia learned how to curl up prettily in a soft chair in the reading room and pour over books. Both legs pulled up, clean feet tucked away. She wasn't allowed to sprawl or spread her knees in a horrid, unladylike way, lest she spend the rest of the day in the closet.

One day, as a young teen, she appeared in her mother's doorway. Her pale face had two bright spots of color on her cheeks.

"Mother, I am reading Hamlet."

Brigitte's eyes were stars.

"My favorite. What a powerful story, yes? Family and betrayal and murder and madness."

Ophelia's pretty mouth twisted.

"Let's talk about this madness. It's an epidemic."

"It seems to be."

"Everybody loses their lives."

Brigitte nodded.

"Hamlet is Shakespeare's greatest tragedy."

Ophelia shifted uncomfortably in her flowing nightdress. It had long bell sleeves which fell demurely over the leather book she held. All of her books were bound in leather. She wore a nightdress day and night, her feet kept bare or perhaps slippered in soft-soled velvet shoes if the night was especially cold.

Except for lessons. Her mother allowed her to change into corseted dresses for lessons. Ophelia's teachers had commented on the strangeness of a thirteen-year-old girl showing up for singing, piano, and dance lessons in a nightgown.

"Mother, I want to ask you about Ophelia. In the story."

Brigitte's eyes glittered, and her unpainted lips showed strong teeth.

"Isn't she lovely? So charming. So tragic. Do you see how everybody responds when she hands them flowers? Isn't she the most wonderful thing? Their hearts go to her. Their mouths tremble. They accept her gifts and wear them near their hearts. She brings them together."

Ophelia's jaw set, and Brigitte had never seen such an ugly thing on a child.

"She's mad, mother. She isn't charming. She's crazy. She needs a psychiatrist and somebody to watch over her. She needs medications to stabilize her moods. She needs to get help and live somewhere other than that wretched place where they just let her pinwheel off into the water to die."

Sturdy, Firm Brigitte stood up. Her legs were strong, her dark eyes imposing. She filled them with steel. Ophelia shrank back, her white fingers fluttering to her face as they should.

"None of this unseemly talk, Ophelia. You will not abuse your namesake. Heaven knows the dear girl has had enough of that."

Ophelia blinked large, dewy eyes and peered at her mother's face.

"You do realize that she is just a character in a story, Mother. She isn't... real."

She asked so beautifully. She asked so charmingly. Brigitte smiled and brought her rough hands to rest on Ophelia's feminine shoulder.

"Such sweetness in you, my child," she murmured, kissing Ophelia's forehead. "You will be remembered."

"Was I going to be forgotten?" Ophelia asked, but her mother was already hard at work, head bent low over a new pair of slippers for her charming daughter.

More than anything in the world, Ophelia longed for a friend. She didn't want to spend her evenings staring at the giant moon, which looked low, and fat, and rather carnivorous. Her mother got her a kitten, a fluffy white thing with a feminine ribbon tied around his neck, but he escaped into the night.

Ophelia wished she could follow.

"You should," Brigitte urged, her eyes glowing hotly. "Flee across the moors, shouting his name. You won't find him, of course, but won't you be such a sight? Your tears will shine in the moonlight. Sadness makes a woman extraordinarily lovely. Grief is the finest of jewels."

"Did you flee across the moors into the darkness once, Mother?" Ophelia asked, and Brigitte's face became an old house. It was a rugged thing, weathered, and shutters fell over her eyes to protect them.

"The midnight moors are not kind to a woman named Brigitte," she said simply and left. Ophelia did not go out to search for her kitten that night, although the front door was left not only unlocked but standing open. The moon ran a tongue over its teeth outside.

Brigitte plaited Ophelia's hair, twining flowers here and there. Ophelia couldn't lie down or rest her head for fear of smashing the pansies, rosemary, and violets.

"They make me weary, Mother," she said.

"There's rue for you, and here's some for me," her mother answered.

Ophelia touched Brigitte's brown locks. They were shot through with silver, wiry and looking somewhat wild.

"Shall I plait flowers into your hair, Mother?" She asked.

Brigitte's hands flew to her hair, patting it far too quickly like a dying bird. Her fingernails slid down and cut deep furrows in her cheeks. Blood bubbled up like the clear brook Shakespeare's Ophelia drowned in.

"Go read, child," she said. Ophelia's cornflower eyes grew wide, and she flew prettily to her room. Brigitte smiled after her.

Ophelia the Lonely grew quieter, paler, sadder. The air inside her home changed, as if the house itself was holding its breath in dark anticipation. She began feeling unwell, her stomach hurting after she ate, and she caught her mother heaping spoonful after spoonful of strange herbs into Ophelia's food and drink. She ceased eating, and her cheeks hollowed. Her head drooped like the thirsty flowers in her hair.

Her caring dance teacher slipped her a note. She patted Ophelia's cheek and looked her in the eye meaningfully. Ophelia read the spidery handwriting, and color returned to her face. She slipped the note between her lips, and it was the first thing she had eaten in days.

Brigitte didn't notice that her sturdiest pair of shoes went missing from her closet. She lost the scissors from her mending kit. Ophelia ghosted about the house, a winning thing, all hair and robes and silver secrets.

"Do you remember what my name means?" Ophelia asked Brigitte one evening. They were reading in the study. Brigitte was humming, repeating the same stanza over and over.

"Of course I do. Ophelia means *help*. You are a helpless, darling thing, and the world needs to take care of you before you go mad."

"*If* I go mad, don't you mean?"

Brigitte looked at her. Or, more correctly, she looked through her into the future where Ophelia's exquisite corpse lay.

"I'll surround you with flowers. With pearls. Your tresses will be arranged around your face in such a pleasing way. I can see it now."

Ophelia paled. "What do you mean? Surround me with flowers? Do you mean after I am dead?"

Brigitte closed her eyes. "The plaiting was practice, don't you see. Now, I'll be able to do it just right. I have the most beautiful pale gown for you. The palest of blue with silver threads dotting it like stars. So lovely, so tragic."

Ophelia's voice sounded ethereal already. The wind and her mother's words had swept it away.

"A…a gown? A funeral gown?"

"Ah, it's so lovely, Ophelia! I made it myself with such care. It fits you perfectly. You will be such a wonder."

"What if I grow, mother? And the gown no longer fits?"

Brigitte's laughter sounded like broken bells, like the car horns that blared in the Walmart parking lot as she threaded her way on foot to work.

"It is nearly time, my sweet girl. There's no need to grow anymore. You will never be more beautiful than you are right at this moment. I have some herbs that I have gathered to make a draught. You will die in the epitome of loveliness. This is my gift to you, my darling."

Ophelia's stomach grew hard and heavy at the thought.

"Mother," she asked, "what of you during this? While I lie there pretty and dead, what will happen to you?"

Brigitte's lips trembled, but only for a minute.

"I will adore you. I will throw myself on your casket, weeping, but only for a moment. You will be buried, and I will put flowers and small gifts on your grave. I will never forget you. I am Brigitte, and Brigittes are faithful. We are durable. I will trek out to see you morning, noon, and night. I will work my fingers to the bone to ensure I can bring you the loveliest of things for your grave. Your headstone will be marble. I will keep it clean and free from soil and weeds. For I love you, my darling."

She did. She did, and Ophelia knew she did, but she realized this love was a sickness, an abomination, and no matter how she loved her mother, this resolute Brigitte, she could not stay here lest she die.

That night, Ophelia brewed her mother a cup of tea. It was filled with the secret herbs, and honey, and sweet things that made one sleepy.

She led her mother to bed and tucked her scratchy wool blanket around her.

"Why don't you use my blanket, Mother?" She asked. "It's so very soft and fine."

"It's not for me," Brigitte murmured, and then she was asleep. The tight line of her mouth softened. Her dark hair was loose.

Ophelia stole to her room to fetch her blanket. It was of the finest of linen, embroidered beautifully by Brigitte's worn hand. She spread it over her mother with careful fingers. She slid the flowers from her own hair and gently tucked them into her mother's curls.

Ophelia pressed her pink lips to her mother's cheek. Brigitte's skin was soft, and the bloody furrows were beginning to heal.

The girl padded to the bathroom. She stepped out of her nightdress and into a practical outfit stolen from Brigitte's closet. She slipped out of her satin slippers and into Brigitte's functional shoes, the toes stuffed with paper so they would fit.

Ophelia looked into the mirror and took the scissors to her long hair. She sobbed as she cut, one hand over her mouth, chopping and hacking until she had tresses no longer but a short, uneven cut that made her eyes too wide and her runny nose far too big.

She smiled.

The stranger in the mirror grinned back.

She did what her mother had always hoped and fled across the moors, but her footsteps weren't graceful. She clomped across the land in oversized shoes, dodging the parked cars in the dark and breathing hard. The parking lot pavement was hard and unfamiliar under her feet, but she still ran through the rain that began to fall. Shorn bits of her clipped hair fell into her eyes and plastered themselves onto her reddened cheeks. She ran toward a woman who had three daughters and two sons, and she had been invited to become one of them, whichever she wanted, as winsome or slovenly as she liked. Her name, Ophelia, meant *help*, after all, and she had the power to help herself.

BRIGITTE'S eyes fluttered open. She turned her head to the side and caught the faint scent of flowers.

"Ophelia?" She called. She sat up in bed, and a daisy fell from her hair. Brigitte reached out to touch it, her hand trembling, and realized she was covered in her daughter's exquisite blanket. She ran her fingers over the expensive fabric, feeling its softness. Her fingers fluttered to her lips.

"Ophelia!"

Brigitte leaped out of bed and rushed down the hall in cold, bare feet. She flung open the door to Ophelia's room.

Her daughter's bed was horrifically cold and empty.

"No," she said, and flew around the room like a frightened bird. She plucked at the curtains and the sheets. She searched the house and made a small sound when she saw that the front door had been left slightly ajar. Brigette snatched one of Ophelia's white robes from the front closet and pulled it over her nightgown as she flew into the night after her child.

The rain hit the ground prettily as she ran. She left the gardens and raced across the moors, her bare feet hitting the ground, splashing through the rainbow-colored puddles of car oil. She gave her discomfort no heed, hands to her terrified face, hair dripping flowers as she raced around, calling for her daughter.

"Ophelia! Ophelia!" She screamed, and she was calling *help, help, help.*

Tragedy brought Brigitte to her knees. A missing child makes its mark on a person, and sadness, as we have learned, makes a woman extraordinarily lovely. A devoted mother caught up in madness can, indeed, die of a broken heart, and she tumbled into a stream, the water rushing up her nose and mouth, flowering inside of her lungs. Her dark hair waved gracefully around her white face, her eyes staring at the hungry moon. Brigitte had never, ever been so beautiful as the night she lost her Ophelia and the moon devoured her whole.

OPHELIA made her way into the Walmart.

OPEN 24 HOURS, it said. The signs were loud and garish, and the lights inside hurt her eyes.

Ophelia hesitated in the doorway, her sopping clothes sticking to her body, and she stared at the horrors around her. Men with hair on their faces who smelled of musk. Women using loud voices and wearing rough pants of scratchy fabric. Jarring voices came out of the air and asked for checkers and aisle cleanups and said there was a great deal of air fresheners.

Sound. Noise. Saturating color. Smells. It was too much, far too overwhelming to a young woman raised on weak tea and quiet afternoons in the library with Proust.

Ophelia raised her fingers to her teeth, biting her fingernails, gnawing at a hangnail until it bled. She backed out of the store and into the rain outside.

A thin woman with suspiciously bright eyes grabbed her arm.

"Hey, have any money?" She asked.

Ophelia yanked her arm away and stepped back. She spun around and ran for the house.

"I'm sorry, I'm sorry, I'm sorry," she repeated. It was a chant, a spell, and it would keep her safe. It would ferry her home and tuck her snug in her bed, where she would be warm and things would be quiet. Her mother would forgive her and weave flowers into a garland to cover her shabby head until her hair grew out. She would eat the delicate soups and drink mugs of warm milk with all of the poisonous herbs, whatever her mother wanted, as long as she didn't have to be out in this world of horrors alone.

The lights of her home glimmered on the other side of the moor. She used her arm to brush tears and rain out of her face as she staggered, weaving in and out of the parked cars, tripping over her too-large shoes. She was nearly there when she caught sight of something in the gutter. Her stomach fell, and her mouth formed a large O.

Her mother, face bloomed with death, lay in the water. It rushed over her, washing the color from her skin and out into the moors. Her dark hair moved gently in the current, jeweled with the remnants of beautiful flowers.

Ophelia fell to her knees and sobbed, the sound ugly in her throat. She reached for her mother with ruddy hands but could not force herself to touch Brigitte's unlined, peaceful face. A violet slipped from Brigitte's curls and floated away.

Ophelia managed to choke out two words.

"Ophelia. Help."

Clocks

Once upon a time, in a land far away, there lived a young boy named Henry.

Now, this land wasn't really so far away. It was in New York. And the time wasn't really so long ago because it was, in fact, last Tuesday. But the young boy's name was still Henry.

Henry was the youngest son in a family of three sons. The eldest son was fast and strong with swift feet and capable hands. He had been an athlete in school and was an athlete as an adult. He had money, and women, and respect and was in all the magazines. He had done quite well for himself and his mother.

The second son was intelligent and wise and knew how to work with computers. He figured things out and built machines that were useful to students and the military, and made computers faster, and smarter and better. He had a beautiful wife and loving children, making his family proud.

Henry was still a teenager. He was in a special class at school that concentrated on communication, applied behavior analysis therapy, and managing his outbursts. When he became upset, he often screamed and flailed his arms, scratching his aides. He hit his head against the wall and the desk. He filled his family with love and anxiety.

The oldest brother was on the news that evening.

"The ball just came my way, and I caught it, you know," he said into the camera. His hair was sweaty, and his smile was loose and easy. "Pretty elated right now. Proud of my team. We came out here to win, and we did it."

The middle brother was being interviewed in a science magazine. "All we did was take the general idea of the machine and make it more powerful but also more intuitive," he said. "We want to bring this into everybody's home and change the world."

Henry's mother asked Henry how his morning was.

"Clock," he said to no one in particular. "Alarm fifteen minutes."

"Which shoes do you want to wear today, sweetie?" Henry's mother asked.

"Aunt Trudi's house. 375 North 700 West. Call first."

Many people called him a fool, and straight to his face, but this wasn't true. He wasn't wistful and dreamy like the lads in old fairytales. He was brilliant and complex. His brain ran like the fine gears of a clock. He had difficulty expressing his emotions. Emotions weren't linear and absolute. They were vague and strange and didn't make any logical sense. And in Henry's beautifully insular world, everything made sense. Complicated things were made simple, understandable, consumable. Mama put them into bite-sized pieces.

"Time to get up, sweet Henry," she said at 6:45. She stood in the doorway of his blue room with white clouds painted on the ceiling.

"6:47," Henry would bargain.

"No, 6:45. Time to get into the bath."

Most fifteen-year-old boys shower by themselves and emerge later, fully dressed and covered (and recovered) in Axe body spray. This was not our Henry.

Mama ran the bath water.

"How is this?" She would ask.

"Too hot," or "Metronome," or "Washer and dryer at Lowes, please," Henry would answer.

The bath was fine because Mama kept it at the same temperature every morning. There was safety in sameness. Henry climbed out of his night-night diaper because he still couldn't control his bladder at night. He eased into the water. Mama washed his hair because Henry couldn't manage to wash and rinse and pour the water over his head himself. She sang "Baa Baa Black Sheep," which she had done every morning for fifteen years, except for once. That was when Daddy had left. Mama didn't do the song, and Henry had screamed, flailing his thin arms and banging his head against the tub until Mama, her voice sounding strange and choked, had sung the song, start to finish, while she poured water over his head to wash the shampoo out. Mama had water on her face, too.

After shampooing, Mama helped Henry put on bath gloves and rub soap onto them. There was another song while she turned away ("Privacy, Henry"), and Henry soaped his body. Then, he was allowed to hum or beat his feet rhythmically on the sides of the bathtub or do anything he wanted until 7:03. 7:00 was too early. 7:05 was too late. But 7:03, the magic number, was just right, and then Mama told him to get out of the tub and into a warm towel.

Henry dressed himself, but Mama made sure the pictures on his shirt were facing the correct way. Mama made him breakfast, the same foods, and sat by him while he ate, or not.

"Three more bites, Henry."

"No."

"Three more."

"No!"

"First three bites, and then we can do a load of laundry."

Three bites. Two bites. One bite. Laundry.

Mama told Henry stories while he measured laundry detergent and pushed buttons.

"I was a free spirit, Henry," Mama said, holding the laundry basket on her hip. "Pick out all of the whites, please. Good job. I moved from place to place, living out of a bag because that was all I needed. A few sundresses and a pair of roller skates. What do we do with whites? Hot water or cold? Good remembering. Then I met your father, and everything changed. One, two, three boys. And last and most intricate of all was my sweet Henry. You taught me what it was to love truly. I thought I knew sacrifice, but I didn't. Yes, fifty-eight minutes for the whites to wash. We'll set the timer. Would that make you happy?"

Henry's eyes lit up. His hands flipped joyfully, and his countenance changed. Sweet Henry had become Delighted Henry, and nothing was more precious or pure.

Mama laughed. "Oh, you. You have my heart. It's all worth it for moments like this."

Henry's life had previously been different therapies. Behavior therapies and physical therapies. Speech therapies. Therapies targeting eating. Texture toleration. But now that he was older, Mama had to let some of them go.

"We can't handle them all," she explained to the therapists. "And I don't understand some of them. I want him to learn how to be safe, speak as clearly as he can, and stop escaping from the house every chance he gets. I don't care if he learns to mimic certain behaviors just because he's supposed to. So what if he spins the wheels on a truck instead of rolling it on a track? How can there be a wrong way to play with a toy?"

She looked Henry in the eyes for as long as he could tolerate, which was exactly six seconds. Six, five, four, three, two, one.

"I love you. There is nothing wrong with being quiet or refusing to shake a stranger's hand. Don't walk into the road. Don't leave the house without Mama. Use enough language to give someone Mama's name and phone number if you need help. This is what is important. Things that will keep you safe, darling. Not what will make others comfortable."

"Bus route?" Henry asked hopefully.

"Boy," people said to him, but only people who didn't matter. People who mattered always called him Henry.

"Boy," they said, "What good are you? What do you contribute? You are a drain on our resources. Will you be able to hold a job when you age, Henry? Will you be able to take care of yourself and others, or will you be sucking up all of my tax dollars?"

"Courtyard Marriott, 2800 North Green Valley Parkway, Henderson," Henry replied. He was right. This was absolutely the correct address, and while truth is truth, this particular truth wasn't the truth they were seeking.

Henry's truth was pure and earnest. But society wants truth that is shaded and nuanced and filtered through a socially acceptable lens. Henry didn't know how to open his mouth and say, "Hey, Mom, I'm feeling a little anxious for some reason I cannot define." He couldn't say, "Oldest brother, I'm feeling that deeply satisfied feeling where my stomach is full, and my eyes are sleepy, and I feel your warm hand resting on the top of my head. This is contentment." He couldn't say those things.

But he *could* tell you how to install a new microwave and tell you its model and serial number while he was at it. He could tell you the date and time of his cardiology appointment and mention the address, in case you need help finding it. He could remember all the phone numbers that you couldn't remember. Grandpa? He knows it. Your best friend? Henry has that one, too. Daddy? He could recite it in his sleep and often does, even though that number hasn't been in use for years and years and years.

Six years seems like an eternity when you are fifteen.

That's seventy-two months.

Three-hundred and twelve weeks.

That's 908,236,800 minutes, not counting leap years, of course.

How many tears had Henry's mother cried during this time?

Clock.

CONVERSATIONS are like puzzle pieces. They're meant to fit together in the most perfect of ways. Sincere questions and truthful answers don't work when they're ill-fitting and pounded together by a fist.

The correct answer to "Henry, why is your mother sobbing at night?" is not "Clock."

The answer to "Which shirt do you want to wear?" shouldn't be "GE stacking washer and dryer."

And no matter how much she understands, a mother's heart fractures every time she says, "Son, I love you. Do you love your mama?" and his answer is, "Dentist appointment on June 12."

This year, however, Henry had to miss his dentist appointment on June 12. It would later be rescheduled for August, but June 12 wasn't going to happen at all. That was the day the three sons lost their mother.

It wasn't clear to Henry what she had been doing. Perhaps she was reading appliance manuals or talking to people on the phone who couldn't be seen or walking out the door and coming back with his favorite box of goldfish crackers. Mama was there, and then she wasn't there, and this didn't make any sense. Henry could set his watch by Mama.

"Mama home at 5:00," Henry informed his oldest brother. The camera crew was set up outside the house, hoping to film tender moments of grief-stricken Americana.

Oldest sobbed and tried to hug Henry, but the boy was having none of it. No constraining hugs. No touching except for on the hand, lightly, to guide the way, and only if Henry initiated contact. Henry sat on an exercise ball in his room, bouncing up and down, up and down, while his brothers conversed downstairs.

"Mama home in 30, 29, 28, 27..." Henry told his middle brother that weekend. Henry's hair was sticking up like chicken feathers, but he looked handsome in his uncomfortable new suit. Middlest sniffled and wiped his glasses.

"Mama isn't coming home, Henry," he said. He nodded toward the casket. "Mama's body is there, but her soul is in Heaven. Heaven is a wonderful place. Do you remember Mama talking about it?"

"Bus ride, 3:15," Henry said resolutely and wandered away.

That night, the brothers spoke in low voices. Henry stood by the front door, flicking the lock back and forth, back and forth, back and forth. Mama wasn't there to feed him dinner, count every bite with him, or make him go to bed, so he didn't do any of these things.

"Henry," Oldest said the next morning. "We love you very much."

Henry didn't answer. His shirt was on backward, and he was biting his fingers. He had bitten through his skin and deep into his flesh, but Mama wasn't here to redirect him.

"You can't stay here without Mama," Oldest continued. "I'd let you live with me, but I'm gone all of the time with practices."

"Not to mention that it will cramp your style. How can you have women over with him around?" Middlest said. He said it rather snidely, but Henry didn't notice that.

"Middlest here would let you live with him, but he's always been pretty selfish."

Middlest made a strangled sound, but Henry didn't notice that, either. "That isn't true. I'd take him but I couldn't do that to my family. It would be too much..."

"Work?" Oldest offered. "Hardship? Inconvenience?"

"Danger," Middlest corrected. "Danger to my family. What will we do when you get violent, huh, Henry? What if you tantrum and hurt my little girl? Things were different when you were two years old, but now that you're so much bigger..."

These are all valid points, thought Oldest.

I'm exhausted just thinking about it, thought Middlest.

Flight HK98 to Hawaii, thought Henry.

THE brothers pooled their money and paid for Henry to stay in a very nice place with very nice bedrooms and very nice staff. None of this mattered to Henry. He simply knew that the doors and windows had loud alarms that went off whenever he tried to open one.

"No running, Henry," the very nice staff said.

The food was varied and had different textures, and he sobbed when they forced him to try creamed spinach. They didn't count the bites like Mama had. The spinach wasn't in cubes or a shape that made sense. It was unkempt and wild. There wasn't any logic to it whatsoever.

"Diversity is good, Henry," the very nice staff said.

He lay awake at night staring at the too-dark ceiling, the room scary-quiet. Without his three iPads all humming different tones, his thoughts were louder than microwave doors slamming shut.

"No screen time at night, Henry," the very nice staff said.

They encouraged him to stand up straight. They showed him how to properly play with toys. They taught him how to shake a stranger's hand.

He didn't like the touch of it. The warmth. The hand grabbed his hand, and his hand couldn't escape. It took his hand, boxed it in, and moved it, high-low, high-low, and Henry scratched his face and bloodied his forehead in terror.

Oldest came by and signed Henry out for a visit. It had been a long time since they had seen each other.

"How's it going, Henry?" Oldest asked.

Henry didn't answer. He followed his brother down the sidewalk. Oldest reached for Henry's hand, but Henry jerked it away.

Oldest began to speak, a sort of rhythmic pattering that sounded like water on rocks. Not unpleasant. Not too loud. He touched Oldest's hand with a ginger finger and then pulled away. Oldest smiled and reached out to ruffle Henry's hair but then thought better of it. No ruffling. Just talking and walking and buying Henry's favorite crackers at the corner store. The ones shaped like goldfish, each and every one, the same, the same, the same.

The bell dinged as they went inside. Oldest and Henry were soon mobbed by fans looking at their demi-god.

"Cool if I do this for a second, Henry?" Oldest asked.

Henry grabbed his crackers to his chest. "Mama at 5:00 p.m.," he said.

Oldest signed and posed and hugged and turned to look for his brother. Henry wasn't there. Henry had run.

HENRY walked and munched his goldfish crackers. No forks. No strange metal in his mouth. No chance it would scrape against his teeth.

His feet walked. Walked. Fifteen minutes. Fourteen. Thirteen. When he reached zero, he reset the timer in his head.

"Are you lost?" A woman asked him.

"June 12," Henry said and continued walking. He walked with assurance. He walked with conviction.

He didn't like the mud or the grass or the way the leaves of the trees touched his shoulder when he moved past. But he liked the steady sound of his sneakers hitting the pavement and the way the concrete was so reliable.

"555 New York Avenue," Henry said.

His thin legs were pistons. Step, step, step.

He wavered at the edge of the lawn. The grass was neat and clean and spongy and strange. He put one foot down, gingerly, and then raised it again.

"Bus route," he reassured himself and pressed on. There were stones and groomed curbs and birds that made startling noises. Flowers and teddy bears and pinwheels that spun and caught the light. Henry stopped and studied a pinwheel for quite some time.

"Mama home at 5:00," he whispered and checked his watch. He still had 90 seconds to go.

He had studied the maps. He remembered the route. His body had the innate, precise coordinates that took him to where he most wanted to be.

26 seconds. 25. 24. 23.

Mama's stone was set neatly into the earth, squared off, and nicely edged. Neat and precise. It was comfortable and uncluttered and just right.

Henry was nearly there. Four seconds. Three seconds. Two seconds. One second.

His watch beeped. It was 5:00 p.m.

Henry sat on the stone, away from the uncertain grass. He set a meticulous line of goldfish on her grave. Orderly. Lovingly. He recited her phone number over and over.

We all pray in different ways.

Henry hummed a strange song, patting the grave and watching the sun go down until Middlest ran up to him, panting and sweating.

"Henry!" Middlest exclaimed. He doubled over, trying to catch his breath. "We were so worried! What were you thinking?"

Henry peered up at him, his eyebrows scrunched together.

"Clock," he answered.

Night's Ivy

Christopher wasn't a dreamer. He was a good, solid man with a good, solid job, and he didn't believe in things like whimsy and love at first sight. At least he didn't until the night he met her.

He was standing in line for the opera. It wasn't something he particularly enjoyed, but his sister gave him tickets every year for Christmas because it gave him something to discuss with his boss. So, he went without protest and even took notes when necessary. Then he went home to take something to alleviate the pain that would starburst over his eye.

This cold January night started like any other. He stomped to keep warm and chuffed a bit, perturbed at seeing his breath dance in the freezing air. Then, a woman knocked into him, and everything changed.

"Oh, please excuse me," she said, and when she pushed her glistening hair out of her face, he saw her eyes had somehow managed to shine even more. "I'm so terribly sorry."

"It's all right," he said, but she had already cried out and dropped to the ground.

"I've lost my ticket," she exclaimed, and Christopher immediately knelt beside her.

The cement was icy, and his fine trousers were getting wet, but he didn't care. What was an uncomfortable wet stain when this dear woman's ticket was concerned? He scrabbled around until he saw a piece of quality paper and took hold of it.

"Here you are," he said and presented it to her.

Her smile lit up the sky. Her eyes became moons.

"Thank you so much," she said, and clutched the ticket in her beautifully gloved hands. They knelt together in a sea of beaded dresses and pressed suit pants, and the stars glittered down on them.

"Your lipstick is applied perfectly," Christopher told her. It was deep and red and reminded him of blood and rubies. Exquisite in color and spread expertly from corner to corner of her mouth. "Too many women think they can wear red lipstick. However, they can't put it on correctly. But you..."

She laughed, and he pondered being embarrassed, but what he said was true and precise. Nothing to be sorry for.

"Let me help you up, my love."

Christopher looked to see who spoke. It was a hardened, corpselike man in a suit two shades poorer than Christopher's. He drew the woman to her feet, but his eyes never left Christopher's.

"Thank you for the assistance," the corpse said icily.

Christopher stood and fixed his tie.

"It was a pleasure," he answered, and the man turned away, holding the woman's arm tightly. She smiled at Christopher once more, dazzling him with more than her diamonds, and then leaned her head on the man's shoulder.

The opera was as operas were. Christopher tapped his foot impatiently and congratulated himself for refusing to check his phone messages. When intermission came, he fled gratefully for the lobby. When his boss appeared from the theater, Christopher was immediately at his side.

"Mr. Edstrom. What a delight to see you here," Christopher said warmly and shook his boss' limp hand. "How are you enjoying the performance so far?"

"It's quite divine," his boss began and then launched into speaking about the exquisite tone quality of the soprano and the complexity of the storyline. "And the costumes," he gushed. "Don't get me started."

Christopher did indeed get him started, and while Mr. Edstrom clapped his hands in glee at the jewel tones used in the garb, Christopher caught the delicate sheen of something ethereal in the crowd.

Her hair. The woman from the ticket line.

He was not a boorish man or the type to stare, but he stood and watched her with unusual intensity. She picked her way through the forest of people like a doe through a glen, her date guiding her. Right before she disappeared into the theater, she turned and met Christopher's eyes from across the room.

He gasped and then coughed quickly to cover it up.

"How right you are," he told Mr. Edstrom, and they made the usual required pleasantries and disconnected.

Christopher allowed his eyes to glaze over for the remaining half since he had already given mouth service to the boss about this particular opera. Every now and then, he searched for the woman with shining hair, but then he flopped back into his seat and stared at the ceiling. The decorative walls. The evil villain or do-gooder or whoever was swooping obnoxiously around the stage at the moment.

And then it ended.

Ah, the play ended, but the downward spiral of his life was just beginning.

He gathered his coat and gloves. Dressed wearily. Proceeded to walk out into the bitter cold.

"Sir," said a voice just behind him. He spun around.

Those eyes. That hair. The perfectly outlined blood-red lips were sinful in their lushness. Her lips curved into a smile that nearly made Christopher groan in the sweetest of ecstasies.

She leaned close, slipped something into his coat pocket, and disappeared into the crowd. She was most likely returning to her lonely corpse. He imagined she'd spoon-feed him some old man's soup before tucking him into his casket for the night.

He reached into his pocket and pulled out a business card. "Ivy," it said, with a phone number scrawled prettily underneath. Best of all was the deep, blooming lipstick kiss that promised all the adventures he could handle.

Christopher smiled. And the very next day, he called. Ivy answered, and he was lost.

IVY'S name fit her perfectly. When she threw her arms around Christopher, she wound around him in impossible ways. He was a tall, straight tree, her hero, and this made Christopher feel useful and needed.

"I'm needed at work," he told her once. They were sitting on the couch, her feet on his lap. He rubbed them gently while speaking. "I'm fairly integral to the entire thing. But people? That's a different story completely."

She snuggled up to him.

"Oh, darling, I knew I needed you from the moment I met you."

"You did?" He was delighted.

"I did. I was so very unhappy with dear old Mr. Frowny Face, but I didn't think I deserved anything better. Why, he sucked me dry! And then I bumped into you…"

"It was like fate," he said.

He felt her lips curve against his ear.

"Something like that," she said.

She moved in quickly, her elegant clothes soon hanging beside his, her shoes overtaking the closet. His perfectly acceptable, prim apartment became a palace of pink and gold pillows.

She owned a horrid little dog that gnawed at his Versace and peed on his Italian loafers. The mutt made her laugh so hard that she opened her red mouth wide, and that was worth it all, right there.

"Will you take me out to dance?" She asked him. Christopher rarely danced, but he said he would. They danced all night, and Ivy would sleep during the day. Christopher seemed to get no sleep at all.

"Would you take me to see the stars?" She begged. The light pollution made that impossible in the city, so Christopher drove her out into the country. They stayed in a little bed and breakfast, and he ate pretentious muffins that he abhorred, but Ivy sighed dreamily.

"I would so love to dine somewhere new," she said, and Christopher obediently dressed into his tuxedo and took her out. They ate tiny portions of something mediocre, but the lightbulbs flashed, and Ivy blushed demurely with the attention. Christopher looked at her lovely skin, flushed with joy, and he quickly downed another glass of wine.

That night, she nestled beside him, her wondrous hair spread out on the bed like fabric, or gold, or diamonds, or all manner of precious things.

"Be with me forever, for eternity," she whispered before falling asleep. Christopher gulped and tried to think of something witty yet heartfelt to say, but she was already slumbering.

Forever is a long time, came to mind. Or perhaps, *Maybe we should see how the next, say, three or so months go.* But at the same time, his heart screamed, *Yes, oh yes! Let us be immortals together.*

Christopher's traitorous heart couldn't be counted upon to protect itself. It was so very new when it came to this thing called love, and he didn't understand that love shouldn't hurt so badly, or drain a man dry.

Ivy wanted, and Christopher gave. It was very nearly like opening a vein, but instead of blood, he gave money, and time, and gifts, and his good sense. He came home when she called him at work.

"I'm frightened," she would say, and her lovely skin would be a terrifying shade of alabaster. "I think there is a mouse/ghost/intruder/certain gloom of loneliness in the house."

He would comfort her, and she'd bury her face into his neck, fitting her mouth ever-so-nicely over his jugular, clinging to him as an Ivy would.

Mr. Edstrom requested a meeting with him.

"Now Christopher," he said, and somewhere in the back of Christopher's mind, he was delighted that his boss remembered his name this time, "we need team players. Are you or are you not a team player?"

"Of course I am, sir."

"I'm not seeing the dedication to this company that I expect from you. You can't keep leaving whenever the mood strikes you. Do you understand?"

Christopher opened his mouth to say something but was interrupted by the ringing of his phone.

Mr. Edstrom raised an eyebrow.

"I'm sorry, sir," Christopher said, and reached down to silence it.

Ivy. Her name flashed on the screen. She was home and frightened or lost and afraid, or perhaps she was being abducted right this very minute!

"Christopher."

Mr. Edstrom's voice held a dangerous note of warning. Christopher's finger hovered over the silence button, but he was suddenly buried under an avalanche of fear. There were so many possibilities concerning his clinging Ivy. Perhaps she cut herself badly and was bleeding. She was overcome with hopelessness and took all her depression medication at one time. She found another man, or perhaps the old corpse had returned to take her back.

The thought of her old lover with his skeletal hand around her dainty wrist was what broke him.

"I'm sorry, sir, but I need to take this. She knows only to call in an emergency."

He bolted from the room and down the hall. His hand shook when he tapped his phone.

"Ivy? What's wrong?"

"Why hello, darling!" She was fairly purring. "I went shopping and found the most charming dresses. One is yellow, and one is blue. Which color do you think, my love? Or both?"

After being let go from work, Christopher started drinking more heavily. He'd sit at the bar, studying his formally immaculate nails, and tried to ignore the phone in his pocket.

She left messages.

"Christopher! The puppy did the most delightful thing. I have to show you."

"Darling, I'm worried about you. You...you aren't mad at me, are you?"

"It's lonely, and you aren't home, and I'm frightened. Where are you?"

"There's another woman, isn't there? Someone younger and prettier than I am. That's where you are right now, isn't it? Oh, Christopher! How could you?"

"I'm sorry. I'm sorry for everything. I love you, and I thought you loved me. I must have been wrong."

"By the time you hear this, I'll be dead."

He rushed home. He always rushed home. He held her and consoled her, watched whatever new trick, heard whatever funny story, or appreciated the newest shiny bauble. He did whatever she wanted. Christopher held her while she cried and ducked while she threw his most precious mementos at his head. He told her she was the only woman he loved and tried not to choke on the "love" part but attempted to say it with conviction.

"Oh, Christopher," she always said, and wrapped herself too tightly around him. He strangled in her desperation and woke up in bed, choking on her lustrous hair. It had worked its way into his mouth and nose, tendrilingtendriling down the neckline of his shirt.

He disentangled himself and slipped from his tiny corner of the bed. He tripped over the stupid dog who nipped at him, drawing blood on his ankle. He staggered to the bathroom and turned on the light.

The man in the mirror blinked back at him. Cheeks hollowed from stress, hair graying rapidly. The skin of his eyelids had gone papery and fragile. He'd lost weight, and his night clothes hung on him almost comically.

Where was his zest for life? Where was his excitement? While his cheeks had never been rosy, by any means, they held color once. He had become nearly cadaverous.

With her beauty and neediness and searching hands, Ivy had buried herself so deeply inside his skin that she was eating him from the inside out. She sucked the dreams and spirit and passion from his soul. The energy from his body. The desire from his loins.

The next morning, she threw her arms around him, and he leaned into the hug. It was a taking hug, not a giving hug, and Ivy received the comfort she sought from him. He almost felt her pull the well-being from his body.

Christopher felt cold and alone. He settled deeper into his dry husk of a body.

"Darling, I miss you. Perhaps we could do something tonight. Would you like to go to a show?"

A show sounded lovely.

"Do you mind picking up tickets?"

Of course, he didn't.

Tickets were purchased, and Ivy swirled around in a new dress. Her hair fell in radiant waves that reminded Christopher of the first time he saw her when he was young and energetic and full of undiscovered hope. Christopher slipped on his pants and cinched the belt two holes tighter than usual. He hung the jacket over his shoulders like dressing a scarecrow. He combed his sparse hair with shaking hands.

They stood at the entrance of the theater. Ivy glittered and spun, full of excitement and stardust and vitality that didn't belong to her. Christopher stared at the ground and shuffled alongside her dutifully.

"Oh, I'm so sorry," he heard her exclaim. "Please forgive me. Goodness, where is my ticket?"

Christopher froze, afraid to look. He finally forced himself to turn around and saw Ivy nose-to-nose on the sidewalk with a handsome young man. The man had dark, radiant skin and the finest of hats. Money, health, and enthusiasm fairly dripped from him like blood. Christopher ached to feast on his vivacity himself.

"Ivy."

Christopher held out his withered hand. Ivy and the man exchanged significant glances, and the man handed her a ticket.

"Thank you so much, sir. Now I really must go."

"Not a problem," the man said, and discreetly eyed Christopher. Christopher stood silently, knowing exactly what the man would see. A corpse in the moonlight. A cadaverous sugar daddy who knew when he was beaten.

Ivy's lunar eyes were unusually dreamy during the show. She inconspicuously took out a card and scrawled something on it. In the hubbub of intermission, she scurried over to the radiant young man and slipped the card into his hand. They both smiled.

Christopher smiled, too, for the first time in a long time. He sighed as he felt Ivy's fangs unfasten from his throat.

He could breathe again. His rusty heart began to beat. His blood flowed.

A Love Not Meant to Outlast the Butterflies

Her hair was a sentient thing. Dark and lovely, it fell past her shoulders and waist, nearly to the ground. It skimmed over her body, tendrils of black vines, wrapping itself around large stones and the ankles of strangers and anything else that caught its interest.

"I'm so sorry," the girl would exclaim, and she would drop to her knees, tugging at her hair as it tugged back. "It does this sometimes. I threatened to cut it, although I never would. But it misbehaves most horribly."

The strangers, when freed, always smiled. Sometimes, they asked the girl's name, which she wouldn't tell. She'd nod swiftly, gathering up her grocery basket and her flowers, and would hurry off, her hair waving morosely behind her.

This morning, ah, it was a special morning. Full of promises and secrets.

"It is a day of miracles," she told herself. She dressed in a simple cotton dress. She brushed and brushed and brushed her hair, which purred and shone and twined around her. She slid her feet into flats and headed out into the sunshine. Her hair plucked pink oleander blooms from the trees and held onto them firmly.

She shopped for sweet tea and lollipops and all manner of things that were light and beautiful and not at all responsible. She was bending down in the bakery aisle, studying all manner of different baking chocolates, when her hair caught fast.

"Not again," she breathed, and straightened. Her hair was wrapped firmly around a tattooed arm, wrist to elbow.

"I do apologize," the girl said, her fingers reaching for the man's wrist. "I can't control it. I hope I didn't disturb…" She stopped. Her hand was on his too-warm skin, her blue eyes locked with his. They were hazel but shone with gold.

She stared. He stared.

"What is your name?" He asked. His voice, there was something about it. Something she recognized, something she wanted to respond to. Perhaps it was something she remembered from generations ago. She closed her eyes briefly, swallowed, and then opened them.

"Mariposa. It's silly. My mother named me for butterflies. But I usually go by Mari."

"I'm Jay. Jay Wall."

"Jay. It's a pleasure to meet you."

"Likewise."

He slid his hand to hers and took it gently. Something roared under his flesh; she could feel it. Steam in his veins. Violence and loneliness and beauty in his blood. She put her other hand up to her lips, then offered him that one, as well. He took both of her hands and held them tightly against his heart. Her hair wrapped around and around and around their joined fingers. It sighed.

HE walked her home. She had never allowed anybody to do so before. They held hands as if it was the most normal, natural thing in the world, and perhaps it was.

"Would you like to come inside? I have something to show you. Something rather beautiful, if you would like to see."

She was being terribly forward, she knew, but something about him made her heart sing. Made her want. She wasn't a woman used to want.

She dropped her eyes. Bit her lip.

Jay smiled and took her chin in his hand. His smile was real and genuine and made her heart do funny things.

"I would very much like to see."

Her laughter was back, her worry gone. Jay was a little afraid at how little it took to soothe her, how sad she must be if so little meant so much, but her hair wrapped itself around his shoulders and drew him inside with her.

A LOVE NOT MEANT TO OUTLAST THE BUTTERFLIES

"This is my home," she sang. She kicked off her shoes and spun in the living room. Her hair released him, and he was able to look around. Mirrors and pictures and tiny birds made out of clockwork pieces hung from the ceiling. Flowers and plants filled every shelf, every corner. Books littered the ground in cheery piles.

It was a place of wonder.

"But what I want to show you, it's back here."

She took his hand, dancing into the backyard. He swallowed hard, his fingers burning at her touch, but he followed.

Trees. Trees and bushes and flowers of all types. Roses and blue poppies, yellow jonquils and irises. She picked a deep purple iris and held it into the air. Her hair surged forward, giggling at the flower, and placed it smoothly behind her ear.

"Irises are my favorite," she confessed. Everything felt like a confession. Inviting this man, this stranger, into her life. Telling him her name and showing him her home. Taking him to her favorite spot, her safe nest, her little corner of the world.

Am I doing the right thing? Her eyes asked him. *Are you going to hurt me?*

Show me your place of wonders, his eyes answered back. *I will never, ever leave you.*

She smiled, and rushed forward to throw her arms around him, to rain kisses on his cheek and neck and face. She took him by the hand again.

"Chimes," she said and pointed. There were several of them, perhaps a dozen, silver and bronze and joyous and tinkling.

The chimes were soothing. The flowers smelled sweet and holy and strangely primitive, in a way.

"I think this is where my soul lives," he said and wondered if it was a stupid thing to say.

Mari stepped into his arms and laid her pale cheek against his brown one. She fit there, fit like she had never fit anywhere else before. He wrapped his arms around her, and her hair wrapped itself around them both.

"I think you are my soul," she whispered into the breeze. The chimes. The flowers. Their breath. Everything was exactly right.

She pulled away and gently tugged him after her.

"There's more?" He asked. He was smiling. He thought he had forgotten how to over the years, but now his lips seemed to remember.

"The best part."

She led him through the garden of flowers. They parted for her, swaying to the left and the right, raining petals upon them. She thanked them prettily and led him through.

He felt too tall, too big, too loud with his heavy boots and heavy steps and heavy thoughts.

She paused as if she could hear him. She touched her forehead to his.

"You're perfect. You're beautiful. Now come."

In the center of the garden was a patch of green, leafy weeds. Tall and unbeautiful. The focal point of the garden. It seemed so out of place, so unusual. He looked at her. She was looking back.

"What do you see?"

Her voice, it was Heavy With Meaning. It was important, somehow, that he see what is meant to be seen.

"I see…is it a weed?"

"Milkweed."

He looked closer. The leaves were ragged and…no, not ragged. Chewed. He knelt in front of the patch of milkweed.

"Something was eating this."

Her smile, it started slow, sliding across her face like the moon coming out. It took his breath away.

He turned back to the milkweed.

"What was it?"

"Keep looking."

Holes. Gnawed edges. He followed the carnage until it stopped. Until he saw something exquisite, something small and perfect and terribly, terribly vulnerable.

Several small, green chrysalises. Pearly and cool to his touch. A thread of gold ran through, sewing them up nicely.

"Butterflies." His breath shook the chrysalises and made them dance in a way that filled him with wonder and horror.

"They're fragile, yes, but stronger than you'd expect. They won't fall."

A LOVE NOT MEANT TO OUTLAST THE BUTTERFLIES

Mari knelt beside him, her voice hushed. Their hands knit together in their now-familiar way. Her hair fussed over the chrysalises, petting and soothing and whispering sweet, charming things.

"Monarchs. They're my favorite. These have a few more days. But there are some over here that... oh! It's hatching."

The chrysalis was completely transparent, the shine of the orange and black wings pressing against the thin membrane. It cracked and tore, and the butterfly struggled to emerge.

"There are others," she said and crept around to a separate section of milkweed. Four butterflies began emerging, drying their wings, tiny legs, and huge eyes and colors that made his stomach twist with the beauty.

She held out her hand, and a young butterfly, body still plump from the chrysalis, stepped on it. It fluttered its wings, testing them.

She took Jay's hand and urged the butterfly to step onto his knuckle. It trembled slightly, unsure on its new, thin legs, but then it clambered onto Jay's rough skin.

"His feet are sharp," Jay said. He tried not to breathe so he didn't scare it.

"Surprisingly so, aren't they? She tastes with her feet. She's tasting you. And this is a female. Do you want to know how to tell?"

And she started to talk, her voice small and delicate, huge and round, as she discussed flowers and butterflies and everything and nothing.

She was a terribly lonely woman, terribly so, and Jay could see this with his calm eyes and still soul.

"What will you do when they all fly away?" he asked her.

Mari smiled at the butterfly on his big hand.

"I know she'll leave. She'd die if she stayed. And she won't survive her migration, either. She'll lay eggs and die on the way. But her children will continue to fly south and will finish the trip for her. Or maybe their children. Several generations later, some of them will return to me, and I'll watch over them, just like I did this one." She searched his eyes. "I know they'll leave, but I love them all the same. It's still worth it, don't you think?"

The butterfly spread her wings. Flapped them. Dried them.

"You may touch her wings, but just once," Mari said. "You don't want to disturb her scales. But a small touch, gently, with your finger...it shouldn't be too much."

He reached out with a finger that trembled slightly. This surprised him.

"I don't want to hurt her," he said, and there were Layers to his words. Meanings.

"Please be careful, then. Please don't hurt her. Just love her, okay? She'll give you everything."

Jay pulled Mari closer for their first kiss, a breathless kiss, the first kiss of her entire life. The butterfly wings, fully unfurled and dry, leaped and fluttered clumsily away.

JAY stayed with her that night. He was set to go, and she was set to let him, but the storm came in, and she began to tremble.

"I hate them," she said, and her mouth turned down. "I can't abide the wind."

There was something to it, something darker and deeper than a woman simply afraid of a little rain, and Jay heard the words before he realized he was the one saying them.

"Would you like me to stay with you? For a while?"

Her face, it was hopeful. Her face, it was a little afraid.

"I...would you? Please. If you don't mind. But just to sleep? Would that be okay?"

She was a woman ready to rabbit, a small thing who might be strong during the day but was now a little girl frightened by the storm. And he, just plain Jay, might be the only thing that could make it better if he only didn't make it worse.

"I'll sleep on top of the covers. How's that, my love?"

Teeth brushed. Hair combed. She wore blue starry pajamas and climbed into bed with a grateful sigh. He took off his socks and shoes, lying beside her on top of the white comforter like he promised.

What am I doing here? He thought. Or at least, that's what he felt he should be thinking. But what he really thought was, *I've never been so happy.*

She wrapped her arms around him and snuggled into his body in a way that made him feel his own butterflies.

"And to think that this morning I didn't even know you," she said. Her breathing slowed, and her voice was heavy. "How did I ever live without you?"

A LOVE NOT MEANT TO OUTLAST THE BUTTERFLIES

"I love you," he answered, but she was already asleep. "I'll always love you."

The words were nearly lost in the wind and rain that raged outside, threatening her flowers and new butterflies. But they had been said. They were real. And in her sleep, Mari turned her face toward him, her hair wrapping around them again and again and again. When she awoke in the morning to find that the comforter was no longer between them but that she was in his arms and he in hers, she buried her face into his shoulder, and his t-shirt was wet with the tears of a woman who realized she was finally loved.

MARI hated being cold. He learned this quickly. With the cold came sorrow and despondency, and her white face lost even more color. He ran his hands up and down her arms to warm them. He took her icy feet between his palms and draped his jacket over her shoulders. She'd look at him and smile. Kiss his mouth with a tenderness that still disarmed him. Threw her arms around his neck with a trust that nearly crushed him under the weight of it.

He was jealous. Of her hair, of the way that it flirted and flounced and was interested in everything that went on around it.

"I don't think you should be twining around other men if you're in love with me," he said. He and Mari were struggling with her unruly locks, trying to release a young businessman with a rather intriguing briefcase.

"I don't have anything to do with it! It does it by itself. Sorry," she called to the young man as he scurried away. "I hope you have a better day!"

"Do you know how I feel?" Jay said to her. He grabbed an elastic band from his newspaper and tried to restrain her black hair. "I'm standing right here, giving you everything, and you're spinning and twirling for other men?"

Mari took both of his hands. Held them close to her heart.

"*You* are my heart," she told him. "You. Only you."

The steam ran under his skin. Anxiety. The fear that he wasn't enough. The fear that he wasn't special.

"I love you," she said and kissed him. It was long and deep and real. After she pulled away, her cheeks were flushed. His breath came fast.

She smiled at him.

"I'll see what I can do with it. Braid it or something. Would that help?"

"Yes. I think so. I'm sorry."

"Don't be sorry. Be with me. Shall we go home and check on the butterflies?"

Two more had hatched. They fluttered around, resting on his shirt, resting in her hair. Mari and Jay spent the night laughing and singing and being desperately, desperately in love. This is the love of legends. It's what the love songs are written about. They both knew this.

IT had been a terrible day. A day full of darkness and anger, and everything made mean.

He was so upset that he nearly didn't go to her house. But he needed to see her. He needed his Mariposa. Needed her like he needed light, like he needed air.

She was lying on her side in the backyard. Her hair had been braided tightly. It reached for him as he came to her. It whimpered.

"Mari? Are you unwell?"

She had more chimes out. Dozens and dozens of chimes. Far too many. The wind had picked up, and they clattered, pierced, and made ugly sounds in his ears. Too many frequencies. Too many tuning forks going at one time. The vibration made him grit his teeth.

"Mari!"

She didn't move. The sound, the day, the anger of being ignored, all of it was too much. He began to sweat. His chest hurt, and he grabbed at it, breathing hard.

A butterfly fluttered around Mari's body. It landed on her arm and her hand, then flew up to her cheek. She reached for it, and it moved away.

"Where are you going? Why...oh!"

She saw Jay fall to his knees. Saw his skin ripple and bunch with the force of the anger and heat beneath it. His beautiful eyes had turned a dull red. He gasped for breath.

"Baby! Baby, breathe for me. Just breathe."

She helped him onto his back. Tugged his shoes off and threw them over her shoulder. Pulled his jacket from his body and loosened his tie around his neck.

A LOVE NOT MEANT TO OUTLAST THE BUTTERFLIES

"Tell me what to do," she begged, but Jay couldn't speak. The wind rose around them, tearing Mari's hair from its braid, and she closed her eyes against it.

The chimes. The wind. Her hair. His breath. His eyes rolled back in his head. He began to choke, and his body seized.

Mari screamed his name, but there was no response. She ran her fingers over his body, paused, and gasped as she felt the heat burning in his neck and chest, radiating out from his heart.

"Steam," she whispered and ran inside for a knife. The sharpest she could find, the one she used for cakes and pies and to reflect against the walls for the cats to chase. She said a prayer and pressed the knife into his skin.

Not hard enough. She brought a thin line of blood to the surface, but it wasn't enough, wasn't enough to release the pain, release the pressure.

She bent over and kissed his lips, her tears mingling with his sweat.

"I love you, baby," she said and plunged the knife into his body.

The steam shrieked out through the hole with a sound higher and louder than even the wind. She wasn't ready for it. It burned her eyes, burned her skin, and she screamed, dropping the knife. Her face was on fire, her hair writhing and whipping around her, the rubber band torn from it, but she felt for Jay; she needed to hold onto him, hold him down if necessary. The steam of his rage whistled in her ears, and she shrieked right back.

She collapsed by him, her hands working their way toward his wound. It felt wet, but not too wet. She felt at her face and then let her hands drop away.

"Baby? My heart?" She asked. She put her face as close to his as she could. "Can you hear me?"

He took a breath. A deep one. And then another. She wrapped her fingers around his, and her hair settled over them like a sheet. She closed her eyes, and there was nothing.

THE last of the butterflies had flown. Mari watched for them every day, although she knew they wouldn't come back, that they couldn't. It wasn't meant to be.

Her scars weren't that terrible, really. She had been blinded in her left eye, and that side of her face was bubbled and burnt from the direct blast of steam that she took.

"I'm so sorry," Jay had told her over and over. He couldn't bear to look at her, to see what had happened. "I'm so very sorry."

"Please don't be. Just love me?"

Her face didn't matter when they closed their eyes during warm, slow kisses. But the kisses ended, and her face was ruined, and he knew he could never forgive himself for what he had done, not really. She had saved him, yes, but at her destruction. Her one blue eye followed him questioningly, and he pretended not to notice when her hair fell in a curtain over her broken side.

"Of course, I love you. Always."

He went to the store alone because she didn't want to go out anymore. Couldn't bear the stares and the whispers. The last time her hair had wrapped around a woman's fine wrist, the woman had screamed and jerked away so hard that she had fallen to the ground.

"I'm sorry," Mari had said, her words automatic but the meaning heartfelt. The woman continued to shriek, and Mari had turned and fled, her hands over her face and her sobs bursting out of her in a way that reminded her of Jay's angry steam, that reminded her of how he had almost died, how close it had been, had reminded her what being alone had been like. As she slept that night, her hair wrapped around her throat so tightly that she could barely breathe. She welcomed it.

So, she stayed home and listened to too many chimes in the backyard that was devoid of butterflies. The noise scattered her thoughts. It kept her from thinking. It kept the fear away, at least temporarily.

Jay wandered the store without her. And that was where he found another woman. She was unashamed to step outside of her house. Her face was unbroken.

HE hit her for the first time. Right across her terrible face, her cheekbone felt like it exploded, but it wasn't nearly as painful as the rending of her heart.

A LOVE NOT MEANT TO OUTLAST THE BUTTERFLIES

Her hair was pulled back, severely tamed with water and sprays and so many hairbands that it choked, but it pulled and writhed and wrapped itself around Jay's wrist and slapped at his jaw. He caught it in his hand and pulled. Her hair screamed. Mari's eyes ran rivers.

"You don't love me. You never go out with me. You don't spend time with me. You just sit here, waiting for your stupid butterflies that will never come back. And now you're attacking me?" He yanked at her hair again. Mari sobbed.

He took a deep breath. "I met somebody else. I wasn't looking for her. It just happened."

Her hand went unconsciously to her swollen cheek and scarred face. Jay's ears burned with shame.

"You said you'd love me forever," Mari said. "That I wasn't too broken to love."

Her eyes went to the window, to the sky. This angered him again.

"You're not even trying," he said. He dropped her hair, and she fell to the ground. He left, and she felt her soul crush under his boots.

She didn't get up for a long time. When she did, she took her sharpest scissors from her drawer, the ones that always made her a little afraid, and looked at herself in the mirror.

"I'm sorry," she whispered, and her hair begged and cried and promised never to touch Jay again, that it didn't mean to, that it had lost control just this once, but it couldn't leave her alone, and without it, she would be so alone.

"I know, but I don't have anything else to give him," she said, and the snipping sounded like murder, sounded like death. She tossed the long, thick braid out into the backyard, where she wouldn't have to hear its soft crying. Then, she tended to her wounds.

She didn't see the butterflies that descended from the sky, a cloud of orange wings, grabbing her braid with their delicate feet and draping it in a tree nearby. Respect by Monarchs. A butterfly burial.

Jay came back that night to see her. To tell her that he was sorry. To say that things were bad, they were hard, but no single moment is unendurable, and he needed her. His soul had been char and ash before, but somehow, she had stoked it to flames. They were meant to be, and he couldn't stay away.

She wasn't in her room. Nowhere inside. He found her in the backyard, asleep in the garden, holding one of his t-shirts in her hands. Her face was horribly swollen, and bruising was setting in. Her hair was short like a boy's, and tears and dirt marked her face. He took her in his arms and was horrified to feel how cold her body was.

"She's not you. This other woman will never be you. We're the stuff of legends," he told her, but she didn't wake. He held her, rocked her, caressed her. He tucked a blue poppy behind her ear. It fell out, and he cried.

Mari awoke warm and stiff in her room, tucked gently under her covers. Flowers filled the bed, every corner. They were beautiful, but she was still alone. She turned her face to the wall and tried to live without him.

She was fairly successful. She didn't sleep, and she forgot to eat, and she threw up whenever she thought of him holding somebody else's hand and sleeping in somebody else's bed, but she somehow managed to breathe. And she remembered his voice. She thought of the night she released the steam from his veins, and she was still glad, even after all this time. He was still in the world, and that gave her hope. The world needed him. She did, too, but she didn't matter anymore.

She put one foot in front of the other. She also bought more chimes and put them around the inside of the house. The sound drove her crazy. She would scream at the chimes, and they'd scream back. But if she was distracted enough, she wouldn't think of her Jay or her hair and that was a blessing.

One night the butterflies came back, one by one. Came back and fluttered around her. They landed on her short hair and touched her devastated face and rested on her blouse. And then they fell to the ground, dead. Every single one.

"No!" she screamed, and gathered their bodies up. Scales fell from their wings, powdering her fingers. They couldn't fly now, even if they were alive. They would have been hobbled. Crippled, even as she was crippled.

"You aren't supposed to be here. You're supposed to be flying south and being happy. This is the wrong place!"

But they had come home to her, even though it meant their migration would never be. Generations of butterflies that wouldn't exist. The end of a line. The end of several.

A LOVE NOT MEANT TO OUTLAST THE BUTTERFLIES

She held them to her breast and sobbed. She was alone. There was nothing. No one.

"Mari?"

His voice. She thought she heard it, but maybe it was the wind. The chimes. Maybe it was the universe mocking her.

"Mari? Are you all right?"

She didn't have the strength to turn, but he came to her and stood before her. He put his hands around hers, and the touch and tingle and spark and rightness were still there.

"They're dead," she said and opened her hands. The butterflies fell to the ground like leaves.

"Oh, baby," he said, and took her in his arms. And things were right for a second. As it should be.

"I need you," she told him, and it hurt her to say it. Took all her dignity and swept it away. She was just a girl, sitting in the dirt, cold and scared and crying. "I need you."

He pulled away. Stood up.

"I don't know why I keep coming. I don't know how to leave you, but I can't do this to her. I shouldn't be here. She told me she loves me tonight."

Mari looked at him, and her eyes blazed blue.

"I don't care if she thinks she's in love with you. You aren't hers to love. She's in love with another woman's man."

His face changed, and that was the moment she knew it was over. Knew it had been over for a long time. Their love, the love of legends, it burned too hot. It wasn't built to last. It wasn't meant to outlast her butterflies.

"I'm sorry. You shouldn't be alone. Call somebody. I shouldn't have come."

His boots stomp through the garden and the house. She didn't turn to look. She couldn't.

He'd be happy. Happy with somebody who could give him what he wants, if only he could make himself stay away from the pull of the butterfly girl's soul. You can love somebody more than life, she thought, but you can't make them love you.

Mari stared at her white hands, stained with the colors of butterfly wings. She looked at the moonless sky and listened to the chimes. Even their dissonance couldn't distract her.

She felt something caress her cheeks. Her scarred one. Her whole one. It wiped tears and whispered soft things. She looked up and saw her hair stretching down to her from the tree. It ran itself across her lips, and she closed her eyes. When she opened them, her hair gently twined around itself one last time, wrapping tightly around the branch, forming a noose. A tear slid down her cheek, but she nodded. Took one last purple iris and held it tightly. Left her dead butterflies at her feet, her lost mariposas.

A Threadbare Shirt

I can't explain my son, Niko's, obsessions. After six years, I don't even try anymore. Perhaps "fixation" is a better word; he passed "obsession" long ago. We never know what it will be: washers, dryers, goldfish crackers, the burners on the stove. Some of his obsessions are sweet and endearing, like Cookie Monster. Some, like turning on the oven, fill me with absolute terror.

His current obsession is Luke's newest white dress shirt. It's a nice, high-quality shirt that my husband bought for business meetings and church. We take special care with it. It hangs as neatly as it can possibly hang.

Niko is rifling through the closet. He discovers this shirt and claims it as his own. He tugs it off its hanger and holds it to his cheek like a blanket. He puts it over his head and feels his way to the laundry room. The shirt is washed with every load of dirty clothes that goes in. Darks, lights, towels. Niko opens the washer door and peeks in to watch the shirt dance in the soapy water. When the load is finished, it goes into the dryer. Niko is anxious to see how his beloved shirt is doing. The dryer door opens again and again and again. What a relief that Niko is now old enough and tall enough to turn the dryer back on by himself. There had been a year's worth of evenings where I was unpleasantly surprised to find wet laundry strewn across the floor.

Luke's shirt isn't white anymore. Some days, after a bout of reds, it is pink. On other days, it is blue. Several of the buttons have fallen off. The fabric is so threadbare that you can see through it. The edges have frayed, and it can't be worn anymore. Instead of being angry, my husband has simply started wearing his second-best shirt. His calm acceptance brings me to tears sometimes. Sometimes they are tears of gratitude, and sometimes they are more bitter. I couldn't exactly tell you why.

Niko crawls onto our master bed and falls asleep. His hand wraps firmly around his daddy's shirt. I stand in the doorway and watch him for a while. He wants to be where we are. He wants to surround himself with the people and things that comfort him.

He's getting too big for me to lift now. I tap Luke on the shoulder, and he doesn't even ask me what I need but stands up and walks to the bedroom. He gathers his son in his arms. He carries him through the dark house and tucks Niko into his own bed. Luke covers him with his Cookie Monster blanket and smooths his hair. He leaves the white dress shirt in Niko's hand, which is where it now belongs.

This shirt is a direct allegory for what our lives have become. It isn't how we always pictured it. It isn't what we expected. Things come into this world, like Luke's shirt, and we expect it to have a specific intent and purpose. The shirt is nice. The shirt is to be worn when Luke needs to look his best. That is how it has been, and that is how it is going to be.

Only that isn't how it's going to be. Something comes along and changes it. Suddenly, the shirt is no longer a plain, serviceable shirt. It has become something much more unique. The shirt spins in the washer. It spins in the dryer. It gives comfort when nothing else can. It reminds Niko that he is truly safe. It is always there. It lets him know that he is loved.

There are days when I want to scream, "Nothing is mine anymore!" My journals have pages torn out. My writing desk, which is supposed to be my little corner of the world, is gouged and used as a step stool. My clothes have peanut butter handprints all over them.

IT'S frustrating when my plans go awry, but that is simply how it's going to be. It doesn't do any good to fight. I can drive myself crazy telling Niko over and over not to touch the CDs and DVDs, or I can choose to store them out of reach. We are no different than any other family in that we need to pick our battles. If I'm battling with the doctor, the dentist, the school district, and everybody else that I can think of, I have to learn to let other things go for the sake of my sanity. My house will not always be perfect. I doubt I'll ever have a completely free night out that won't be tinged with worry. My husband's new dress shirt won't be worn more than twice before it becomes Niko's plaything. Instead of getting angry, I try to follow my husband's gracious example and simply accept it.

As Niko brings his threadbare shirt to his face in his sleep, I know that we have made the right decision on this. The shirt didn't live out its existence as a nice, button-down dress shirt. But it became something a lot more beautiful and infinitely more precious.

Just Beyond
Her Dreaming

She had a lover nobody could see.

    There was nothing strange in this. In fact, it was better this way.

She had a husband, or at least a man she was married to. And this invisible lover that nobody could see or hear or smell or taste (he really was very delicious) was what kept her contented and sane for a while. Until, at last, he didn't.

But nobody likes to talk about that. Not really.

It's disturbing.

Unsavory.

But oh, it was so *glorious*.

SHE had wished for a name of beauty, but that wasn't what was given to her. Perhaps her mother was in poor humor, or ignorant, or simply mad in the throes of childbirth, but she called her "Hester" before she died.

Hester spent years pretending that she had said, "Heather," as the flowers, or "Ether," as the phantasmagoric, or even "Esther," who had been a great and beautiful queen.

But Hester it was, and Hester it had always been, and after she curled up outside in the meadow with bare feet and a dirty shift reading *The Scarlet Letter,* she burned with shame for days. Every time anyone called her by name, she heard the obscene way their teeth closed as they hissed it out.

"I won't be that," she said once to nobody in particular, and naturally, they didn't care.

But several years down the road, when her lover spoke to her? He called her sweet things. Pretty things. "My darling" and "little bird" and her favorite, simply "lover." He never spoke her name, not once in all the time they were together, and that was one of her favorite things about him.

But that was in the future. Now she was a child, now an awkward adolescent. It was all about rules and society and making sure her ankles didn't show. Now, it was about being a lady and having a governess and looking for a father where she really didn't have one. He was a paper doll in a finely cut blue suit. He was a sea captain on an ocean without stars. He was a million different things, and none of them were correct.

He died, and it really was a relief. She went under the care of a relative, and life didn't change so much. She still looked at the moving wallpaper and heard the whisper of dead things. Perhaps they were her parents. Perhaps it was her soul.

Things like that didn't matter so very much to a young woman with coltish knees and hair that didn't know how to settle under a bonnet.

But what did matter? Paint. Her art. Pictures. Dreams.

Ladies didn't paint, but Hester did. Real women sat near the window and sewed intricate little swatches of embroidery. They didn't pull their hair loose and lean into the room's sunlight with an absolutely indecent hunger. They didn't close their eyes and smell the deep, dark scent of the paints and powders and brushes as Hester did.

"What a degenerate," a woman whispered to Hester's aunt. This woman's face was lined and caked and had more paints and powders and brushes on it than any of Hester's canvases ever would.

"Poor thing lost both parents," her aunt sighed. "I really try to do the best I can."

"You're a saint," the Puritan Harlot said, and patted the aunt's hand. "Nobody could expect any more. You've done all you could."

They burbled and cooed about Hester's inevitable future as a spinster, but Hester had already kicked her shoes off and slipped out the back door. The sun fell on her hair as she unlaced the top of her dress, breathing in the good air as she ran for the fields.

Wild things run, and Hester knew she belonged to the grasses and skies.

"I did my best," she whispered to the bees and birds. Her skirt was hiked up far too high. Feral flowers and thistles bit at her pale legs.

"I know," she heard, and she spun around.

Nobody was there.

That was the first time she and her lover never met.

HESTER was shameful, but her hair was rich, and her lips full. She caught the eye of a solid older man whose previous two wives had died young. Young, but hard. They had both been desert girls, their eyes green and squinted against the too-bright sun. Here, the rivers drowned them. The grasses choked them. Like snakes, they had shriveled and died when dragged out of their burrows and left somewhere strange and foreign. Children expelled from their wombs, and life was expelled from their lips. That was all.

William, for that was this man's name, had watched with helpless horror as both wives had passed on. Ineffectual man that he was, he had rung doctors and wrung his hands, but that didn't stop their chests from heaving, their lungs from expanding, and their blood from flowing.

He began with a wife. He ended up with a corpse.

Wife two was also lovely, although a bit swivel-eyed. She made an even spindlier corpse.

Wife three? She would be young and lush. She'd be able to survive the fields and greenery. Half wood-sprite, half fawn, she and William would be stolidly and deliriously happy. Within dignified reason, of course.

He watched Hester's bonnet slip from her head as she tore through the field. Something moved in his chest. Perhaps it was resignation. Perhaps it was joy.

He called upon Hester's aunt that very day. Hester was improper, yes. Impetuous, certainly. But he was a man of fine reputation. He could provide for her. Train her up in the way she should go. He could do all these things, certainly, and what's more, he was perfectly willing to. He had a satisfactory estate, and his children needed a mother. He would be willing to overlook her more girlish nature and raise her into the fine young woman he, and Hester's aunt knew she could be.

The aunt was grateful. Hester, not so much. But her opinion meant nothing in this matter, and she knew it.

The wedding was stiff and fine. She wore a dress too constricting and too good for her. It was trimmed in lace and pearls fetched by the sea.

"You look wonderful, darling," William said. He calculated net worth with his eyes. He found an errant stray of her hair and pushed it back with a thick finger. "As beautiful as any of my other wives were."

"Thank you," she said demurely, but her eyes were full of lions and forget-me-nots and the sea.

William smiled at her.

"Love isn't really so important. You'll see. Standing is. Reputation and luxuries. All of this will be agreeable by and by."

"That comforts me," Hester lied, but it was a lie of kindness, so she was forgiven.

After the wedding, which was simply ordinary, she moved into William's home.

"Good afternoon, children. This is your new mother."

They looked at her, and she looked at them. William nodded, and a servant took Hester's only bag.

"I'll just run this up to the master bedroom," he said, and disappeared. A puff of smoke. A breath. A black cat in the moonlight.

"Does he always move as stealthy as that?" She asked the children, and they nodded.

"I think he is a ghost," one of them whispered. Hester thought perhaps it was a boy, but they were all dressed in such frills and with ringlets spun so tightly that she really couldn't be sure.

"I wouldn't be surprised," she said, and the girl/boy child grinned, showing missing teeth, and Hester smiled back. Perhaps this could be bearable after all.

HOPE deceived her. Three years went by, and it was hardly bearable at all.

"Wear your hair up, darling. You don't want to look unkempt."

"If Sister Alistair invites you for tea, you simply must go. There's no other way to look at it."

"You have new standing, Hester. Mold yourself into the part. This is who you are now."

William's words showered on her skin as falling stars, and they burned just as badly. She twisted her hair into rolls and stabbed it with pins. She crushed her ribs with boned corsets. She pressed her feet into tiny, pointed shoes, tied her bows far too tightly, and always blackened her lashes immediately after her early-morning cry.

"Our other mothers were sad, too," the girl/boy children would tell her. Hester would smile and put her arms around them, nuzzling them as one wild bird does to another.

"I'm not sad, darling ones. Don't you ever think so."

Sadness was feeling, and Hester didn't feel. At least not like she used to. She helped her newish children with their letters and their singing. She supervised the cook in the kitchen, which mostly amounted to saying, "That was lovely, Hilda. Would you please do the beef again soon?" and when William was away, which was often, she sat at the window and stared out.

"You aren't meant to be here," her invisible lover said next to her elbow. She heard him more and more now, but they were not lovers yet, you see. They were still voices caught in the ether. Ephemeral beings that had yet to touch.

"Here is as well as anywhere else, I suppose," she sighed, and the exhalation from her breath fogged the window. Somehow, this made her ache.

"My little bird," he said, and something about the crystalline flavor of his voice made her ache more in the most decadent of ways.

"I want to tell you a story," he said, "but only after you've lived."

She knew he was gone before she turned to look, so she didn't bother. But she put her hand against the glass and wondered.

THE Bible said that Mary, the Holy Mother of God, pondered sacred things in her heart. Hester did the same. Hester and Mary had very little in common besides being young and thrust into overwhelming motherhood, but they treasured up knowledge in their bosoms just the same.

That night, her husband was out on business, as he often was. Hester slipped a cover over her nightdress and wandered the house, peeking in on the children and seeing that everything was set to rights. Of course, it was. It always was. She then retraced her steps, seeing that everything was set slightly off. This picture tilted just so. These papers pushed askew on the old wooden desk. This felt better. This felt more like home.

She took a candle and stepped outside. The cobblestone hurt her feet. She took a deep breath, snuffed the candle, and began to run.

The candle fell from her grip. Her loose hair bounced around her shoulders and elbows. The nightdress flapped like a crow's wings, and she finally felt free. She fled the street, turned down the back way, and raced to the fields of grasses where she belonged.

The moon, being a woman and quite understanding of these things, lit her way graciously. Clouds parted to show the stars. Hester heard the panting of her breath and the slightly sinister sound of her sky-white feet passing through brush unknown. Here, she startled sleeping butterflies, which took to the air behind her. There, she tripped and fell but clambered to her feet in a sea of fabric and dew-damp leaves. Her breath came in gasps, nearly sobs, but she ran and ran and ran. Away from something or toward, she wasn't sure, but what she knew for sure was that she had something to feel.

Fear.

Relief.

Desire.

Desire to shed her entrapments, desire to be free. Desire to be something other than a china doll with mechanical gears inside, grinding to starts and stops with elegant handwriting and a fine Sunday bonnet.

"You came," whispered the voice, and this time, when she turned to look, he was there. A young man. Thin, with clothes whose lace rivaled that of her most opulent of dresses. He wore a mask pale as starlight, with holes cut for eyes and a tiny slit for a mouth. Hester felt as though she should be frightened, but she wasn't, not at all.

"I didn't mean to come," she said. "I simply ran."

"And here you are. As it was meant to be."

"Who are you?" She asked, and although she couldn't see it, she felt he was smiling under his mask.

"I am here for you. A gift from the universe, perhaps. Or maybe a punishment. But you are here, and I am here, and that isn't any coincidence."

There was truth in his words, a primordial conviction that thrummed through her veins as he spoke.

"I don't mind being unhappy," she told him. His body faded away in the shadows until only the mask could be seen in the moonlight. "Unhappiness is acceptable. But I don't want to be..."

"Imprisoned," he answered for her. She would have nodded, but it wasn't necessary. None of it was necessary. The stations and etiquettes and things typically required of her suddenly had no bearing at all.

"You want to hunt," he said, and this was true. "You want rain in your hair and blood on your lips."

"I suppose I want a lot of things."

"Then take them."

His hands were warm on her skin, and his lips pressed against hers with the slim filter of the mask between them. She ran her hands through his hair and over the porcelain of his face.

"Will you ever take it off?"

"Perhaps."

"I'll wait."

The sun rose, and Hester rose with it. Her lips were deliciously swollen, and her nightgown and cover were askew in the most scandalous of ways. She felt more clear-eyed and lucid than she had been in years.

The way back to the house was far longer and more treacherous than the way out. But she smiled to herself and loosely linked her fingers with a tall, reedy man that nobody else could see.

IT was strange having an imperceptible man around the house. He stood in corners while Hester brushed her hair. He leaned against doorjambs when she spoke to her husband. He sat quietly on the parlor couch while Hester and William argued.

"If you were here just a little bit more," she would say, and William would cut her off. It was an argument so well-worn that she could mouth the words alongside him. Sometimes, the man in the porcelain mask *did* mouth along, and Hester had to put her hand to her lips to keep from laughing at its absurdity.

"Hester, my work is important and keeps you in the comforts you so well enjoy. It is necessary that I take these business trips. Why don't you busy yourself with the women's charity or host a few more garden parties? After all, your standing in the community requires..."

His words tasted like soot and hemlock. They sounded like the unseemly shriek of carriage wheels and grimy harlots. She let them rain over her while she studied her white gloves. Not a speck of dirt on them. So pristine. So pure.

She caught her lover's gaze and blushed.

"What's this? You redden? "William said, and his voice softened. "I don't mean to speak so harshly, my dear. I only want you to be content and respectable. Are you not happy? Do you want for anything?"

"I want for nothing, my husband," she said, and he patted her on the head as he did his children.

"Will you try harder?" He asked.

Hester swallowed, and it hurt.

"Yes. I will try harder."

She performed her duties with a diligence that would have floored William had he been paying attention. Each day, more and more color fled from her face.

From her soul.

"Darling," her lover whispered, and when she turned to fully look at him, he saw that her blue eyes had gone nearly ice clear.

"Did you say something?" She asked.

"You're losing yourself."

"I'm afraid there isn't much to lose."

She took to painting reserved little landscapes on prim canvases up in the upstairs sunroom. Sea shores. Neat rows of breathless houses lined up like soldiers or unhappy housewives.

Her lover didn't say a word, but he brushed the wetness from her cheeks with his hand.

"At least I am painting, yes?"

He leaned over and kissed her trembling mouth.

"Shall I tell you a story?" He asked. He released her hair from its pins and began to speak, telling her of sunshine and suicides and other things of beauty.

"I wish you could tell me all the stories in the world," she said, and he smiled behind the mask.

"I can. Perhaps one day I will, my love."

Another year came and went. Hester did needlepoint and kept her knees primly together at all times. She spoke carefully in dulcet tones. Her heart turned its face to the wall and died. She feared her soul and body were not long to follow.

"Would you miss me if I were gone?" She asked William. Her hands twisted over themselves. Her eyes never left the carpet.

"What's that?" He asked. He was sitting at his desk, working on figures. Figures or bonds or letters or enchanted conversations with the stars, it didn't matter. Whatever he was working on took his full attention. As always.

"It doesn't matter," she said and slipped away. For the first time in many, many moons, she crept into her old solace, the fields. She didn't run. She had not the energy. She walked. Staggered. At one point, she dropped to hands and knees, crawling.

"How can I help you, lost little bird?"

Her lover had appeared beside her, his neutral mask lined with worry.

"I want to go home," she whispered. She continued pushing her way through the brush.

"Where is home, exactly?"

"I don't know," she said, and curled up into a little ball. Something chittered in the darkness. Something else hooted in reply.

"I don't know where home is," she said again, and covered her face with her hands.

"Shh, darling, my love. Don't cry."

Her lover sat beside her and caressed her hair, her face.

"Your home is with me," he said. "Wherever you are, that's where I want to be. Wherever I am, you should be there also. I love you. I've never told you this, yes, but it's true. I love you, my sweet little bird. You're with me. You are home."

She thought of her house, stricken of all color. She thought of William, who had stolen her very self away, piece by piece. She thought of their children, of their warm skin and big, bright ideas as fresh as the spring.

"You and the children are home," she slurred, eyes suddenly heavy. And then she was asleep.

SHE awoke with her head cushioned in her lover's lap. The sun shone in that gentle way it has in the early morning before it remembers how horrid and loathsome humanity can be.

"Are you feeling better?" He asked.

She replied by lifting her mouth so he could kiss her. It was as if a first kiss, shy and searching and oh-so-wonderful.

"I meant it," he told her, his voice warm behind the cold mask. "I love you with everything I have."

"Thank you," she said.

There was more, and she meant to speak it, but the words made her shudder inside as though she had swallowed moths.

He kissed her again.

"You don't need to say anything more," he promised, and she knew he meant it.

He helped her breathe. It made her really feel that she could be enough for him without the ropes of pearls and chains of gold. Never had finery felt so constraining. She realized now that's what it had always intended to be: leashes of silver and jewels.

"Your children are coming," he said, and Hester started at his words.

"Here?" She wondered, but the girl/boy children were already upon them.

"Mother. We thought you would be here. Are you well?"

Hester lay in the grasses, her fingers entwined with her lover, who could not be seen. The children looked past him, although one seemed to notice a subtle glint of something like stone or porcelain.

"I'm fine, my darlings. I was simply restless last night. How did you know this is where I would be?"

The oldest child shrugged.

"Father often talks about how he found you running through the fields. You know, *before*. He says we should stay far away from here."

Hester sat up, her cheeks burning.

"Why is that?"

"He says it's unseemly."

Hester looked at her lover, and he looked at her. She cupped each child's chin in her hand in turn.

"It is *not* unseemly. It's a place of beauty. Would you like to see?"

The children nodded, and she took their hands in her own.

"Then come with me, my loves. See what draws me."

Flowers. Red ones. Blue. Butterflies with painted wings. Tiny frogs and crickets and the sound of the wind laughing in the greenery.

Vines in their hair. Bluebells in their eyes. The taste of nature was on their lips and between their teeth.

They laughed. Oh, heavens, her children laughed. They played and rolled, and their glee was as sweet as bells to her, as cold mountain water on parched roots.

"They, too, are wild things," she said to her lover, her king, and he kissed the tips of her fingers.

The sun finally swooned in the sky, and their bellies told them they had missed far too many meals that day. The walk home was one of sweetness. She had a child holding each hand. Her lover ghosted alongside them, humming something vaguely familiar but still altogether new.

Life was perfect. She was home.

And then, right before darkness fell, she really was home. Back to the stately house on the refined street, with her very dignified and righteously angry husband staring at her as though she were a filthy thing.

"Children. To your rooms."

"Father, but we haven't eaten supper and…"

"Go."

They had dandelion fluff in their ringlets and fear in their eyes. Wise children, they fled.

William turned to Hester.

"What have you done?"

His voice was hard and cold. It matched his eyes, the shiny pate of his head.

"Nothing, my dear. We were only in the field today."

"Never. Never again. You are never to take those children from this home."

"But darling, I only—"

"Do you not understand what you have done? How soiled they are? Why, after looking at them for only one instant, I could see the dirt ground into their cloth, the tears in their clothes."

"William, they are only children."

His eyes hurt her. The way he stared hurt her.

"They are my children. My children, Hester. You have borne me no children. These belong to me."

He said more horrible things that would have shaken her to her marrow had she heard, but she was incapable of that. She had lost all sense earlier at what he had said about the children. Their children.

His children.

"And you are not to be near them, do you understand? You shan't influence them in any way. I'll see that the governess knows."

She blinked at him.

"Surely you don't...what did you say?"

He sighed and checked his watch.

"I believe I made myself perfectly clear."

"But William—"

"Go to bed, Hester."

He left. Turned sharply on his heel like a solider and walked into his study as if it were an armory. He shut the door. Locked it with a key.

Hester stood in the parlor, quite alone.

"I have the most magnificent of stories to tell you, my darling."

Her lover was so gifted at stories, telling her about fancies and things that lived just beyond her dreaming. She so wished she could tell the children. They would find such amusement in it. She missed them bitterly. The governess shepherded them away from her at every opportunity. She hadn't so much as spoken to them in several weeks.

"Yes?"

"This is a very special story. It is extraordinary."

"Will you tell me?"

"I would. But there is something you must know."

He spoke with gravity, and Hester turned to look at him. The smooth face of his mask betrayed nothing, and for the first time, she was frightened.

"What must I know?"

His eyes, which nobody but Hester could see, were the clearest of blues, of greens, of browns, of yellows.

"It's a grand story, my darling, but I can only whisper it during the night before the sunrise. And the person I whisper it to must be my wife."

Hester's white skin, bleached even whiter after she stayed indoors at William's request, paled until the blood ran blue beneath it. Like paints. Like the colors she had given up in order to be an acceptable helpmate to her husband.

"But I cannot—"

He grabbed her arm then, the first time he had ever done so, and his lips moved oh so quickly, oh so passionately beneath the mask.

"I love you, my darling. Do you understand that? I love you exactly as you are, as you were meant to be. I take nothing from you. Your freedom, your children, your desires. Can't you see it?"

She wanted to wrench her arm away, but something inside her couldn't. If she was too rough, he would disappear. Or maybe part of her wanted to stay, to listen to what he was telling her. To ask him to say his words again more slowly so she could close her eyes and let them cover her like the sea.

This made her pull her arm away quite firmly.

"I can't," she said, and the misery in her tone surprised her. She tried again, more regally.

"I'm sorry. I can't."

He stood there, her only joy, in his ruffles and frills and silly mask. He stood there, with his strange stories and songs and declarations of love. He stood there and her heart beat too hard, too fast, and then it felt like it suddenly stopped.

"I understand. Of course. Forgive me, my lady," he said and bowed.

Hester's dear lover, whom nobody else could see, disappeared. She gasped and then cried.

She had become just like everyone else. She couldn't see him, either.

"WILLIAM! William!"

Hester raced into the spare room that had now become his. She pushed the door open and set her candle upon the table.

"William, I need to speak to you urgently!"

He mumbled and snorted, then sat up in bed.

"Hester? What is it? Is it the children?"

She sat on the corner of his bed, pressing her hands tightly together as if in prayer.

"My dear William, I have done my very best for you all these years. You do know that, don't you?"

His brows pulled together in a way that made her cringe inside, but she continued on.

"I wear these clothes. I hold those vapid parties. I stay in our home, and even when you took my paints away and my meadows away—"

"It's the middle of the night."

"Even when you took my children away, I said nothing. Nothing! I have tried my very best to hold my tongue and be the wife you want me to be. Now I need to know, my darling husband and I need you to tell me truthfully. Do you have anything in your heart for me?"

"Hester."

She grabbed at his hands and pulled them to her breast. She kissed his fingers fervently.

"Please, William. Please. If there is any feeling for me at all, even the tiniest bit, I need to know. I'm begging you."

He looked at her. He really looked. He took in her hair and the tears that ran down her face without shame. He saw her eyes and the wounded animal expression in them. Her fingernails, shaped and shined so carefully. Her night dress, mended so delicately.

"Of course, my love," he said, and she fell into his arms in such a way that he was embarrassed at first and then merely stunned.

"Then I need you to do something for me," she whispered, and the tears made her voice sound hollow and strange. "Something to prove that I mean something to you. Do this one thing, and I shall stay."

"Whatever you wish," he said, and held her fragile little bird bones tightly. "What is it that you need?"

She swallowed hard.

"Fetch me a flower from the fields. A red one. One that I can wear in my hair. Such a little thing, but it is so very important to me. Will you?"

"You want a flower?"

"A wildflower from the fields."

"And this will sate you?"

"Please."

William smiled at her, and she found herself smiling back. Hope is such a silly little thing.

"I shall fetch it tomorrow morning, my dear."

Hester nodded and slipped from the room, but she could not sleep. She found herself in the sunroom where she had put her paints and canvases away.

Her tidy little homes. Her squalid little landscapes. Her choked little seashores.

She threw the horrid paintings to the floor, one by one. Pastels and grays and sedate, starched things without any soul. She rifled through her paints until she found what she was looking for.

Reds.

Yellows.

Greens and blues and all the colors of her lost lover's eyes.

She dipped the brush into the paints, but soon it was too little. Too small. Insignificant. She smeared the colors onto her hands and gasped at their opulence. Jewels! Treasures! She swooped her hands across the walls, creating rainbows and daydreams and stories most magnificent. She stood on her tiptoes, climbed onto the stool, and jumped as high and hard as she could to reach the ceiling. It was a dance. It was a military drill. She arched and stretched and crumpled, and soon, the walls and Hester and the room were one delirious kaleidoscope of everything that was right and beautiful and far too precious to exist in this world.

She spread out on the floor, staring at the art that spun around her like the universe on its kindest of days. She closed her eyes. She slumbered.

Light woke her. She blinked and rubbed her eyes with crimson and cobalt hands. Her mouth tasted of yellow.

William, she thought and struggled to her feet. She hurried down the stairs and out the front door.

He was just returning home. His eyebrows rose when he saw her.

"Hester! What on earth?"

"Did you get it?" She asked, and pressed into him. He pulled away and examined his suit carefully.

She paid that no mind.

"Did you fetch my flower, dear husband? The red one for my hair?"

He took her in, her breathlessness, her outstretched, painted hands, and was filled with benevolence. Such a child beneath all of her womanly ways! Such a young thing with endearing enthusiasm!

"I have it, my child," he said. "Now close your eyes."

Hester did as he bid, biting her lip with anticipation. She felt something alight in her hair. A tear slid out from under her lashes, but she didn't bother to wipe the treacherous thing away.

"There," William said. "Now you look beautiful."

She opened her eyes. Reached up into her hair. Felt something stiff and cold and sharp.

She pulled it out with trembling fingers.

"Just the thing for you," her husband said, beaming. "Quite expensive. The pearls are the largest I have seen, but it's such a lovely pin, and you wanted something for your hair. I'm sure it pleases you, my dear. I've seen few things finer."

She stared at the pin in her hand. She stared at her husband's pleased face. She put the pin in his hand and walked slowly into the house.

"CHILDREN," she said, and they pushed into her arms like warm puppies, like baby rabbits, like squirmy little wild things made of feathers and bones and fur.

"We've missed you, Mother," they sang.

"And I have missed you. Darlings, I would like you to meet someone. He is somebody very special. Will you say hello?"

"Hello, sir," they chorused, and her lover smiled.

"It is a pleasure to meet you," he said, and when he bowed, they giggled.

"He has the most magnificent story," Hester said, and although her voice sounded a little different through the mask, the children could still understand her clearly. "It's a very special story for very special children. Would you like to hear it?"

"Oh, yes," the children squealed. One looked carefully at Hester's eyes, pinwheeling behind the cut-out holes in the porcelain, spinning like a color wheel of madness, but then the story began, and the child was transfixed.

"This story," said the man, "is a fine story indeed."

"What is it called?" Asked the youngest child.

"It is called 'The King in Yellow.' Your mother enjoyed this story, didn't you, my little bird?"

"Yes," Hester agreed. "It changes everything. Absolutely everything."

"Are you ready to hear it?"

The children nodded. Hester pulled them close around herself and kissed them through her mask.

"We're ready," she told him.

Her lover slowly removed his mask and began to speak.

Mean Girls

I **was** tired of it. Tired of being talked about and laughed at. Tired of being slammed into lockers so hard that I felt the jolt in my teeth. Hate burrowed into my bones like worms. It kept me warm in a way that nothing else did.

"You know what you can do," the demon said. She had high cheekbones and would have been beautiful if she didn't reek of demonic viscera and revenge. She was wispy, wavering around the edges like a dark mirage.

"Get lost," I told her. "I don't have time for something like you."

The demon sighed heavily. "Oh, Luna. You have all the time in the world. What else are you going to do tonight?"

Probably paint my nails and then chew the polish right off again. Make a gourmet meal of spaghetti and canned sauce for my brother and me. Feign reading a schoolbook and go out for a bike ride instead. It was my night off from work, and that meant I had to figure out what to do with myself.

"I have lots of things to do. Tons. So many things," I told the demon. "It isn't easy being this in demand. Later."

"Losers have time," she called after me. "You're no exception. Next time you want to get back at them, any of them, let me know."

I told Seth that my black eye came from a volleyball game. He was so stressed about college that he actually believed me.

"Glad to see you going for it," he said over his books. His brow was furrowed in that familiar way. "Glad you're fitting in."

"Sure," I said, grinning toothily. "Love it. The sport. The team. The uniforms we all wear are a set of kind, inclusive girls. High school rocks."

"I have to admit that I was kind of worried about, you know…"

"What?" I asked frostily. "What were you worried about?"

He eyed me over his calculus.

"That I'd go off about demons again," I said. "No worries. Only crazy girls do that."

"They call you Luna the Lunatic."

"That's because they're jerks!" I shouted and then caught the look in his eyes. "Joking, I meant to say. They're joking. Because we tease each other all the time, the softball team and I."

"Didn't you say you played volleyball?" He asked me. He started to close his book, dark eyes shaded with concern. I laughed a little too heartily.

"Volleyball. That's right. Slip of the tongue, Seth. Worn out from school and practice and all." I yawned, a real jaw-cracker, and looked at my wrist. Yeah, as if I'd ever wear a watch. "Gotta go to bed. Super tired."

He looked like he wanted to say something, but I kissed him on his head.

"Goodnight, big brother. You'll do great on your test. You always do."

He frowned. "I hope so. It's the best way I know to get a real job and support us. I'm sorry it's taking so long."

I smacked him in the shoulder, which was a sure sign of sisterly love.

"Hey. Look at me. We're doing fine. You are, and I am. There's nothing to worry about."

He scoffed, but I took his head in both of my hands and forced him to look at me.

"Don't be an idiot, Seth. We have a place to live. We're not starving."

"Practically. You're a growing girl, Luna. You shouldn't be living on Ramen."

I rolled my eyes. "I get free food at work. Don't worry about me. Besides, I'm pretty sure teenagers everywhere live on Ramen. It's a requirement."

"And we throw some extra frozen veggies in there," he muttered, going back to his books.

"We do. That makes all the difference."

I crept into the bathroom and popped an aspirin. The pain in my head screamed louder than the pain in my eye socket, but the rage was the loudest of all. It buzzed like bees. I caught my expression in the mirror and didn't like what I saw.

I grabbed the side of the sink with both hands, studying my face. Bruises became me, I decided. They meant I was still kicking. They meant I was still alive.

"Luna," a voice called. It sounded soft and sincere. I didn't trust it. "Luna, lonely girl."

"Really?" I said aloud, peering down the sink. "You're going to do the drain thing? Everybody's seen *IT.* You can't scare me with something so unoriginal."

"We hate to see you so alone," the voice gurgled. It was getting closer.

I shoved the rubber stopper into the drain. "Yeah, that's where we differ. I do just fine alone."

I kicked off to my room, but I was restless. There was too much on my mind, and the aspirin didn't touch the pain in my head. I realized that my jaw ached, as well. I was clenching it, grinding my teeth against each other. Great. I'd grind my molars to dust, and we'd never have enough money to replace them. I'd be a freak in yet another way.

Why does everything come to money? I was sick of it. Sick of wearing old band tees and torn jeans, telling everyone I liked them that way. Maybe I could do with a frivolous pair of high heels instead of my Doc Martins that I bought secondhand. Perhaps kids would treat me better at school if I wasn't the poor girl.

"The poor thing is only part of it," the stuffed monkey on my bed said. Its glass eyes looked shifty. "Poor is hard enough. But poor *and* crazy? I'm afraid you just don't have a chance, my girl."

I felt my muscles bunch.

"I'm not crazy," I spit out.

The monkey laughed. "You're not?" It practically purred, lashing its tail. "Do all sixteen-year-olds talk to their toys?"

The monkey's hard eyes made a satisfying clang when they hit the inside of the trash can. I stomped to the phone in the kitchen and punched some numbers. "Hey, Kent? Yeah, it's Luna. Do you happen to be short-handed tonight? Great. I'll be right in."

I threw on my work uniform, an embarrassing dusty rose diner dress that made me look like some freak from the 1950s. I'm pretty sure my nose ring and black eyeliner didn't help.

"Going to work," I yelled at Seth as I bolted for the door. "Good luck with tomorrow's test!" I slammed the door, hopped on my bicycle, and pedaled my way to Sunny Ray's Sunshine Diner. Everyone just called it The Dive, but we'd never let poor Sunny Ray know that.

A snaky demon slid itself between the spokes of my bike like a ribbon, creating a dark blur as I pedaled. I steadily ignored it.

Less than fifteen minutes later, I was chaining my bike up at work. Honestly, if somebody else felt the need to steal it, I'd probably let it go. They would have to be even harder up than I was.

"Here," I said, pushing to the back of the diner and clocking in. "What do you need me to do?"

Gina, the manager, looked harried. "Wash up and take table four. They're on one today. The other servers can't handle them."

I tried not to groan. "But I can, huh?"

"You can. Skedaddle."

I've never skedaddled in my life, but I liked Gina. To tell you the truth, I liked most of the staff at The Dive, and if handling some handsy old man at table four meant their lives would be a bit easier, I'd do it. Never let it be said that Luna Masterson was selfish.

I scrubbed my hands and arms, blew my bangs out of my eyes, and grabbed the order. I set toward the table with a big, stupid smile plastered on my face.

Oh no. No.

I nearly spun on my foot back to the safety of the kitchen, but the diner was full of people. I decided to soldier on.

"Here's your meal," I said, and busied myself putting down plates and soft drinks. I stared at my hands with their chipped nail polish instead of at the faces all turned my way.

"That's some shiner," a girl's voice trilled. I tried not to wince openly.

"And here's some salt and ketchup," I said. "Do you need anything else?"

"I don't know how I feel about a crazy girl touching my food," a boy said. He was the mouth breather in my biology class. He didn't like me so much after I asked if it hurt cutting his family up during frog dissection. "She may have done something to it."

I sighed. "I didn't do anything to it, Rob. I just brought it out. Are you good here?"

The trilling girl shook out her hair. It looked so soft that she must have spent my entire month's food budget simply on conditioner. "I bet you're right, Rob. Luna the Lunatic did something to it."

Another girl with too-big teeth grimaced. "She probably spit in it."

I put my hands on my hips. "Listen, Chompers, I did no such thing. You ordered, I brought it, end of story. If you need something, holler. Otherwise, enjoy."

I started to turn back toward the kitchen, but a wheat roll bounced off the side of my head. The table burst into laughter. I swallowed hard.

"Oh, server," the triller said. "I dropped my roll. Could you please pick it up for me?"

"It's okay," I said through gritted teeth. "I'll bring you a new one."

"No, I want that one. The one on the ground. Get down and pick it up for me. Please."

I wanted to scream at her. I wanted to smash her face down into her mashed potatoes until she stopped screaming. But I thought of Seth, falling asleep over his books, and how I would explain Miss Trill's murder to our case worker. I needed to stay with Seth and not be sent back to the group home. I wasn't going back there again. I waited for years until Seth was old enough to legally become my guardian. I couldn't screw it up.

"Sure," I said, so brightly that I could scream. "Not a problem." I slowly got down on my knees, careful not to flash the people behind me in my short skirt. I have standards.

"Whoops," Rob the Frog Boy said, kicking the roll. "It rolled under the table. Get it? Rolled?"

I didn't curse or set the place on fire. I simply stretched my arm through the dark jungle of teenage legs.

They're going to do something.

My fingers touched the roll. Yellow, snake-slit demonic eyes met mine under the table. I gasped and reared back just as my back and legs began to burn.

"Sor-ry," Chompers sing-songed above me. "I spilled my soup all over you!"

"Let me help you out of there," Rob said. He grabbed me by the waist, yanking me backward, hard. The demon under the table clawed at my hand, leaving bloodied red scratches. Rob left carpet burns on my knees and legs.

Burning macaroni and cheese rained down the back of my neck. I yelped with pain.

"I'm so clumsy," Chompers said.

"You're a mess," The triller said with faux sympathy. "Let me help clean you up."

She poured a pitcher of ice water over my head. I curled up on the floor, gasping, eye-to-eye with the diner demon, while the kids above me laughed.

"Luna the Lunatic can't handle it," one of them sneered. "Crazy girl with a crazy dead daddy. Quick, somebody take a picture."

"Out!" I heard my manager's voice sizzle with anger. "Get out, and you will never come back, do you understand?" She chased the trio away while I tried to pull myself together. Everybody was looking at me. The diner had gone horrendously silent.

"They're gone," Gina said and knelt beside me. "Oh, Luna, you need someone to look at those burns. Let me help you up."

The tenderness of her hands nearly broke me. I avoided her soft brown eyes, knowing the kindness in them would make me break down and cry.

"No, I can do it," I said, and jerked away. "Thank you," I said, and scrabbled to my feet. "I'll be okay. Let me get a broom."

"No, dear, you're going straight to a hospital. And then you'll come back and file a police report, do you understand?"

I reflexively grabbed her hand. "Please, no. I can't do a police report. I'll never hear the end of it if I do something like that."

She looked concerned. The demon perched on the table behind her looked sly.

"It burns, doesn't it?" It warbled. It knew nobody else could hear it, could see it. Just Luna the Lunatic burned and shivering in the diner. "The skin. The body. The soul. Humiliation burns, too, doesn't it? Do you see everybody *looking?* Shaking their heads with pity? At you, Luna. At you."

"Do you have trouble with these guys regularly?" Gina asked. I fluttered my hand to my neck tenderly, feeling the rawness of my skin. Her eyes darkened. "Never mind. Now isn't the time for that. To the doctor with you, and then home. You're scheduled for tomorrow, but why don't you take the day off, okay?"

I cradled my bloody hand. "I'll be okay, Gina. Please let me come in."

Her eyebrows raised. "Why on earth would you want to?"

My cheeks felt like they were on fire, and the demon was right. Humiliation burns.

"I need the money," I whispered and looked away.

Gina nodded. "All right. See you tomorrow if you're feeling well enough. I'll keep you back in the stockroom, though."

It sounded great. I nodded, apologized again for the mess, and tried to hold my head high as I walked through the door. Unlocking my bike with my clawed hand was difficult, but it was nothing compared to my shredded pride. I was covered in Sunny Ray's Vegetable Soup, Homemade Macaroni and Cheese, and the desire for the most destructive revenge.

"Home so early?" Seth called out. "What happened?"

"Didn't need me after all. Gotta shower," I answered and scurried for the bathroom. I hissed as the cool water hit my body. My back, legs, and neck couldn't stand the temperature warmer than "uncomfortably cool." The burns were red and angry, but what would a doctor do besides charge money I didn't have? I washed delicious, delicious food from my hair, dried off gingerly, and taped some gauze over the burns. Unless I wore a jumpsuit and turtleneck, Seth was going to notice this. I had to stay out of sight.

"I'm beat. Going to bed. Goodnight, Seth," I called to the kitchen.

"Are you okay? It's early," he yelled back.

I tried to sound chipper. "Big day tomorrow with friends and, uh, volleyball. Sleep well."

I waited until he bid me goodnight, and then I headed for my room. The demon with the glorious cheekbones was waiting outside of my window. Her lips turned up when she saw me, and she pressed a taloned hand against the glass.

"Invite me in," she whispered.

I opened the window and sat on my bed. "You're invited," I said as she swirled inside. "Let's talk."

HER idea was simple.

"Make them suffer," she cooed, and licked her sharp teeth. "They obviously delight in making you hurt. It's time to see *them* hurt."

I wish I could say that I was 100% against it from the start, but that wasn't true. Some hidden part of me, the dark Luna that raged, seethed, and hated, hungered for retribution. I couldn't take the torment anymore. The old newspaper articles about my father's suicide taped to my locker, being pushed down in the hallways, and the whispers and looks. I'd almost rather deal with the physical abuse than the rumors. They killed me.

"I don't think I can take it anymore," I whispered to the demon. She grinned at me, and while part of me blanched, the other part secretly thrilled.

"You don't have to," she said. "There are ways to make them pay."

"Yeah? How?"

She turned her eyes upon me, and the hunger made me catch my breath. "I'll show you. But first, you need to be ready. Absolutely ready, Luna. I can't have you backing out when you're so close to revenge."

I touched the searing welt on my neck and thought of the laughter while I cowered on the diner's floor.

"I'm ready," I told her, and I'm sure the dark light of her eyes was reflected in my own. "Teach me what I need to know."

We spent all night talking, the demoness and I. When my alarm went off in the morning, I was already awake, lying in bed and pondering everything.

"We can wait," she had said, "but why would you want to do that, really? What if you could make them sorry tomorrow? Wouldn't it be...delicious?"

It would be delicious. My hands shook as I shrugged into my clothes. I grabbed a piece of toast and was out the door before Seth came out of his room.

Seth. He was my main concern.

"I don't want to do anything to get him in trouble," I had told her. "None of this blows back on him."

"If we do it correctly, none of it will even blow back on you," she promised me, and I hugged my books to myself as I hurried to school.

My locker was pasted with pictures of last night in the diner. Food in my hair, lying in a puddle on the floor. My jaw clenched, but I thought of today and tried to breathe.

"Use it," the demon whispered in my ear. Her tongue nearly touched my lobe. "This anger? It's so sweet. This hatred? Pure energy. Bathe in it, darling. Dine on it."

The hate felt so good. It bloomed in my stomach, taking root deep inside, unfurling and filling the holes where fear and sadness used to be.

"Isn't that better?" The demon mewled. I nodded. It was. So much better. Anger is easier to feel than sorrow.

"Yes," I said out loud. I felt woozy, drunk on the power. "Better."

"Are you talking to yourself? She's talking to herself!" It was the girl who had given me the black eye days before, a tall brunette with a mean left hook. She looked at my locker and laughed. "What happened here? Stupid girl. Food is for eating, or didn't they teach you that in your foster homes?"

Normally, this is where my eyes would dart around for help. Another student, a teacher, or heck, even God. A guardian angel, a blue fairy. Whatever could help a desperate girl to avoid another beating, another jibe. My bones could take it, but my psyche couldn't.

But today? It was different. I felt warm and detached, floating in a place of misery and pain that she couldn't touch. How could she break my soul when I didn't have any soul left?

"Yessss," the demon said, and her eyes were half closed in ugly rapture. "Shall we make her pay, Luna? Shall we make them all suffer?"

Yes.

"Do you want to taste their pain, Luna? Feel it on your tongue?"

Yes.

My schoolbooks were knocked from my hands and kicked down the hall. Chompers and Rob. The Triller was close behind them.

"Careful," Chompers said in mock earnestness. "Don't ruin her books. She won't be able to afford new ones."

"Maybe we can take up a collection," Triller said. "Like we did earlier to help pay for her daddy's funeral. My father paid lots of money for that."

"Didn't think it would cost so much to put a crazy old man in the ground," Rob said. "You can bury a dead animal for free."

"Maybe it cost extra to take the rope off his neck first."

My hands clenched into fists. "Don't talk about my father."

The kids grinned wider. The demon showed her teeth.

"Why not, Luna? Does it make you sad? Are you going to cry?"

Chompers touched the bandage on my neck. I flinched.

"Looks like that hurts. You really ought to be more careful. Maybe Daddy can kiss it better...oh, ouch. I forgot."

The blooming plant in my stomach turned into a cactus, into rose bushes, into stinging nettles, and everything that spewed thorns and poison.

"Do it," the demoness whispered. She slid her long fingers down Rob's arm, through Chomper's hair, across the Triller's throat. "Let me go, Luna."

My breathing was coming quick and fast. I wanted to hurt, to burn, to maim. My parents had taught me better. They had taught me to be kind. They had shown me how to look for the best in people. But that was before everything, before growing up alone and scared, hearing the doors creak open in the strange houses at night, before learning that demons weren't the only monsters.

"I'm warning you," I managed. It was all I could say. My throat was closing; my body was tense. The demoness writhed where she stood, her skin going gray and savage with want.

"Warning us of what? What's a poor, dirty orphan like you going to do anyway? Just go insane like everyone else in your family? Do it."

"I'm w-warning..."

"Do it."

The demon's eyes were slits. "Do it."

"Do it," Rob said again. He put his hand on my chest and pushed me hard into the locker. "Do it, Luna the Lunatic."

"Don't touch me again," I spat.

He touched me.

I blew.

I opened my mouth and screamed. Screamed long and hard, letting all of the pent-up emotion swirl around me in a firestorm of sound. The demoness leaned her head back and shrieked as well. It was a cacophony of dissonant sound, a song of hatred, the death melody of a siren.

"Give it to me," the demon wailed, lust and need making her voice ragged. I did what she had taught me the night before, taking the very essence of my soul and braiding it into a rope, an ephemeral thing that she could grab and hold on to. She took it, and I pushed myself, the very being of me, through the coil and into her.

She solidified, becoming sharp and defined before my eyes. More than that, she had *power*. I felt my energy slipping away as she became stronger.

"Yes," she cried, and the sheer wantonness of her voice made me turn away. Her unworldly eyes glittered as she turned her gaze on the kids staring at me.

There were no words, only grunts and groans and screams. I saw the demon's razor claws slashing, her teeth tearing into cloth and skin and throats. Blood splashed on the walls and floor. I felt it splatter across my face.

"No," I said weakly, and was horrified at how my voice tremored. I tried to make it stronger. "No!"

"No?" She asked, and she was an animal in a swirl of screams. Flashing, shredding, taking. Students ran down the halls away from her, panicking and trampling each other. I saw a boy fall and not stand up again, his hair running red under the horde of Keds and Adidas.

Bones broke. Teeth were knocked out.

"No!" I screamed and tried to reel my essence back in. She weakened, slowing down, and I tugged with all my might.

"You invited me in," the demon shrieked, and gnashed her gnarled teeth. She was foaming at the mouth, pink from the blood of my classmates, and I was sickened at what I had done.

"You're uninvited, then! Uninvited!" I slipped in blood and went down, scrambling over the still bodies of Rob and Chomper. "Unwelcome! You can't be here. Get out!" The rope of essence between us snapped, and the recoil threw me back hard, smashing my head against the floor.

THERE was beeping and whirring and pain. So much pain. I groaned and tried to lift my hand to my head, but it wouldn't move.

"Luna! You're awake."

I knew that voice. I loved that voice. I turned my head to it and struggled to open my eyes. "Seth?"

Warm hands clasped mine, and I was filled with relief.

"Seth, it's you."

"Of course it is, dork? Who else would it be?"

His face came into focus, and he was smiling everywhere but with his eyes. His eyes were worried.

"How did your test go?" I asked.

His eyebrows shot up, but then he laughed. "I missed it. Something more important came along like my sister being rushed to the ER."

I looked around me and frowned. "Gosh darn it, I'm in the stupid hospital."

"Yeah, and for good reason. The school called and said there had been some wild animal attack in the halls. I'm sorry to tell you…some of your friends are dead."

I felt sick. I thought my stomach was going to revolt. I closed my eyes and breathed in the cool, dry hospital air. It stunk like chemicals.

"Dead?"

"You barely made it. You're pretty banged up yourself. You're lucky, Luna." He ran his hands through his hair. "No, we're lucky. What would I do without you? You're all I have."

I thought of the demon's teeth sinking into skin, the smell of blood, and the pattering as it fell on the school floor. A tear squeezed out from under my lashes.

"No, don't cry. I'm sorry, Luna. I'm so sorry this happened."

"Did anybody see this animal?"

Seth grabbed a tissue and dabbed awkwardly at my face. "Not really, no. It sounded like you saw it first and started screaming, and then it just attacked. What was it?"

I shuddered. "Teeth and claws. A demon. Something dark."

He patted my shoulder awkwardly. "It's okay if you don't remember. You've undergone trauma. That's what the doctor said."

I grabbed at his hand. "It's all my fault, Seth. This happened because of me."

"Why is it your fault?"

The tears came faster now. My heart rate quickened, and an alarm went off. "I wanted them dead," I said, and then I was sobbing. Seth sat on the bed and threw his arms around me. He rocked me like a child and said soothing things into my hair, the kinds of things Mom or Dad would have said.

"It isn't your fault. You had nothing to do with this. Nothing."

The nurse rushed in and made him step back while she checked my vitals. He released my hand, and I wanted nothing more than to hold it again, to hear him comfort me even though I knew it was a lie. It was my fault. The demon couldn't have done it without me, and I gave her permission easily.

People had died. I was the cause of it. I'd have to live with that for the rest of my life.

I turned away to look out the window. The demoness was there, and her unholy eyes met mine.

She smiled. Her teeth were sharp.

"Invite me in," she cooed.

Heart of Fire,
Body of Stone

Italia's stomach twisted in a strange way. It wasn't hurting, necessarily, but grinding. The contractions were different from her earlier Braxton Hicks. Her body had become a mortar and a pestle, a modern-day Baba Yaga, crushing away stone and cervix and everything that kept the baby at bay.

It might be the modern day, certainly, but childbirth is as old as time. Italia had been to plenty of births and had caught every baby, but it was different when your own child was going to burst.

Too soon, she thought. *He has months yet.* The next contract was more than a grind, more than a warning. It pulled her tummy tight like there was a metal band around it, and the sheer force made her gasp. She went up on her bare toes in response, like she was pulled from the sky by a wire, like granny kicking in the air above her young head.

No, she wouldn't think of that now. There wasn't time.

If she had friends, she'd call friends. If the town had a midwife, she would have phoned her. But the hospital was out of the question, and what more could anyone do, really, than Italia could do herself?

She prepared pots of boiling water. She chewed herbs. She bathed in her tub until the water ran red with different fluids, but still the baby wasn't born. Italia paced the floor of her home, her bare skin reflecting the moonlight. She knelt. She walked. She squatted. She walked. She lay on the bed, she knelt on all fours, she curled on the ground, and screamed.

"Come to me."

The voice was earthy, and Italia turned her head toward it. Her dark hair hung in sweaty knots around her face, and her face was sheened with perspiration.

"Italia. Come."

The voice was vaguely familiar. She didn't know if it was her grandmother or God or the butcher from town or the woman who tried to steal her when she was a child. It was made up of wind and sticks and twigs and flowers. It spoke to the blood running through the umbilical cord and dripping from between her legs. She pushed herself slowly to her feet, careful not to slip in the pool of blood and amniotic fluid puddled around her feet. Her legs shook with the effort.

"Outside."

Your child will not be born here, the voice meant. *It won't be born indoors in the dwelling of men. Your child is one of us. It belongs to the wild things, the things of beauty.*

"No," she whispered and wrapped her arms around her stomach. Something supped and writhed inside. "No, I don't want to give it up."

You have no choice.

"I can choose not to go outside," she answered, and tried to tip her chin up even now. Wetness ran down her leg, and a contraction rolled forward, pressing her soul down like the sea.

"Then you will die," the voice said, and it wasn't cruel. It wasn't kind. It simply *was.*

It was this honest *wasness* that made her move. The voice didn't threaten or cajole but told her how things were. It wasn't the way of man but of the earth and the sky. The nature in Italia recognized the truthfulness of what was being said and that primitive, elemental belief in things that stayed just out of sight by the campfire and darted in and out of your peripheral vision. The soul knows things that the mind doesn't, and the body responds to what you cannot fully see. She took a tired step forward. Then another.

The night was chilly, but she didn't pull a coat onto her nude frame. She slid her feet into the heavy boots beside the door and staggered into the night.

"Good girl," the moon said, and took a bite out of her left shoulder. It left a section ringed with teeth and moonlight. The stars themselves zipped down like silver fish, piranhas of the sky, and nipped at her body with sharp teeth. They darted this way and that, tearing away small chunks of flesh on her hands and her arms, her breasts and thighs. Tears ran down her face, and the stars drank them like thirsty butterflies.

Blood pattered from her wounds and ran into the earth. Flowers and briars sprang up behind her where they landed.

The moon took another generous mouthful. Italia's teeth and jawbone shone in the moonlight.

"I'm sorry," the moon whispered gently. "I am a carnivorous thing. And we must take before we can give."

Italia couldn't speak well with her missing cheek and lips. "Take what? Give what?" The wind whistled through the hole in her face, filling her mouth with wonder.

The moon ignored her and turned its face to the sky. "It's almost time," it said.

Italia stumbled, and a series of stars shot down to steady her. They glowed, buzzing in her hair like fireflies and nipping at her wounds. An especially tiny star peeked through her cheek and set her face alight from the inside. It climbed inside the hole and perched on her tongue.

She was cold. The pricking of the stars burned with an icy fire. The red flowers blooming in her path warmed the ground with her body heat. She was shivering badly but continued through the grasses, through the bushes that pulled at her skin and tore great furrows into her body. After tasting her blood, buds unfurled, and berries sprouted.

She walked. She walked. Vines reached out to guide her to the correct path, to cut at her skin with their sharp teeth, to smooth her hair as she passed. She felt the baby dropping lower, lower, lower. Her skin began to stretch and burn. She touched between her legs and felt her baby's head pressing against her fingers.

She fell, exhausted, into the soft grass. The coos of the night flowers filled the air.

"Help me," she whispered. She was speaking to the moon, to the air, to the universe. "Please help me."

"Just breathe," the universe answered back.

There was a second, one perfect moment, where Italia smelled the moon-flowers and heard the stars chattering to each other in their strange, chiming language. The earth held its breath for just that one brief instance, and Italia took a deep breath in. She let that soothing breath out. Her hand fluttered to her abdomen.

The moon opened its mouth and shrieked. It was a piercing scream, sending animals fleeing into the wilds, and it blazed brighter than the sun ever could. Italia screwed her eyes shut and realized that her ruined mouth was also open, was also screaming, as her body tore itself apart. The very stars themselves pulled her eyelids open and swarmed into her eyes, bursting like grapes and veins and filling her eye sockets with light. Her stomach churned and tightened and went soft again, but there was no baby.

There was no child.

"You're going to die," the moon said again, and its voice still wasn't unkind. "Unless…"

"Unless?" Italia asked weakly. She was covered in mud and blood and bruises and sores, surrounded by the flowers that sprung from each blood drop. They dipped their leaves into her wounds and feasted.

"We must take before we can give."

"I have nothing left…to take."

Her eyes rolled back in her head. Her breathing was fast and shallow. The baby was firmly caught inside and would not be budged.

The moon looked at the stars. It looked at the animals and vines. It looked at Italia, who was one of its own. There was another glorious silence.

It snicked its teeth.

This was the sign, the permission they needed. Tendrils of tender flowers and vines wrapped around Italia's body. They raised her carefully into the air, blooming furiously. The stars swirled in the sky, gathering momentum, and then they coursed down to the earth, raining on her body. They burned where they hit, filling her with coldness, searching for each wound, each lesion, and burrowing inside like insects. They rode her blood like disease, shining through her skin as they found exactly where they needed to be. They patched holes. They grew new skin. They healed and cauterized and gathered around her uterus, where they found the heavy, gray baby quite literally made of stone, and they pushed, they pushed, they pushed.

Handmaidens of the moon. Doulas of starlight. The baby slid, wet and cold, onto the soft grass. Its face was carved out of limestone. Its body was small, not fully developed, and it was as thick and heavy as any marble angel you'd see in the cemetery.

Italia's body came to rest gently beside it. The stars left her to perch on the hard, rock hands of her mysterious child.

Out of the two, only one of them began breathing.

The moon looked on.

The Bone-Shaker's Daughter

"**B**reilig. Close your eyes and hold out your hands."

"What kind of silliness is this, Tema? We are not children. There is no time for such games."

Tema laughed, and it was the sound of freedom, of birds flying free through clear skies, nothing at all like their daily lives in Redoubt.

"You're always so serious," she teased. "We have nothing but time. Let's live out our weak little lives here, shall we? Waiting for something to happen, waiting to die. From one day to the next, we wait and wait. Let's fill those hours with a little bit of joy, yes? A little bit of shine. Now, hold out your hands."

Breilig did so. His hands were dark with the sun, scarred and calloused from daily work within the city walls. Not the graceful hands of an elf at all.

He scowled at them.

"Close your eyes, I said. You never listen."

Breilig squeezed his eyes shut, and Tema laughed again.

"There, see? For one second, life isn't so bad, is it? This feeling? It's expectation. It's knowing that something surprising and good waits just around the corner. This, my dear one, is how life is supposed to be."

Tema took his dark hands in her pale ones and slipped something inside his palms.

"Tell me what you're holding. This glorious surprise."

"I don't know."

"Keep your eyes closed and feel, Breilig. Let that brain of yours rest for a second. This isn't about thinking at all. Keep that part out of it."

She slipped her hands from his, sat on a piece of rubble, and watched.

Breilig turned his face to the sun like a blind man. He ran his fingers over the treasures in his hands.

"Smooth. Surprisingly cool. Very light."

"Yes."

"Are they beads?"

"No, they're not."

"Game pieces?"

"No. What do you think they're made out of?"

Breilig felt the pieces between his thumb and forefinger.

"I'd guess wood."

"You'd be wrong."

He sighed.

"Why do you make this so difficult, Tema? Why don't you just tell me?"

"Don't you dare open your eyes! What, and spoil the surprise? What else must you do today, except clearing rubble out of the city streets and worrying about your madness."

He snapped his eyes open and handed the pieces back to Tema. He stood up to go.

She grabbed his hands and pulled them to her.

"I'm so sorry. My friend, please forgive me. I didn't mean to bring something so dear up in such a callous manner. I just…please. I'm trying to help. I only want you to be happy."

He took a deep breath.

"I know you do. I know I spend time worrying when I could be spending it doing other things." He closed his eyes again and held out his hand. "Let's try it again, yes?"

Tema grinned and swept the tiny white pieces out of the dust. She dropped them into his palm.

"You know what these are. I want you to feel it. They'll call out to you. You'll feel it deep inside, darling. Let me know when you do."

Breilig held the small pieces of…

"Stone?"

"Not stone."

...*not* stone in one hand and caressed them with the other.

"You're an elf. You're in touch with all this deep inside. Just let yourself realize it."

Breilig took a deep breath and held the pieces. There was something to them.

"A deepness."

"Yes."

He hadn't realized he'd said it out loud, but there it was. A deepness. A sense of vitality. He held the pieces and knew they were important, somehow, in a way that all life was important, certainly, but...

All life. That was it. He had it.

"It's bone," he said, opening his eyes and grinning. "The pieces are made out of bone."

Tema smiled back at him.

"Yes! I knew you'd be able to tell. What do you think of them?"

His eyebrows immediately furrowed, his smile dropping away.

"Is that safe? You know, with the undead. Does it not invite danger to have their bones lying around?"

Tema shook her head and collected the small pieces from him.

"It's safe. Do you think I'd be messing around with something that wouldn't be? That I leap onto the corpse-men's cart and take whatever I can find? Of course not. Once the body is reduced to bone, it catches the sun, which soothes the soul. But these pieces are meant for music. Let me show you."

She took a small, dried gourd from a pocket hidden inside her dress and dropped the bits of bone inside.

"Now shake it," she said, and handed it to the elf.

He shook his head.

"No. I don't want to invite something."

Tema rolled her eyes.

"You won't invite anything except for a little amusement, and heavens knows you don't want *that* around."

She shook the gourd, and the round balls of bone rattled gently.

"Softly," she said, and shook the gourd in a light rhythm. "Hear that? It's not conjuring up hordes of undead, is it? Are your elders coming after you for some unforgiven slight? No. It's music. Music, Breilig, and it's a wonderful thing! Do you feel your heart fly?"

He wanted to say he did. He wanted to say that her confidence gave him strength, that seeing her creating music out of old bones was the most meaningful experience of his life. She started to hum and dance the delicate, elegant ways of her people, bending and weaving before him like a plant moving in the wind and stream.

But he couldn't say these things. He felt the weight of his elven blood and the grandeur they had once experienced. That greatness was there, deep inside, riding around his circulatory system like his familial madness, and then he was ashamed again, looking at his soft shoes covered in dust and scat and filthy puddles of water that made up the alleyways of Redoubt.

"We are nothing," he whispered, and the sheer starkness of it made him ball up his fists. "We were made for more than this."

Tema stopped dancing, and the sound and beauty of the morning were gone. She studied Breilig carefully before putting the gourd back into the folds of her robe.

"We escaped for a minute, didn't we," she said. It wasn't a question but a fact. She pushed her fine hair out of her eyes and turned her lips up, but the smile wouldn't come. "For just a second, we were somewhere else, you and I. And then you were somewhere else, all alone."

"I was here," he said. He refused to look at her. "Always here. There's nowhere else for me to be. Nowhere to escape to."

He stood there, tall and broken. Scarred inside and out. Tema reached out and took his hand. She held it in hers and then brought it to her lips.

"How long have we known each other?" She asked him. Her pale eyes were full of moons and stars and secrets. He had looked at those eyes his whole life, wondering what swam in them.

"Always," he answered. "We've known each other always. Since before time, I sometimes think."

"How many years have I sneaked away from my father to come visit you? To ask about your ways and run my fingers through your dark hair and escape, however briefly, from the life of a bone-shaker's daughter?"

"Many."

"And you, Breilig. How many years have you crept away from your people, slipping through the alleyways and past the marketplace to meet me? To sit on the walls of the city and watch the undead howl outside, to talk about despair and beauty and all the things that make life worth living? How many?"

"Many."

"Many, and many, and many again. And, if the Gods allow, even more years."

"Perhaps the Gods will have pity, and there will be no more years at all. The dead will overcome all of us. We won't be able to dump them outside of the walls fast enough. It will be the end to civilization that already ended years ago."

Tema's eyes, full of stars and moons earlier, began to fill with storms and lightning and the angry, shaking spears of her people. She slipped her hands from his and put them on her hips, standing upright and proud and strong, although she still only hit his shoulders.

"Breilig, son of Ca'an, I will not hear you speak in such a manner! Cease feeling sorry for yourself! There is life here. It may not be a very easy life, but it's life, and it is worth fighting for. Every morning, I arise and see the sun. Yes, I see rats and refuse and children who have starved through the night. I see another loved one thrown on the corpse-men's cart to be taken away before she can rise and harm us all. I see the same things you see, and what's more, I see a wonderful, caring elf wallowing in his own sadness when he could be using his time to create something. Make something beautiful. Make life worth living for somebody else if not for yourself. Make an effort for me. I spent time harvesting and grinding, breaking and polishing this bone to make music for you. For just a brief time, I wanted you to think of something besides the disgrace and shame of your people. I don't care about that. I defy my father and spend time with you because I see something of value inside of you. Don't you dare disrespect that! Don't tell me my time and my love is wasted because some silly, morose, straw-for-brains elf can't see outside of himself for one moment. Don't you dare!"

She turned and fled, the sounds of chiming bells and rattling bone fleeing with her. She disappeared into the shadows of the city.

Her time and her...love? Breilig thought. Never had she been so bold. Never had she spoken of something so blasphemous to her people. Yet it was so thrilling to his heart. Words he thought he would never hear and would certainly never dare speak first.

He turned back to the wall, watching the crowds of risen dead clamoring and pushing their faces against each other. Such a sea of inhumanity, but he thought of Tema's tearful retreat, of her words, and he smiled.

TEMA stumbled through the crowded alleyway, pushing her way through the nameless, faceless people that blocked her path. That stupid elf. Stupid her for falling in love with him years ago when she knew so much better. Maybe finally saying something was the right thing to do, however. It would make him take her seriously for once. It would douse her in enough shame to leave him behind and focus on a more agreeable future.

She turned a corner and ran smack into a tall brick of a man the size of a doorway. The air was knocked out of her, and she fell into the street's filth.

"Look where you're going," the man growled, but his face changed when he saw the young woman sprawled on the ground. He reached down and hauled her to her feet.

"Th-thank you," she managed, still out of breath. She used the sleeve of her robe to wipe her tears away. She flushed and stared at the ground. "I'm sorry."

"Watch where you're going, miss. It's dangerous."

"I didn't mean to run into you, sir. I wasn't–"

"No, look," he said and pointed. Tema stood on her tiptoes to see what he meant.

"The old woman?" She asked.

"She refuses to give up her dead."

"But she can't do that."

"No, she can't."

The man's voice sounded heavy, tired, and sorrowful, like every other person in Redoubt. She wanted to shake him, tell him to fight for his life, but after what had just happened with Breilig, she felt weary and sorrowful as well.

An old woman whose face must have been gentle once was clinging to the body of a man. The way she curled her fingers into his clothing told her that he must have been her son.

"Don't take him from me," she screamed. "I can't let him go like this?"

A slim man with scars across his face gently touched her shoulder. She shook it off and spat at him.

"You know the ways, Hannah. You know this must be. We can't allow him to stay."

"He's all I have," she wailed, and Tema's heart hurt at the sound of it. "Don't take away the only thing I have."

"Hannah, he's gone. He's already dead. Now we just need–"

Tema heard the bells of the Undertakers. The corpse-men as they came near. The sound was loud, jarring, painful, and unholy.

"No," the old woman said, and threw herself atop her son's body again. "They're coming to take him!"

"They must take him. You know there is no other choice."

"He's a good boy. A sweet boy. He would never hurt anybody. That isn't his way."

The man shook his head.

"My wife was good, too. Never hurt a soul when she was alive. But after death, she wasn't herself anymore. None of them are. This thing, this curse, it's stronger than we are. If it was a matter of will, we wouldn't all be walled up in this stinking city, would we?"

Tema hid behind the tall man she had run into.

"Doesn't she know it's better to give the body willingly?"

"Love blinds us when it comes to our dead," he answered. "Common sense doesn't always prevail."

The first of the corpse-men came by. He was shaped like a barrel and most likely had just as much ale in him most nights. Who wouldn't, seeing what he had seen?

"Bring me your dead," he called, and his voice was hoarse and weary behind the words. He was a man who had said this phrase far too many times. "Bring me your dead."

"Here," the man called and easily pulled the old woman away. Her scream sounded like death itself. "We have one here."

The rest of the corpse-men arrived, big men with swords and spears and clubs. Two ragged horses dragged an iron gate behind them, with bodies flung on top.

Two of the corpse-men wordlessly grabbed the body and tossed it with the others. It settled heavily, indiscreetly, its leg turning at an odd angle.

"My boy," shrieked the old woman as she was held back. "My son."

"We all must deal with loss," the barrel-shaped man said and turned. "Bring me your dead," he called, and the grim parade passed on.

"I feel sorry for her," Tema whispered to the tall man, but he quickly held out his hand.

"Look," he said, and something in his tone chilled her, made her shiver all the way down to her thin fabric slippers. A wrongness crept through the air, dug its way to her marrow, and she faintly wondered if she'd be sick.

The son's body began to move.

Just a little, at first, so slowly that Tema wondered if she hadn't really seen it at all. A curl of the fingers. A jostle of the leg.

But then the head turned slowly, much farther than any neck should allow it, and the snap of bone didn't sound clean like her father's work but a dark, loathsome thing.

"Quickly," shouted one of the Undertakers, and he roughly pushed the crowd aside while two other men rushed the cart.

The old woman screamed and stepped in front of them. They slowed, but only barely, shoving her out of their path. She was nothing more than sinew and linen. An ancient relic from old times. She stood between them and the thing that was now growing strong, now scuttling from the cart like a thing only seen in the depths of hell, now climbing the side of the building like a hissing lizard.

That's the sight that would stay with Tema for all her days. The man with his head turned around completely backward, scaling the wall like an insect, his tongue hanging from his dislocated jaw.

"Move, girl!" The tall man pushed her back toward the way she had come when she had fled Breilig. "Run!"

She couldn't move. She couldn't do anything more than stand and stare as the now-alive dead thing zipped toward her. How it moved so fast, she didn't know. What unholy arcana made it stick to the walls like that, she would never be able to say, but right now, all that mattered was that she was screaming at her feet to run, and they simply couldn't do so.

She closed her eyes. Covered her face so the last thing she saw would be her bone-shaker's fingers instead of some crazy woman's dead son.

There were roars and shouts. Thuds, and the sound of steel against stone. The old woman shrieked again until suddenly, her voice cut off in a way that made Tema drop a hand to her throat without thinking.

"Look," the tall man said, and grabbed Tema roughly by the shoulders. "They subdued it. Hacked it apart. Next, they'll throw it over the walls before it has a chance to do anything again."

"Move," shouted the head corpse-man, and the cart jangled and clanged unmusically as it rolled forward. Tema turned her face away from the dismembered limbs on the rusty iron gate and the shine of fresh blood on the Undertaker's weapons.

Corpses didn't bleed. She knew that. She continued to look away from the carnage but instead looked at where the old woman had been standing.

"It's a shame," the tall man said, "but she needed to let him go. We have to release the dead."

"And remember the living," Tema said, but the man had already moved on. She heard chickens and running feet, vendors hawking their wares, and the corpse-men's bells fading into the distance. Just another day in the city, trying to find a reason to stay alive.

"Tema."

She heard her name and turned. There stood her reason right in front of her.

"Are you all right?" Breilig asked. He dusted the dirt from her clothes and briefly took her hand before pulling away. "I saw what happened. I couldn't get here fast enough."

"Do you ever feel," she asked him a bit dazedly, "that maybe we spend our time on trivial things when something very important is right in front of us?"

"I do," he said, and this time, when he took her hand, he didn't let go.

BREILIG spent that night with Tema and several after. They had been together since they were children, but only covertly and never in such an intimate way.

"A human and an elf?" He mused, tracing ancient Elvin words on her bare shoulder with his finger. "Father wouldn't stand for it, of course. How am I to," he deepened his voice to impersonate his father, "restore the former glory of our race without a proper heir?"

Tema shrugged.

"I would like children, too. I always thought I would have them. But in the end, I need to choose what is best for me, Breilig, and that is you. Children would be a joy. But they would also be a concern and a heartache. I want more than anything to be yours and have your child, but that cannot be. So, do I choose you, without children, or life without you? It's no choice, really."

She kissed him, and her mouth was a wonder. He wondered why he had taken so long to sample it.

Fear. Shame. All the heavy words he loathed to think of.

"Darling, I'm losing you. Where are you going?"

"I'm here," he said and smiled. "I'm right here."

"Exactly where you're supposed to be, yes?"

"Yes."

"Stay with me," she said, and wrapped her arms around his neck. She laced her fingers in his dark hair. "Promise me that, my brooding elf. Can you?"

"I will," he said. "There's nothing I want more."

When he returned home, he crept into the scant wooden hovel like a child who had done something wrong.

"Where have you been?" His father demanded. "You've been gone for days!"

"I think I have discovered love, Father," Breilig said, but his father turned away.

"We have no time for such silly trivialities. You were with that whore, weren't you? The human girl."

"She is no such thing, and you will never speak of her in such a way again."

"My son," his father said, and his eyes shone with an intensity that belied his sanity, "You know what you must do. Bring honor to this once proud race. We can be great again."

"Father."

"And not just for me. For all your brothers and sisters. All of your people who are forced to bear the humiliation of our fall."

"I love Tema. That won't change. She's always understood me."

"A human woman cannot bear an elf child. You would provide no heir. Our line would stop."

"I want to marry her."

His father glared at him.

"I wouldn't begrudge you a dalliance with this human girl. But you will marry one of your own and sire a leader for our people. We are not meant to live scrubbing filth off the streets. We were destined for greatness, and you will make that possible, my son. A bride has already been chosen for you."

Breilig opened his mouth to argue, but his father was already walking away, leaning heavily on his staff for support.

"She'll be presented to you this evening. I suggest you clean up. Your bride won't want to smell another woman on you, no matter how base this human may be."

Breilig went about his day, scavenging for food, thinking about Tema's soft, white hands. No other fingers could ever compare. The way she created music this morning to move his soul...he washed the stench of Redoubt from his skin and dressed into clean linens with a sigh. His father was old, and it would not harm him to please the old man and at least meet the girl.

She smelled of sunlight. She stood tall and slim, her dark hair pulled back and pinned with vines and flowers somehow found within the city walls. She had dark eyes full of secrets that he found himself wanting to learn. Her eyes matched his own.

"My name is Pristlin," she said, and dipped her head briefly. He did the same. Stood. Didn't know what to say.

Pristlin licked her lips.

"Your father told me...he said that..." She took a deep breath. "Your father told me that you are to be my groom. If this pleases you, of course."

Still, Breilig stared.

"I know how strange this must be for you," she continued. "It's certainly strange for me. But I believe in this race and our strength. I believe we can band together and achieve our former glory. Be powerful again. I believe we can do this, you and I."

She took his hand in both of hers. Her fingers were long and tan. They intertwined beautifully within his. She held them to her breast, and her eyes glowed with a passion that made him catch his breath. Something moved within his soul.

"Will you accept me, Breilig, son of Ca'an? Allow me to be your wife, and together, we will raise the new Elvin King of Redoubt?"

She was slim where Tema was round. Lean where Tema was soft. Elegant where Tema now seemed like a clumsy colt, frolicking through the streets without a care. Pristlin was a woman concerned about the resurgence of their people. She wouldn't tell him not to worry. She wouldn't think he was being far too serious.

"Do you really believe we can raise our child to greatness?" He asked.

Her beautiful eyes shone, and Breilig swallowed hard.

"Oh, I do. There's no doubt in my mind that we will. I hope this isn't too forward, but when I see you like this and hold your hands in mine, I feel so much hope. Hope, Breilig. Here. Isn't that exquisite? Isn't it a thing of wonder?"

"It is, indeed," he agreed, and then he smiled at her. A full smile, unchecked. She smiled back, and he laughed.

"What's so funny?" She asked him, her wonderful eyes searching his, her beautiful smile not faltering in the least.

"I think this must be that feeling you mentioned, my dear. This might be hope."

Her smile grew even wider, but then color touched her cheeks. He was charmed. It was the loveliest thing he had ever seen. He desired to see it a hundred times. A hundred times a hundred.

"Then do you think that, just perhaps, you might choose to take me as your wife?"

He clasped her hands and brought them to his lips.

"With pleasure," he murmured. He saw their future together. Their children playing in a clean land with trees and flowers and no city walls ever to be seen. "I will give you anything you desire."

She lowered her eyelids shyly.

"I hope that in time, sir, you will give me your heart."

Breilig tipped her face back so she would meet his eyes.

"My love," he said truthfully, "I think that you already have it."

Their wedding date came quickly. Tema stole away with several pieces of beautiful cloth her father wouldn't miss. It was made into a dress that suited Pristlin's tall, delicate frame and golden coloring.

"What a dear you are to do this for me," Pristlin exclaimed, and kissed Tema on the cheek.

"Yes, well, anything for Breilig. He's my best friend," Tema said. Her white fingers twisted around in her dress.

"Yes, he told me all about how you were sweet childhood friends. I'm so glad he had you while growing up."

"So was I," Tema said, and then she excused herself to run to the city wall. Breilig and his new bride wrapped their hands together and said their vows in the old Elven tongue. Tema sat on the filthy stone wall and cried, her tears falling on her short, pasty human hands.

Time is a wicked thing, uncaring and forlorn, and it stops for no one. Years passed, and Breilig, his eyes sparking with madness behind the irises, and pretty Pristlin conceived their first child. He was a boy, a strong, healthy heir, and from the day of his birth, he was the crowning glory of the elves.

He was dark and quick, sensitive and strong. He was taught manners, skills, and just enough ruthlessness to ensure his success. His black curls licked around his ears, just like his father's.

His smile? That was his mother's, and it tore Tema apart every time she saw it.

Breilig bedded her occasionally when he was upset or tired, or the weight of his responsibility was too much to bear.

"Shhh," Tema would say, brushing his hair out as they hid away. "You are not Breilig, son of Ca'an, Husband of Pristlin, Father of The Elven Heir to me. You are only my dear friend, my only love, and always have been. Peace. Think of us tonight and nothing more."

But he couldn't think of Tema without thinking of her father and his arrogance. Or of his finery and the fact that he unknowingly provided scraps to clothe Breilig's bride on their wedding day. He lost himself in this arrogant man's daughter and quietly delighted in the horror he knew it would bring if Tema's father ever found out.

One afternoon, Tema was sitting on one of the walls protecting Redoubt. She was humming, using a small knife to carve holes in a bleached piece of bone.

"Hello, Tema," Pristlin said quietly. She gathered her rough clothes around her and peered over the wall. "Oh, it's certainly high. Aren't you ever afraid you'll fall?"

"Not at all," Tema answered. She didn't look up but continued carving. "And if I did, what of it? We'll all end up outside the walls, eventually."

Pristlin brought her finger to her lips, chewing her nail. It wasn't something that Tema had ever seen her do, so she put her carving down.

"Is something bothering you, Pristlin?"

"No. Well, yes. Yes, it is."

Tema patted the wall beside her.

"Sit and talk with me. Would you like to carve? I have another piece of bone."

Pristlin cautiously climbed onto the wall, holding Tema's hand. After she was settled, Tema handed her a second piece of bone and a small knife.

"What shall I do with it?" Pristlin asked.

"Whatever your soul sings to you. Feel the life that used to be there. Draw it out. It's its own form of arcana."

Pristlin chipped away at the bone.

"I want to talk to you about my husband."

"I suppose you do."

"I want to know what he means to you, Tema."

Tema looked out at the clear sky over the crowded undead that seethed below.

"He means everything to me, I suppose," she said. "He was my sun. His light touched my life like the sun touches the trees outside, the frightening allies, even the dead below. He made things bearable."

"And now that you no longer feel his light?"

Tema shrugged, smiling bitterly down at the instrument she carved.

"Perhaps life isn't quite as bearable as it was before. But we survive. Now listen to this."

She put the newly created bone flute to her lips and blew. It created a haunting sound that moved the very blood in her veins.

"Mournful," Pristlin said.

"Bone flutes usually are. But they're strong, too." She turned to Pristlin. "I'm the Bone-Shaker's daughter. Do you know what that means?"

"I'm not that familiar with humans, no. Tell me."

Tema's pale eyes, so different from Pristlin's dark ones, filled with tears.

"It means that we take scraps, pieces of others. We take their bones before they are tossed from the city walls and make something of them. Instruments, mostly, but sometimes knives. Beads. Pieces for our hair. Useful things. Beautiful things. I polish these bones until my fingers bleed to change them from a thing of horrors to something that brings joy. Even a second of joy is worth all the work."

"It sounds selfless."

"It is," Tema said, and realized her voice was raising. She lowered it. "It is. All my life has been spent trying to give others a chance at peace. Like Breilig. I don't know if you've seen what you've done to him."

"What I've done to him?" Pristlin was taken aback. "What have I *done* to him?"

Tema stood on the wall and began to pace.

"You've changed him into something darker than he was before. He seldom smiles, and when he does, it's an ugly thing. He's so obsessed with your son and his pure blood—"

"Don't you mention our son."

"—that he's forgotten who he used to be. He's forgotten about anyone but himself."

"That's untrue," Pristlin cried. Her hands shook in her lap, holding far too hard to the bone and knife. "He thinks of our people all of the time. But do you know who he doesn't think about? He doesn't think about you, Tema. I know it hurts, but you must accept it. You only hold him back. Let him go."

"I can't let him go. Don't you see he's all I have? The only thing I ever wanted for myself?"

Pristlin's eyes sparked.

"You will let him go, or I will make you. Do you understand? You don't know what I'm capable of."

With one quick pull, Tema ran her knife across Pristlin's throat and then pushed her from the wall. The elf didn't make a single sound as she fell. The wandering dead fell upon her body, tearing and raking and feasting.

Tema turned away and cleaned her knife.

"You don't know what I'm capable of, either," she said aloud. "And I'm tired of sating myself on other people's scraps."

She tossed the bone flute down to Pristlin's ravaged body.

BREILIG mourned the disappearance of his wife. He didn't eat or sleep but searched Redoubt by foot, walking for days as he searched the inner areas, the orchards, asking clan after clan, race after race, if they had perhaps seen a beautiful elf maiden pass by.

"Must have been killed if she's missing," a dwarf told him, his mustaches drooping in sorrow. "Sorry to hear it."

Tema stopped by his ratty room with a bone bowl full of hot broth.

"You need to eat something," she told him. Her voice was soft as she placed the bowl before him. "If not for yourself, then for your son. He needs you."

"He needs his mother."

Tema's pale eyes normally held the moon and stars. Today they held worry.

"He doesn't have his mother. She left for whatever reason. He needs you, darling. You must be strong for him."

"I can't." His eyes nearly pinwheeled in his head as he looked at her. "You do it, Tema. Pretend he's our child, yours and mine. Remember when we thought we had to choose? Each other or a child?" He laughed, and the sound was far too wild, much too loud. Tema drew back from him.

"I don't like seeing you this way," she said, and Breilig howled.

"Be strong. Calm down. Be a father. Be a leader. Everybody wants something from me," he growled, and his voice changed into something feral and ugly. "Leave me alone." He hurled the soup, and the bowl crashed against the wall. "Leave me be!"

Tema turned and fled into the night.

BREILIG slipped into a fever that wouldn't loosen its grasp on him. He saw his wife bending over his bed, speaking to him. She told him stories of the old ways, of their former glory.

"It will come again, my husband," she whispered to him. Her voice was like rain on parched roots. "You and our son will raise our people to glory again."

After the fever broke, he lay weak and stinking upon the rags he used for a bed. He called feebly for his son, but nobody came to his door.

"Pristlin? Tema?"

He stood and stumbled, catching himself on a rough piece of wood that he used for a table. A too-soft apple was there, and he took a bite. Another. He realized the flesh was delicious, and the juice was heaven on his tongue.

He staggered into the alleyway. Life flowed around him, almost as perceptible as death usually was. A woman walked by with flowers in her hair. A child pranced past with a crudely carved toy.

He followed the woman and child slowly and for no reason. He was awake. He was wandering. He breathed in the air, and it was full of dust and smoke, brick and sewage. He tasted traces of honey and freshly baked bread, the sweat of the laborers and the galley girls.

He found himself near the wall where he used to meet Tema, and it was no surprise to him that she was there.

"Tema," he breathed and sat down heavily next to her. "It has been days since I saw you last."

"Weeks," she said. She didn't face him but stared out into the desolate lands beyond the city.

"I'm sorry for how I was to you. You didn't deserve it. You've done nothing but be a friend."

"Friend," she repeated, and the way she said the word, high and tuneless, made Breilig give her a second glance.

"Are you well, my dear one?" He asked her.

She laughed, and it reminded him of the corpse-men's bells, such a cacophony of sound. The wrongness made his stomach tighten, and he reached for her.

"Don't touch me," she hissed, and Breilig drew his hand back in surprise.

"You aren't well," he said, and he wondered briefly what he should do. If his family's madness had managed to touch his lover or if she had been touched by the unholy and undead. He wondered if he should call for help or perhaps flee, but then he saw the tears on her cheeks and he was immediately ashamed.

"I have wronged you," he said quietly, "and for that I am—"

"Does your every sentence begin with the word *I,* Breilig? Is that all you can think of? Yourself?"

Her words were cutting. The voice didn't even sound like hers, but shrill and dead, choked out of her throat by emotions not of her own.

"I didn't mean—"

"And there you go again. It's always about you. Your honor, your people. Your wife, your child. But what about me? I always loved you, and you never saw. Then when I told you, you threw me away as soon as an elf maiden came along."

"It wasn't right."

"No, it wasn't. But I forgave you because that's what you do for the ones you love. *Love,* Breilig. Not tolerate or use. Those are different things entirely."

The wailing of the undead grew louder. They were gathered at the base of the wall, pushing against the stone and iron. Tema looked down at them with pity.

"They are my children," she said sadly. "They are the ones we will join. I will, you will. All of us, eventually. Whether the walls fall or the undead overrun us from the inside out, this is how it will be. You must see it as surely as I do."

"But what is it that you always say? Every second of hope or joy is worth it? Have you forgotten that?"

"You never believed it," she said. "Don't pretend to believe it now."

She pulled a long bone flute from her billowing sleeve. It shone in the last rays of the sun, so beautiful and intricately carved that he gasped.

"You like it?" She asked and smiled. Her smile was sweet and genuine and reminded him of all the smiles they had shared since childhood. "It's my greatest treasure. A true thing of beauty. Shall I play for you?"

"Yes," he breathed.

She yelled down at the frenzied masses outside of the walls.

"I'll play for you, too, shall I?"

Her song was soft and sweet. The clearness through the flute of bone filled Breilig with joy and loss. Sorrow and whimsy. He wanted to weep and sing and dance.

"Your wife is down there," Tema said, and put the flute back to her lips.

"What is that?" He asked her. "I must have heard you incorrectly."

"I see her sometimes. A flash of her hair, a bit of fabric from her clothes. Of course, it could be my mind playing tricks on me, but I like to think it's her. I play for her, you know."

The song she played was melancholy. He remembered binding hands with his bride and promising to be by her side forever.

"Is this what forever means?" He wondered aloud.

"Do you know what else I can do?"

She stood on the wall, her back against the blazing sunset as it turned the clouds orange. She was a thing of glory, then. The Bone-Shaker's Daughter. Creator of magic, unifier of souls. Breilig had never seen anything so wondrous or so terrifying. Her hair turned orange in the fading light. She was aflame.

"What else can you do?" He was almost afraid to ask.

She bared her teeth in what might have passed for a smile, but Breilig realized with a coldness that reached into his belly that she wasn't really there at all. Her eyes took in nothing and everything. Instead of moonbeams, they held broken belongings and shattered pottery and slinking things with sharp teeth. They held the madness he had always feared in himself. Was he mad, and she reflected it back, or was she mad, and he drew it into himself?

"How would you like not to be alone anymore? To be a family again. With me, with your wife, your son, or whoever you choose. Your father, perhaps? The man down the alley who sells trinkets and false gems? Or your mother, long dead. How would that be?"

"I don't understand what you're saying."

"I can make them come."

She put the flute to her lips, a long, straight flute, something so very precious and dear about it, and she played. Her fingers moved quickly, stirring the blood in his body until it moved faster, cleaner. He wanted to get up. He wanted to snap a bone in half with his jaws, wanted to leap off the wall into the melee below, wanted to succumb to love and lust and murder all in one moment.

The dead below howled and surged, a frenzy of motion. Lightning cracked down among them, zipping from body to body. Some cried out with voices that sounded strangely human. Others had scales as though they were fish.

"They're attracted to the music," Breilig realized. He leaned over and saw the masses were starting to hurl themselves more forcefully against the wall.

"No," he shouted. "You mustn't stir them up."

The sun came out of the clouds and silhouetted Tema so sharply that Breilig threw his hand up to shield his face.

"They come. They climb. I call, and they listen," Tema said between notes. Riled undead began to scale the walls. Unholy screams and hisses rose from the city around them as corpses reanimated. He heard men calling each other to arms, screaming for their weapons, and begging the corpse-men to aid them.

"The dead call to the dead," Tema said and laughed. She laughed and wiped away tears, and Breilig saw madness as he had always feared it.

"It isn't time for us to all be dead," he said. "Please, stop this. We can still fight."

"There's nothing left to fight for," she screamed, and she let the flute fall limply at her side. "Nothing, Breilig. You were what I lived for. You were my sunlight."

"I can still be your sunlight if that's what you want," he pleaded. "Stay with me. Help me raise my son. I know you feel despair now, but we can change it."

Tema closed her eyes.

"Your son. Such a beautiful boy."

"He is. And he's probably scared. He lost his mother and probably thought he was losing his father, too. But he can have both of us, you and me. We can take care of him. But first, I need to find him. Will you help me?"

"I know where he is."

She held her hand out, and Breilig took it. Instead of helping her off the wall, she pulled him onto it.

"He's free," she said, and pulled him to face the sunset together. "Free and happy, without burden or sorrow. He's with his mother and soon his father and Tema."

Breilig's golden skin paled. Tema nodded.

"You...you saw him go?" He asked.

Tema laced her white fingers with his dark ones.

"He went quietly and without pain. Afterward, I did as my father would have me do. I turned his tragedy into a thing of joy. And for a moment, we all felt that joy, didn't we?"

She smiled brokenly and handed him the flute. The bone was warm and beautiful and heartbreakingly familiar.

"Oh gods," he whispered.

She pressed her mouth to his and spoke against his lips.

"They don't exist."

She wrapped her arms around him and let them fall.

This Broken Love Story

She loves him in pieces, in separate parts. A sliver of this, a morsel of that. He is tasty and delicious, and she savors him bit by bit by bit. There could always be enough to go around, maybe. If she is careful. If she only sups a little at a time, just enough to whet her taste. If she keeps her hunger sharp enough to appreciate but never to devour whole. She keeps a spare collarbone in her back pocket. She warms her hands on it and nibbles it delicately with sharp teeth. When the desire becomes too strong, she puts it away again. Anything else would be untoward. Anything else would be far too terrifying.

He doesn't nibble, or take dainty sips, or deny himself. He takes mouthfuls of bone, of meat, of soul. When you're starving, it's difficult to hold back. When the gas tank or stomach or heart is empty, nipping away at a brandy snifter is ineffectual. Better to gulp great big lungfuls before it's gone. Take the loss. Take the teasing. Take it before it's rescinded, or before he grows tired of the game, or before they both wake up and realize that this isn't reality.

"It isn't ideal," she murmurs, mouthing the underside of his jaw. Just enough for a taste. Just enough to keep the bloodlust at bay.

"It isn't ideal," he agrees, and when he pulls away, she's missing her right shoulder and most of her ribs.

This story is broken, and they both know it. But it is their story. It is still a story of love.

Water
Thy Bones

There's a loveliness to bones. Their shape. Their weight. Their strength and fragility.

A body uses them to run. Uses them to stand timidly against a wall. They hold a person upright if they're working correctly. They're a framework for an entire system, a complete body, and the significance of that is very nearly overwhelming.

Yet, at the same time, bones are so exceptionally frail. They can be broken. Sawed through. Pulverized. Bleached. Painted. Kept. Valued. Destroyed.

Remembered.

Taken.

Oh, yes, they can be taken. While the victim still hangs on them, a skin-sack of meat. Veins still connect, blood still curries oxygen back and forth like it's a precious thing, and at that point, it still is.

That's when their beauty becomes something real. When bone is exposed to the air for the first time, the marrow gasps as it breathes in deep. The rest of it, the tissue, gristle, and muscle, is pulled away, and the skeleton is allowed to be free.

That's the part Michael Harrison liked the best. Peeling away the stinking red refuse and letting the white parts glitter and shine through. It's the most awe-inspiring kind of birth, the most natural. Give all of us time, and nature will do it for us. But sometimes, nature needs a push.

NIKILIE was a strong, beautiful thing. She suffered from pain that pressed behind her eyes like delphiniums, but she still got out of bed and moved around the world as living things do. Her tongue was red, and her eyes the warmest of browns. Eyes you could fall into, dark skin smooth as butter. It invited the unwanted stares and hands of men and women everywhere she went. At least it used to until she started taking razor blades and serrated knives to her body in the dim quiet of her bathroom.

"You're so lovely, Nikilie," friends told her. She cut and sawed at the skin on her thigh, leaving tight, slim lines beaded with blood. Jewels on the skin of a goddess. That was beauty. That was purity right there.

"Baby, come here." Cat calls on the street, and lascivious glances turned into something genteel, something finer under her blade.

"I want you," her boss told her behind his office door. He was one of many, simply another person abusing authority. His hand slid up and under her shirt. "A gorgeous woman such as yourself should never be lonely."

"I never am," she replied, but her whispers disappeared under the sound of fabric ripping, her favorite top turned into refuse. Her words, though, shone as she carved them into her skin in the silence of night.

Never lonely. Never. Never, never, never.

Fabric can be rent, and so can skin, but at least she made the choice this time. Pried under the coating. She saw what lay underneath.

She wasn't simply her face or her skin or the smooth Island accent of her words. She was herself. Nikilie. She was what ran under her skin, not merely the features built out of it. She wanted somebody who would love her from the inside out.

The first time Michael saw Nikilie, he stopped and stared at the aggressive way her skull pressed against the paper-thin skin of her face. She pursed her lips and worked her jaw, the bones moving in such a way that Michael had to stifle a groan.

"What is your name?" He asked her. She sat on the hard, plastic seat of the subway, an exotic flower growing from the cracks in the pavement. He stood next to her, holding loosely to the straps above.

"Stacee," she said, not meeting his eyes.

"I don't blame you for lying. I'm a stranger on the subway. My intentions may not be honorable."

Her eyes flicked up, then warm and wet. He saw moss and flowers and lovely things growing in their humidity. A tropical paradise.

"You're not from New York," he said and then blushed.

This made her laugh, and she scratched at her wrist.

"No, I'm not. But you are. And yet, you're easily embarrassed. How can this be?"

He shrugged, grinning, and she smiled back. Beautiful white teeth, strong, and one overlapped the other just a bit. Perfection.

He wanted to run his fingers across them. He wished to wear them as pearls.

"I'm awkward," he said, and lifted his shoulders again. A *what can I do?* gesture. The self-realization of a different man. "I say what I think instead of saying what I should. I don't mean to make people uncomfortable. I just do. I'm no good at small talk."

"Why is that? You seem to realize it makes it difficult to fit in."

The subway's movement shook them, making him dance and sway with unusual grace. His suit coat looked like bird feathers. He was something exotic, something from the islands, and for a second, a look of recognition and delight shone from Nikilie's eyes. *Ah, yes,* her eyes seemed to say. *This is something I've seen before.*

"Life is too short, I suppose," he answered. "There seems to be so little time. Yet we're supposed to dance around this and barely mention that. I don't understand it. In two minutes, I'll step off this platform and will most likely never see you again, so why shouldn't I say what I'm thinking instead of wasting that time with faux pleasantries?"

"And what are you thinking?"

He could read her expectations in the lift of her brow, in the tiredness that suddenly came into her eyes. *You're beautiful. Could we go out for coffee?* Or perhaps, *what an exquisite face you have.* Something about her face, her lips, her eyes. About her body or long, long limbs. But he had caught sight of the black, healed skin on her wrists, under her bangles, and when her shirt fell off her shoulder just a bit before she automatically pushed it back up, he saw the fresher wounds there.

"Your bones," he said, and gestured with one hand. "Your elbows and knees. The things that make you *you,* underneath everything else. I've never seen anything more striking."

The subway stopped, and Michael was gone in a flurry of suit coats and umbrellas, moon boots and patchouli.

Nikilie stared at the floor for the remainder of her ride. That night she took a razorblade to her inner thigh, but the cuts were heartless and shallow.

THEY had coffee at a safe, generic, neutral spot. Nikilie thought about discussing the weather, but Michael had no interest in such niceties.

"Did you ever break your leg?" He asked. "You have a slight limp."

She had, indeed, broken her leg a few years ago. Skiing, she told him.

"An island girl on skis is just as tragic as you'd think," she told him, and when he laughed, she saw the fillings in his teeth. It made her heart hug close, just a little.

"When you are dead and gone," he said, "they'll look at your skeleton and be able to see that break, how it healed itself over. People will hold your bones and wonder what caused it. Running from a predator, perhaps? Or something that happened as a child? No, it didn't heal correctly for that. It must have happened when you were a strong, adult woman. I bet they wonder. I bet they speculate. You'll give them pause, and joy, and something to puzzle over."

Nikilie's mouth fell open. Michael talked so tenderly, so gently, of strangers holding and caressing her bones. It nearly made her frown. It made her want, and she wasn't a woman accustomed to wanting.

"What's wrong, Nikilie? Am I disturbing you with this talk?"

His eyes were brown and open and very nearly alarming in their earnestness. She should be demure. She should excuse herself and go back to her hopeless, helpless life. That's the way society worked. That's the way the script played out.

"No, you're not," she said, and the boldness and sheer honesty of her words shocked her. "It sounds strangely wonderful. Isn't that an odd thing?"

"Not at all," he said reverently. "You want to be loved and worshiped the way a person should be. Not because of your airs or your face. Not because of the fine clothes and jewelry you wear. But because of you. Who you are at the heart. At your very center."

His talk tasted so sweet that she turned down her boss the next time he made advances.

"What's wrong, baby?" He asked. "Don't be like this, a beautiful woman like you."

"This bag of flesh is the very least of me," she said, and quitting her job felt like the best thing in the world. She walked out of the building and blinked in the cold New York sunshine. She took her high heels off and walked all the way home.

Nikilie and Michael began to visit zoos and aquariums. Cemeteries. They twined their thin fingers close, bone rubbing against bone. When she curled up with her feet in his lap, he ran his hand down her ankles, caressing the tendons and scarring there.

"Tell me why you cut yourself."

No judgment. No sad-eyed face of faux concern. Her Michael Harrison wasn't like that, and he would never be like that. He just wanted to know, and Nikilie found she wanted to tell him.

"A few reasons, I guess. It makes me feel better."

"How so?"

"My skin itches, for one thing. It tickles from underneath. Like there's something below that is trying to break through the crust."

"Like what?" His eyes were bright, dilated with interest and the strangest type of arousal. Nikilie briefly thought she should feel stupid or embarrassed, but she didn't. She watched Michael run his tongue over his lips unconsciously, and she swallowed any would-be embarrassment away.

"Rivers, perhaps? Oceans. Stars. Lianas, maybe. May I have a drink of water?"

"Of course," he said, and he poured her a glass from the pitcher he always kept nearby for her. "Why else?"

She drank the entire glass of water without pausing and then held the cool cup to her cheek.

"What? Oh. I…"

The words really did fade away, then, because she simply didn't know what to say. *Beauty is a curse,* perhaps, although that sounded so terribly arrogant. More importantly, it wasn't what she meant. *I hate all the trappings of being human.* It didn't make sense, either, although it was closer. *I want to scrape it all off and be free.* That was the closest yet, but it made her feel quite mad and restless inside, even as the thought thrilled her.

So instead, she sighed, and that was the best she could do. Sighed and fluttered her hand to her scars uselessly. She shook her head and searched out Michael's eyes.

They were blazing. They contained passion and desire and exquisite care and something so akin to purpose that Nikilie's breath caught in her throat with hope.

"You're trapped by something that covers you. Beauty, yes, but it's like a cold, wet blanket draped over your true self. There's something superb inside, the true you, but it's shrouded in fluff and perfume and bubbles. Is this how you feel?"

Nikilie felt something move deep within her bones. Her marrow uncurled and stretched. Something bloomed. It felt like Hibiscus.

"Yes," she whispered, and her voice didn't shake. It felt *alive.* It climbed from her throat and wound around Michael's hand, searching for sunlight.

"Beneath your skin, which is indeed fine, and subcutaneous layers of fat, there are veins and ropes of nerves. Meat and muscle. All this excess. So much bloat! Ah, but under that? At the very core of you?"

If her eyes were alight, then his were on fire. They burned. Sparked. Two delirious, gorgeous infernos of famine and desire, burning away the refuse of her body to get to the bare essence underneath.

This was what true longing was. He saw the basics of her, the very base, and that's what he wanted. Not the trappings. Not the prettiness. He wanted the deep and dark and ugly. The most honest and primal parts.

You are everything I ever wanted, she told him. She didn't say a word, but she felt his grip tighten on her bony wrist and knew he understood.

Her hand shook, but not in self-loathing this time. It was a wondrous thing. She cleared her throat.

"Could you hand me my purse?"

He did, his eyes never leaving hers. They blazed sunlight, and she felt a physical itch under the skin on her wrist.

She reached into her bag and pulled out a small box. Inside was a tissue-wrapped razor.

"Just in case," she said, and when she smiled, the island erupted in full bloom.

He was hungry, starving, and watched her like any predator watches its prey. It was, perhaps, the first time she had ever desired to be consumed.

The razor glistened in the light like ice in a polar cave. The aurora borealis held between her fingers. A wishing star fallen to earth and seeking to sup from her veins.

"Shall I feed it?"

Nikilie's voice held the slightest hint of teasing, but underneath the playfulness, it carried so much more.

Shall I? Shall I do this now, here with you, and will we both accept the consequences that come with it?

He didn't reply, but touched her face softly. He traced her jawline, felt down her neck, and ran his fingers across her collarbone. That's where he let his fingers rest, and their warmth felt volcanic to Nikilie.

"There," she said and placed her hand atop his. "This bone specifically belongs to you. It's yours, always."

"You know I'll treasure it," he said, and his voice was thick and heavy.

"I know you will. You genuinely will. You're the only one who loves me from the inside out."

The first cut went deeper than planned, the blade ice cold and giving her that momentary instant of surprise. Her mind went blank, her body confused, her nerves short-circuiting, and her mouth curling in a soft "oh" of surprise. Then the pain hit, and she closed her eyes against the glorious rush.

Michael sank to the ground and held his arms out to her. She crawled into his lap, and he wrapped himself around her. Blood soaked into his sweater.

"Are you all right, my love?" He asked, and her lips curved in response.

"I have never felt so alive," she answered, and cut again.

No holding back. No fits of guilt or shame, of wondering how she should hide her wounds, of holding her head in her bloody hands and sobbing. She only felt euphoria. Excitement. She was unearthing the deepest, best parts of herself, and most precious of all, she wasn't doing it alone.

She grew too weak to cut with the force necessary, and she blinked sunny, Caribbean eyes at Michael.

"Would you?"

She spoke so softly that he leaned forward to hear her but with such love that her words reverberated through him.

"Of course."

He guided her fingers, and they both gasped as something green and fresh unfurled from her vein.

"I knew it," she breathed.

She was fading fast, her voice nearly gone, and Michael helped her go deeper, discovering the cosmos and garden of Eden hidden away all these years. Before the light in her eyes went out, she wanted to see everything, to see the value and gold hidden at her very center.

"Hang on just a little longer, love," he said, and worked furiously until lilies spilled from her wrists, and heliconias, orange and gay, and vines, and all the flowers she had ever seen. Cereus bloomed furiously, reminding her of the moon at night.

"You make me feel not so alone," she said, and then the vines overtook her, covering her frail neck, twisting into her mouth, and twirling over her eyes. Petals bloomed and fell. Michael was left holding something delicate and wonderful, beautiful from within as well as without.

"You'll never be alone. Never. I'll always, always be with you. I promise."

A girl missing in the city didn't retain the public's attention for long. But Michael was a man who cherished a special thing, the inner wholeness of a person. He tenderly unwrapped flowers and leaves until he found skin and flesh, and then he looked deeper. He cut, scraped, and boiled until he was left with bone. It was white and fresh and pure, with life blooming from the marrow. He held each flowering vertebra gently in his hands and kissed each and every rib.

His garden was exquisite, a thing of wonder and beauty. Flowers bloomed from eye sockets and thrived from femurs. Nikilie was broken down into the most astounding of parts. True to his word, Michael never forgot her. He watered her bones daily.

Unpretty Monster

The Titanic was a grand ship full of beautiful things and people. There were fine ladies and handsome gentlemen dressed in their best. Men and women with gowns and furs and threadbare knickers and skirts. There were children with scrubbed faces and perfectly brushed hair and other children who wore their poverty like dirt on their faces. They were perfect in every way for what she and her sisters needed.

She met a human man on this ship. He had a strong, white smile and brown eyes that didn't shy away from her. She realized her gait was awkward, and her fingers were too long, almost otherworldly. She wrapped them around the ship's railing and looked out to the sea, which called to her bones in a way that made her breath catch.

"Are you all right?" This man asked. He put his hand on the small of her back, kindly, protectively, an easy gesture that had been bred into him from years of impressive schools. She automatically tensed up under his touch but then tried to remember the ways of humans.

"I don't mean any harm," he said, and drew his hand away.

She smiled demurely, careful not to show her teeth.

"No harm. I'm simply a bit… unsteady."

His hand jumped to her back again. "Shall we sit down? Please, let's do that. My name is Murdock. Will you tell me yours?"

She had a name centuries ago, long and deliciously difficult, but that was a more complex time. It was a time when gods left thunderous footsteps on top of the mountains and monsters openly vaulted against the sky. They didn't need to hide or blend in or secret themselves away. They didn't don the skins and trappings of their prey and move amongst them. Things were simple now. There was no grandeur or nuance in the way that things were. The earth belonged to artless creatures, and she had also let her wondrous name slip away.

"Call me Nim," she said, and she liked the way he tasted her new name in his mouth like the finest fish in the sea.

"It is unusual," he said and nodded. "Where are you from? I can't quite place your accent."

She started. "My accent? Do I not speak just like you? Do I not use the same words?"

He was quick to placate. "The same words, certainly. You speak beautifully. But the way you pronounce your words is unique. Quite lovely. I'm certain I've never heard such an accent, but at the same time, it sounds utterly familiar." He blushed, a strangely human thing, and Nim wanted to reach up and feel the tips of his red ears to see if they were indeed as hot as they looked, but she kept her strange fingers to herself.

"English is not natural to me," she said and shrugged. It felt good to sit, to tuck her legs under her as easily as she would have tucked her tail. "I spoke many things first. Greek was what I remember most, I think. After a while, they all run together."

His attention was starting to drift, his pupils dilating at the sound of her voice, the cadence of her words, and she didn't want to lose him yet to the siren's curse. She cleared her throat.

"What about you? What can you tell me about this ship?"

She tapped her foot sharply on the deck, and his eyes focused.

"I...what? Oh, the ship. Yes. Well, it's very new. Very special. Unsinkable, they say, and filled to the brim with the nicest things."

"Like what?" She asked him. "What do you consider nice things?"

He hesitated. "Well, it's not what I consider nice, I suppose. It's what they consider nice."

"Who are they?

"You know. *They*. The ones who make the decisions."

"Like your king, then? King of the humans?"

He blinked at her.

"I suppose I never understand the concept of *they*. Others telling you what to do. Then again, I never listened to the gods themselves," she said and smiled. This time, she forgot herself and showed all her teeth. They were sharp and pointed at the ends. "This has been both my freedom and my bane."

Her smile was unlovely, she knew. She was always the homeliest of her sisters, the unpretty siren, but it wasn't about appearances, was it? It was about the song. The desire. The raw need that she and her kind tapped into.

She quickly covered her mouth with her hand, hiding her teeth. She wanted to talk more, to ask questions, and more than that, to actually speak. To talk about sailors breaking against the rocks and the taste of men's blood, certainly, but to speak of other things, too. Of her lost brothers, of sea foam, of the wonders far below the waves that so few humans had the chance to see. There were horrors and terrors and so much beauty their souls would ache.

She couldn't speak of these things, of course. She couldn't speak of anything, because opening her mouth for more than a few sentences would seduce anyone who listened and would drive them mad. While she would be expressing her love for the sea or her fascination with the birds who float above it in their personal ocean of stars, they would be slitting their own throats or throwing themselves from their bows to quiet the madness inside their heads.

A siren is meant to sing but must silence herself in order to not be a monster.

"Do you find me to be a monster, Murdock?" She asked, but his fingers were already walking themselves to his throat, ready to thrust themselves inside and suffocate him with his own flesh.

She took his hands in hers, firmly, and held them until his fingers stopped twitching. His brows furrowed, and he blinked rapidly.

"I'm sorry," he said, and his words were slightly slurred." I can't recall what we were talking about. Perhaps it is too much sun."

She nodded and released his hands. She missed the feel of them, strong and warm with bones and blood. She heard his heartbeat. A single heart, such a simple organism. Her three hearts were a perfect percussion in her body. Too ornate. Too intricate.

"The ship," she nudged, and his eyes refocused.

"Ah, yes. Let us go inside, and we'll explore, you and I."

There was a grand staircase made of burnished wood. It reminded her of the ships of old, where the wooden figureheads were polished and painted, shining like the sun until the salt of the sea wore them down.

"Show me more, please," Nim said, and Murdock showed her different tables and dishes with beautiful cloths and silverware. He showed her how the joints of the ship were fitted tightly together, and, most of all, he showed her how the people walked around in wonder.

The humans! They had dry skin and bright smiles and walked so smoothly in their stilted shoes. Children ran around, chasing each other and not caring when they bumped into her.

"S'cuse me, Miss," one called before scurrying away. Nim eyed him hungrily.

"They can be little terrors," Murdock said apologetically.

Nim shook her head. "Little wonders, you mean. We have no children at home. They're so difficult to come by. They're like tiny breaths of spring."

"No children? But where do you—"

Murdock was interrupted by the long, low sound of the ship's foghorn. Nim was relieved. His questions were getting a bit too close.

"Let's watch more people, shall we?" She chirped. She followed a woman with a feathered hat and reached out to touch it, cooing with delight.

Men were for eating. Their bones were sometimes sharpened and used for tools, but other than that, they were for nourishment and perhaps a few hours of fancy. But human women? They were rare. They weren't allowed on ships at first, angering the gods and cursing the sailors. They were exquisite, their skin dewy, and their dresses were both ridiculous and magical. Nim looked down at her own dusky gown, pilfered from an unattended piece of luggage. It was better than the human rags she was wearing previously, tattered and full of salt. She wanted to fit in, just for a day to see something different. That was all. Was it too much to ask?

"I wish I could stay with you all forever," Nim told Murdock. Her eyes were full of lights, she could feel them, but she couldn't shut them off even if she wanted to. She was far too happy. "This is where I want to be."

"Why can't you?" He asked, puzzled, but then his eyes unfocused again. Something dark and deadly swam across his irises, and Nim gasped.

"No," she said, and picked up her unfamiliar, heavy skirts. She burst through the doors and ran outside to the railing of the ship.

The beautiful, hellacious voice of her sisters rang from the sea. They were hungry. They were so lonely. Wouldn't somebody join them and keep them company? Wouldn't somebody offer their delicious souls, their toothsome sorrows, the firm meat of their body to satiate their hunger?

"Not this ship," Nim shouted, but her voice was only one of many, lost in the swirl of sound.

"Nim?" Murdock asked. He had come up from behind her, his face pale and sweating despite the cold air. He looked into the water below.

"Don't look. Don't listen," Nim said, and grabbed his face between her hands. "They will kill you. They have no love for you, do you understand?"

Join us. The waves themselves seemed to echo the song. *Forget your troubles. Be free.*

"I wish to be free," Murdock murmured. Nim held him fast.

"It isn't freedom. It's death," she said, and was surprised to find her face wet. *It must be the sea spray,* she thought. Tears were for humans.

"So beautiful," a woman next to her said. Her dark eyes swam with madness. She pointed into the sea. "Look."

Nim knew what she would see. Her sister's faces rose from the ocean as they swam easily alongside the ship. They were stunning, their mouths open in song. Long hair wound around them like seaweed, moving in the water luxuriously. Now it covered their nakedness, now it demurely hid it. They splashed their tails and reached longingly toward the ship.

Join us. Please. We are ever so hungry.

The woman beside them nodded once. She removed her fine hat and slid her dress over her head.

"No, please," Nim said, but she didn't dare let go of Murdock.

The woman slipped silently over the railing. There was a quiet splash, and then the water frothed. Nim's sisters sliced the water with their tails and ripped their prey apart with pointed teeth. The sea bloomed red.

"Let me go," Murdock said dreamily, and stretched his hand towards the sea. "I need to go. They're so lonely."

"They're hungry, Murdock. There's a difference. A terrible difference."

The siren's song increased in volume and urgency.

Come. Join us. Jump to your deaths. Impale yourself on our teeth and claws. Let us wrap our tails around your throats until you are dead. Oh, so wonderful! Oh, so wanton!

Murdock's muscles bunched as he pushed Nim away. But she refused to let go. She, too, was a monster of the deep, and she knew how to get what she wanted.

She captured his eyes with hers and opened her mouth.

Stay with me, she sang. Her teeth were sharp and white and glorious. *There is nowhere but here, no one but me. Stay.*

Murdock struggled, his fingers reaching for the railing even as he seemed to go boneless in Nim's arms. She nodded and covered his mouth with hers.

The kiss was final. He would never heed another siren's voice again. He belonged to her.

There was a scraping and a great groaning as the ship listed violently to one side. Nim stumbled, and Murdock grabbed her, pulling her safely to the railing.

"What was that?" She asked.

Murdock's eyes were full of Nim's lights, but his voice was clear enough. "I think we ran into something. What would we possibly run into out here?"

The sisters in the water laughed triumphantly.

Not this ship, Nim sang down to them. *Any others, but I told you to leave this one alone.*

Who are you to tell us anything, weak one? They answered back, fangs glinting. Nim had been on the receiving end of them more than once. *We lust little ugly one. We feel greed. There are so many on board, and soon they will be in the water. We will feast on their hands and their hearts and their eyes...*

Stop it.

...and we will especially enjoy the one you cling to now. He will scream your name as we tear him apart. He will beg you for help, but what will you be able to do about it? You will do nothing but watch him perish.

Their ugly laughter was the worst part. It always was.

Yelling filled the night. The crew ran this way and that, inspecting the boat and equipment. Nim could taste their terror, their franticness.

"We are going to sink," she said.

Murdock smiled at her. "Impossible. This ship is unsinkable, after all."

Sweet human. Trying so hard to calm her terror even as he was realizing the true horror of it all. Was this the way of man? Is this what humans did?

She took his hand and held his fingers to her lips. "You will not be allowed to live," she said simply and turned away.

He pulled her back. "What do you mean?"

She felt the sadness in her smile. Oh, she wanted this kind person to survive, to marry and have more little humans and tell them the stories of his childhood and perhaps even stories of her. But that wasn't to be. He had heard her call and would never fully be free from it. He could live in the desert but would long for the sea, crawling on hands and knees through the dunes until he could make his way to the coastline. He would look for her all of his life, forgetting to eat and drink and sleep until his body gave up. Even then, his soul would be trapped if she didn't come for him.

"I'll do what I can for you. I think you're a good man."

She stepped away and fell backward over the railing. She heard Murdock scream her name and closed her eyes so she wouldn't see his horrified face. She hit the water and took a deep breath. The sea caressed her skin more gently than any lover ever had. She twisted free from the binding human dress, and her awkward legs became a graceful tail once more.

We brought the entire ship down, her sister said. She swam around Nim with glee. *All we need to do is wait. We'll have them all in the end.*

It was what sirens did. It was what they have always done. It was a curse and a gift, this craven desire, this jubilation for carnage, but Nim had grown tired. History repeated and repeated and repeated. The gods had died and forgotten them. They were simply more predators in the sea, sharks with higher senses of self-importance.

She watched the ship break in half. The lights went out, and the screaming onboard increased. She thought of the beautiful staircase, of the marvels of human creation, and felt empty sorrow when the bodies plummeted into the sea en masse.

Her sisters began their feeding frenzy. Tails whipped the surface and churned the water into foam. They feasted on those in the water and beat at the windows to get to the terrified passengers inside. Their seductive songs ceased as they filled their bellies.

After a few hours, there was an aching silence. The screams and chatter died down, and the sirens, fat and lazy, sank to the bottom of the sea to rest. Nim swam quietly to and fro in the dark.

She found Murdock clinging to a floating barrel, listless and barely moving in the cold. The hollows of his cheeks stuck out pitifully. Nim looked closer and saw a gash on his head. His soul oozed illness and pain.

"My friend," she said, surprised at how relieved she was to find him.

"Nim?" His voice quivered in the dark. "Is that you? You're alive."

"I am. I'm so glad I found you. You're terribly hurt, aren't you?"

"I think my back is broken, Nim. Something hit me on the deck. But the water is so cold that I can't feel much. That's a blessing."

He was so dear, this brave man. She swam closer and pushed his hair out of his face.

"Look at me, Murdock."

His eyelids fluttered, but he managed to meet her eyes. His face lit up, and a smile rested on his lips.

"May I sing you a song, my human? It will make everything go away."

He nodded as best he could, and Nim pulled him to her. He released his grip on the barrel and tangled his fingers in her hair. She touched her forehead to his and sang him a song of freedom, of peace, of love and desire as she pulled him down to the beautiful depths below.

Salt

Her son was a small thing with twiggy fingers and thin vertebras pushing against the skin of his back. He was all eyes, nervous energy, and kinetic movement. His brain didn't function quite right, and his thoughts got lost in neural pathways.

They called him a crayon-eater, a window-licker. Jokes about a short bus, but he didn't understand.

His mother's tears tasted like salt, so he never ate salty foods. No goldfish crackers or potato chips. No pizzas or chicken nuggets shaped like dinosaurs.

He survived heart attacks and bad arteries and too much calcium in his blood. His body tried to destroy him, but his mother knew each jack-knifed beat of his heart, knew what it sounded like when his lungs constricted, knew what to do when his lips turned blue. She used CPR. She used herbs and prayers and drugs and rosary beads. MRIs and cardiograms and candles and runes. His heart continued to beat because she willed it. She brushed his teeth and washed his hair, bathed his body and dressed him. He was four.

Five.

Ten.

Twelve.

He was a four-year-old boy in a fourteen-year-old body. He needed help using the public restroom. The flushing toilet scared him, and it was difficult to wash his hands when he used them to cover his ears.

A too-loud man yelled at his mother for bringing a teenage boy into the ladies' room. The man raised his fists high and brought them down with a bad sound. The boy saw salt on his mother's face.

His body was stronger, his muscles bigger, his anger and fear unchecked. He had no sense of holding back or softening his blows. He swung and screamed, and things cracked under his clenched hands, but his mother was safe, still crying. She was holding him and his bloody hands and telling him she loved him, he was a brave boy, the bad man would never bother them again, she loved him, she loved him, she loved him, but stop now, please, her little hero.

Stanley Tutelage's Two-Year Shiny-Life Plan

S<u>tanley</u> Tutelage was destined to be a great, big Nobody. He was astronomical in his mediocrity. From his very boyhood, he excelled at flying under the radar, of being the person voted Least Likely to Be Noticed and being the personification of mayo on white, no crust.

Mayo on white, no crust the child grew into mayo on white, no crust the man.

One evening, Stanley had a date. She was a lackluster thing with her hair pulled back in a responsible hairstyle. She was just Stanley's type.

"Do you ever feel like there's more to life?" He asked her.

"More? Whatever do you mean?" She took careful bites of her chicken and snow peas on rice. Every forkful was the same size. Each bite was chewed exactly seven times. Stanley counted.

"There has to be some sparkle. Some shine to life. It can't always be like this, can it?"

Stanley's date peered at him over her glasses. "You want a sparkly, shiny life?" She gave the words a grimy quality. Her mouth turned down, and she chewed her food too hastily this time. Six chews instead of seven, and then she swallowed it down. Stanley was afraid the shock to her system would be too much for her dutiful, pumping heart.

"That's not what I meant. A shiny life. How ridiculous." Stanley laughed, a forced sound like the braying of a donkey, and then quickly took a drink of water. But as the waiter dropped off their check with two fortune cookies, Stanley let himself ponder it for just a second. A shiny life. What a beautiful, wondrous thing.

"What is your fortune?" He asked his date. "Anything good?"

She very nearly harrumphed. "I don't believe in things like magic or fortunes."

"Oh, I don't either," Stanley reassured her, "but they're still fun to read sometimes."

She pulled her cookie out of the crinkling wrapper and opened it.

"You will have good financial gain," she read. She flicked her eyes to Stanley's. "I'll accept that. Now read me yours."

Stanley's fingers were, strangely enough, trembling. He opened his cookie with reverence. *Please, please,* he thought, although he had no idea what he was asking for, exactly. Something to come to him, perhaps. Something that would make everything in his life better. If lives could have shine, he wanted it.

The cookie read, "Make a plan."

Make a plan. He had been making plans since boyhood and a lot of good that had done. He worked in an office, stuffed into a cubicle with everyone else in Massachusetts. Every day, his plan was to get up, eat lunch, work, and come home before the world caved in on him. It was the saddest and simplest of plans. Make a plan, indeed!

He let his date take home both of their meals in a doggy bag. He drove to her apartment in silence while she stared resolutely ahead, the Styrofoam containers of food warming her lap. At the front door, he received no kiss.

HIS coworker's suicide changed everything.

They were working practically elbow to elbow. Close enough to complain about the music if anybody had been listening to it. They could have shared breath mints if they were on that level of friendship. Stanley and Quiet Jeff worked side-by-side, listening to each other's chairs roll back and forth as they bustled around their separate cubicles doing the Being Busy dance.

"I must make this phone call," Quiet Jeff's squeaky chair announced. "I am Being Busy."

"I, too, am Being Busy," Stanley's rolling chair answered. "I'm doing important things on the computer. Do you hear my keys? Clickety-Clack!"

"Pardon me while I Busily roll over to get a notebook and pen," Quiet Jeff's chair apologized.

"Absolutely, if you'll forgive me while I roll over to the whiteboard. Notes, you see," Stanley's chair squeaked Busily.

To and fro. Hither and yon. They rolled and worked, and Stanley's soul fell farther and farther from his body. It was ready to crash onto the floor in a million little pieces when suddenly he realized that Quiet Jeff's chair had been stopped for quite some time.

Stanley continued to display his Business, but Quiet Jeff didn't move. Stanley saw the top of his head over the cubicle walls, his hair sticking up in the back like a bird of paradise. He sat, and the silence of his chair nearly deafened Stanley.

Should Stanley move faster? Should he roll harder? Was he supposed to make up for Quiet Jeff dropping out of the game and keep the movement on an even keel? He was pondering this when Quiet Jeff stood up, threw a folding chair through the company window, and stepped through.

People screamed and rushed to see the last of Quiet Jeff. Stanley knew it was fifteen floors down to the sidewalk, which seemed like a trivial fact before this, but took on a Great Big Meaning afterward.

Every time he pressed the elevator's call button, he counted the floors as he went up, up, up. It certainly took much longer than it took for Quiet Jeff to fall down, down, down.

But on this day, people dabbed at their eyes with tissues and told stories about how close they were to Quiet Jeff. They bonded while handing each other sugar packets in the break room or said hello every morning when they saw each other in the gray, dour office. None of these things were true. Sirens sounded, and the room was full of people when Stanley switched his chair with Quiet Jeff's. He rolled a few times in his cubicle.

"I'm Busy," Quiet Jeff's old chair chirped.

"Yes, you are, friend," Stanley answered aloud.

MAKE a plan.

He found the fortune folded up in his wallet, put away neatly like his dollar bills. He took it out and stared at it.

Make a plan.

Quiet Jeff had been replaced with Body Odor Cindy, who wasn't as nearly as Busy or quiet as her predecessor. Rumors had trickled down saying that Quiet Jeff's carefully earned bank account had gone to his ex-wife, who blew it on a shopping trip in New York.

And that was it.

That was *it* for Quiet Jeff, who had rolled with such diligence and purpose. His life amounted to a swan dive to the pavement and knock-off Jimmy Choos for a woman he detested. This bothered Stanley.

This bothered him while he sat in his dull white apartment that he wasn't allowed to paint. He thought it over while eating his breakfast of oatmeal and almond milk, which didn't aggravate his stomach like dairy. He mourned Quiet Jeff's sad end while cleaning his bathroom and studiously avoiding the mirror so he didn't see his receding hairline and worker's pallor.

"There has to be more to life than this," he told his reflection. His gaze drifted to the fortune taped on the mirror. Make a plan.

Stanley's eyes went wide and round as the wheels in his head turned. He had an idea, a small grain of one. What if he could change things? What if he could make his life…shine?

He blinked. He looked at himself in the mirror. There was wonderment in his reflection's eyes. His face looked younger, his expression hopeful.

"Should I?" He asked himself. He put his hand on the clean mirror and studied himself intensely. "Would I even dare?"

The reflection nodded, slowly and with purpose, but then faster and with joy. Its mouth fell open, and a strange sound came out. It was only afterward that Stanley realized it was laughter.

That night, he sat down and went over his finances. He wrote a list of everything he had ever wanted to do. He checked both lists, did some calculations, and wrote something down clearly at the top of the page. His handwriting, usually casual and standard and mundane, turned into something beautiful and powerful.

TWO YEARS, he wrote. TWO YEARS.

STANLEY TUTELAGE'S TWO-YEAR SHINY-LIFE PLAN

HE went to work on Monday like usual, only this time, he was wearing his favorite blue T-shirt and khakis instead of a button-down and tie.

He was called into his boss' office, which was exactly where he wanted to go.

"You can't come to work dressed like that," his boss told him. His boss was a man with pictures of a family on his desk, but the family didn't really belong to him. They had, once, many years ago, but they had drifted away like dandelions on the wind.

"I quit," Stanley said in response.

The boss' eyelids didn't understand the conversation because they didn't blink. Not once.

"The dress code states that—"

"I just wanted to tell you in person," Stanley said. "I quit. I'm out of here. I have wondrous things to do in my life, and it doesn't include slaving away in this place."

"—you're required to wear appropriate attire in the workplace. This isn't appropriate, Mr. Tutelage."

This was when Stanley realized that nobody really listened to one another. They used their mouths and said words, but those words had nothing to do with what the other person meant. It was a game, a "say what you have to say and get it out first" game that wasn't played with two people at all. Stanley didn't want to be part of that type of game.

"I want a life that shines," he said, and walked out of the office. It felt good. He used the stairs instead of the elevator, thinking of Quiet Jeff with each floor, and when he arrived tired and sweaty on the street, he looked at the sun. It was going to be a good day. Unlike Quiet Jeff, Stanley had survived when he hit the pavement. The key to survival, he surmised, was obviously taking it slow.

He took it slow down the street. There were birds and a stray cat and people wearing interesting hats. He took it slowly to the bank, where he slowly emptied his bank account. Every single penny and the feeling was heady.

"I don't have a safety net now," he told the banker in wonder. "I've always had a net."

"If you'd like to redeposit," the banker began, but Stanley cut her off.

MERCEDES M. YARDLEY

"I have all I need for two years of the most wonderful life I could possibly live."

"And after those two years?" She asked.

Stanley smiled cheerfully. "Then I die. Have a great day," he said and slowly, gloriously, walked home.

He hated his apartment. He always had. It was the mayo on white, no crust of apartments, and he needed more than that now. He packed his non-work clothing into a bag. They didn't take much room. He packed his phone and an e-reader. Breaking his lease was easy with the amount of money he now had on hand.

"I'm moving out," he said to his landlord.

"I'm getting on a plane," he said to the person at the airline.

"I'm buying this place," he said to an old woman who lived by the sea. The house was made of poorly stacked stones, but the vines and moss made love to the walls in such a way that it held together beautifully. It smelled of sea and corpses. He hoped the salt would weather him like it did everything else, taking bits and pieces to the ocean to feed the fish.

"I can do anything I want to it?" Stanley asked the old woman, who smiled.

"It's yours, Stanley," she said.

Stanley was living his life slowly, but his feet rushed as he hurried to the hardware store. He bought a ladder and brushes and paints, as many as he wanted. Burnished orange and gold and blues and greens. His life would be full of color. It would be full of whimsy and miracles. He painted the kitchen until it was a glorious sunset. The living room was stone gray, and the bedroom was a pool of wonders. He slept with paint flecking his face, and when he awoke, he painted each closet a different color.

It was magnificent.

The first six months rushed by ridiculously fast. Stanley learned how to bake bread and ride a bicycle. His quality of life, now that he knew exactly how long he would enjoy his life, was better than he could have hoped. If he wanted steak and eggs, he had steak and eggs. He had a year and a half to live, and that was a finite time. There was nothing to prolong, no future to hope for. He went for walks if he desired. He stayed home if he didn't. If he wanted a duck, he would go out and get a duck. He didn't wish for this mysterious duck, actually, but it felt good to realize that for the first time in his entire humdrum existence, Stanley Tutelage was a man who got what he wanted.

He marked the days off on his calendar with big black X's. They were like the X's on the eyes of dead cartoon characters, and one day, they would be the X's over his own eyes. This made him smile. He would be a glorious corpse. Death gave him life in a way that he had never expected, and he worked in his garden that evening, humming an off-key and happy tune.

Happy Stanley was a friend to everyone in his new village. Happy Stanley attracted women, quite a few, and finally the throng of ladies was narrowed down to simply one. Her name was Christine.

Christine's eyes were moons and her hands were far too long and thin, but she smiled easily, and it lit up the brightly colored rooms. When Stanley had a year left, she shyly held his hand. When he had nine months left, she moved in. At six months, they discussed the final steps of his two-year plan.

"Quiet Jeff jumped," Stanley pointed out. He was bent over the kitchen table, making a neat list. "So, there's jumping or bullets or hanging. Since we live by the sea, drowning is an option. There's car exhaust or cutting or pills. A car accident. I could leap in front of a train or a bus or a semi. Let's see. Hypothermia. Arsenic. There's always immolation, but I don't want to set myself on fire. Let's set that one aside."

"Darling," Christine said, running her fingers through Stanley's hair.

"What, dearest?"

"Perhaps you could scrap your plan. Perhaps you could live."

The mind doesn't make a sound when it comes to full stop. It's a deliciously quiet thing, in reality. But inside of Stanley's head, bricks tumbled to the ground and kicked up clouds of dust. His brain was a construction site, and it was too dangerous to walk through the rubble. Far better to go around it.

"What's that?" He asked.

Christine kissed his temple gently. "I'm sure it was a lovely plan when it started, but things have changed. You're happy. You have a beautiful home and friends. You have me." She batted her eyelids shyly, and Stanley's heart dinged like a typewriter. "There's no need to go through with it now."

Stanley's eyes traveled to the refrigerator, where his fortune was stuck to the door with a magnet. "Make a plan."

"This plan is everything to me," he said.

Christine looked hurt. "I thought I was everything to you."

"But I only have you because of the plan."

"I don't love you because of some plan, my darling. I love you because of you."

Stanley sighed. "You wouldn't have loved pre-plan me. I was miserable and horrifyingly average. It breaks every mother's heart to know her child is average."

That night, Christine slept easily, but Stanley hardly slept at all.

CHRISTINE'S morning hair was in full glory.

"Darling, would you consider living?"

Stanley had spent another few nights awake. He crossed off each day on his calendar. One, two, three days wasted on concern. Three ducks not purchased. Three days lost in his two-year plan.

"I love you," he told her simply, and her smile tasted like sky.

"Then live for me," she said, and he had nodded. Her tears of joy were wonderful things. Stanley also had tears, but they were bottled up inside and weren't quite as sweet.

Now that Stanley was going to live, he needed to find a job. The money would run out shortly, so what would Stanley and Christine do? He spent nearly three weeks on a job hunt. Those days would have been precious if he had stuck to the plan, but now they were simply days. There weren't many job openings on the island, but one of the restaurants did need a busboy.

Stanley Tutelage became a 44-year-old busboy.

His smile turned upside down, and he worked hard, picking up after children who ate crackers and spewed them on the ground. He cleaned up spilled drinks and wiped sticky things from the table. The restaurant had a dress code. Stanley wore a terrible cheesy shirt to his job every day. He had preferred his button-up from his old cubicle job.

Christine worried about his health, so they cut back on rich foods. They also worried about money, so now they had Meatless Mondays and tacos made with lentils and oatmeal with no sugar.

STANLEY TUTELAGE'S TWO-YEAR SHINY-LIFE PLAN

"If we're going to be in this house long-term, Stanley, we need to do some renovations. The walls are practically falling down around us."

Renovations on his salary were nearly impossible. Stanley kept his eyes open for a second job, which he found. He helped wash down the fishing docks in the evenings. He sprayed off fish scales and dislocated eyes and chased the yowling cats away. Usually, he just stayed in his stupid shirt from the restaurant. Why go home and change first? It only meant more laundry, more work, and more money for hot water.

"I love you, Stanley Tutelage," Christine whispered one night. She was soft and warm in his arms. "I love you so much, but you're a different man than you used to be. I miss Happy Stanley. We'll have to talk about it tomorrow."

"I love you, too," he answered. He meant it as deeply as he had ever meant anything and held her long after she fell asleep. Then he crept away, restless and aching from being on his feet for both jobs that day. He poured himself a glass of water and sat at the kitchen table, looking at the fridge door that was clean of all fortunes. He sighed and glanced at his calendar. It was full of normal, painful, average days that stretched on and on and on. He nearly wept.

Unless.

He stood and flipped the calendar, seeing a day that was circled in bold red. That was The Day, the final step of his two-year plan. It was one month and seven days away, exactly.

Thirty-seven days. Thirty-seven days where he could spend the mornings in warm sunshine and the nights under the covers with the woman he loved. He could be happy and healthy and live with zest and verve again. Years of misery or days of joy. Should he trade? Could he decide?

He pulled out his notebook and wrote in his careful hand. "Make a plan." He ripped out the page and stuck it to the fridge. It looked like salvation. It told him everything he needed to know.

Stanley knew who he was, and he was a man with a plan. That's the plan, Stan. He liked order, he liked lists, and he liked knowing what was coming up. His anxiety spiraled to the ground and disappeared like smoke. The smile curled up and up until he was grinning like a loon. He began making his list, refining the steps of his plan for a shiny life.

Step 1. Go out and buy that duck. Every man deserves one.

Urban Moon

Pen fluffed and primped and preened with her friends. She used a steady hand to blacken her eyeliner. She rouged her lips and pressed them together. Her outfit was chosen with care, showing her long legs, but not so short or low-cut that her mama would have disapproved.

She topped it off with a long jacket, her favorite piece of clothing, made of leather and feathers and metallic odds and ends that caught the light in wondrous ways.

"It feels so good to go out," her sister, Tia, said. They sat in the back seat of the car, crammed in with the other beautiful girls. The car was awash in perfume and body glitter. It was a car of giddy happiness.

"It's been too long," Pen agreed. She leaned back gingerly, careful not to crush her feathered jacket. Her sister reached out and took her hand.

"Are you doing better?" Tia asked.

Pen nodded and squeezed her hand back.

"Much. Thank you."

The women in the car chattered cheerily, but Pen and Tia leaned their heads together and were silent for the rest of the trip.

At the club, they stood in line, checking out each other's outfits and hair. The men looked good. The women looked fabulous. They showed their IDs and entered. Music pumped loudly, and Pen closed her eyes to absorb it all.

"Let's go," Tia said, and threaded her way through dancing bodies.

The girls ordered drinks. They shrugged out of their jackets. Pen draped hers gently over the back of a chair.

"Let's dance!" Her sister shouted into her ear, and Pen nodded. The girls moved onto the dance floor. Magic took over.

The flashing lights and music took Pen away. She moved her body, extending her arms and graceful neck. It took her away. She was no longer grinding her way through school, trying to hold down a job and study at the same time. She was no longer a woman with a broken body who had miscarried the son her boyfriend of five years hadn't wanted. She was no longer a nobody who was all alone after breaking up with him. He had turned ugly. He told her nobody would ever want used goods. He had reminded her that swans mate for life, but humans were different.

She turned on the floor, dancing with her sister, dancing with her friends, dancing with strangers. Eyes fell upon her, taking in her dark skin and the flash of her fine teeth, but she didn't know this. Swans didn't concern themselves with the hungry eyes of strangers.

The music changed to something less frantic, something slower, and Pen pointed at her throat.

"I'm going to get a drink," she mouthed, and her sister nodded.

She returned to the table and noticed her chair was empty. The jacket was gone.

She searched. She searched. She peered under the table and looked around. She asked if anybody had seen it, if they had run across it in the night, because it was oh so special, oh so dear, and reminded her of a better time. Things have significance, you know, and things can be so very precious, and this jacket was one of those things. "Could you help me find it, please?"

Her friends flew from the dance floor and winged around. They twittered and asked.

"Jacket? With feathers and gold and all wonder of magic? Have you seen it at all?"

Nobody had. It was soon time to go, and her friends gathered up their glorious jackets, each one perfect, each one tailored to their bodies, and Pen was left alone.

"Come home with me," her sister sang, holding out her hand. "It's late, and I don't want you to be by yourself. Stay at my place tonight."

Pen shook her head and kissed her sister. "It's just a few blocks away. I'm happy to walk. And I'd like to look for my jacket a little longer. Perhaps I can find it."

I need to find it, her eyes said. *I need this sense of normalcy. I need to dress myself in its feathers and float away, knowing that even if everything falls apart, this one thing will be right with the world.*

Her sister didn't like it but she had to get home to her husband and son.

"Be safe," she said and left with her friends. They swanned into the night in their finery.

Pen stooped and peered under the table again, just in case the jacket had somehow faded into the dark. A pair of leather shoes appeared beside her. She slowly stood up.

He was gorgeous, his jaw lean, his eyes concerned.

"Excuse me, miss. You seem to be looking for something. Will you allow me to help you?"

Pen's hand wanted to fly to her throat. She wanted to fluff her hair and soothe her nerves. She held her hand carefully at her side.

"I'm looking for my jacket. It has feathers and gold. It's very important to me."

The man's eyes were warm.

"It sounds lovely. In fact, I think I may have seen it. There are many fine coats here, but not so many with feathers. Would you come with me and see if it's yours?"

Something in Pen trumpeted in alarm. He was a stranger, and she was unused to other men after being with her boyfriend for so long. But it was cold outside, and, more than that, she wouldn't be herself if she wasn't wrapped up in her feathers.

She followed him cautiously, but it turned out that it was only to the other side of the club, not down some dark alleyway or behind a dirty gas station. She calmed somewhat.

"Is this it?" He asked, and held up a denim jacket with a feather stenciled on the back.

Pen's heart sank.

"No, it isn't," she said and nearly started to cry.

"Hey, hey," he said soothingly, and put his arm around her. She nearly jerked away by reflex, but she was so sad and so tired, and his voice was calm and quiet.

"My mother gave it to me before she died," she said. Her eyes glimmered with tears she had been trying to hold back for months now. "It's all I have of her. I can't lose it. I'll be naked without it." She didn't know why she was telling him this.

His eyes were kind. He nodded.

"I see. Naturally, that makes it even more important. Listen, I have a friend here who has a keen eye. Let me text him in case he's seen it around. Feathers, you said? Actual feathers? And gold?"

She described it, and his quick fingers jabbed at his phone. He grinned at her, and his smile gave her hope.

"Just a second. He's usually pretty quick to answer. Maybe we'll get lucky. What's your name?"

"Pen," she answered automatically and smiled back. "Thank you so much…"

"Tom," he said. "Call me Tom."

His phone lit up, and so did his eyes.

"Sounds like he might have a hit on it," he said. "Feathers with metal accents. He says some girl is wearing it out back and showing it to her friends. Maybe she lifted it?"

"Oh please," Pen said, and this time she couldn't keep her hands from fluttering to her throat. "I need it back so desperately. Can he get it from her?"

Tom typed something, and the phone dinged almost immediately.

"He says he doesn't want to pull it off of her without you making sure it's the right one. Want to run back and take a peek?"

She faltered. She faltered, and her nerves betrayed her. Tom nodded his head again, and he looked hurt.

"I get it. You're a beautiful girl who doesn't want to put yourself in a bad situation. I understand. I'd have him take a picture of it if the camera on his phone worked, but it doesn't. I could take a picture with mine and send it to you, but I haven't seen you with a phone in your hand. Do you have one on you?"

"No," she said and sighed. "I don't."

"My only concern is that she might leave and take your jacket with her. It seems important to you. But whatever you want to do. I want you to be comfortable."

Nice words were said in a nice manner. He seemed calm and open. And more than ever, Pen needed to wrap herself in her mother's love.

"Okay," she said and stood up. "Where is it?"

Tom guided her with his hand at her elbow, not pushy or possessively at the small of her back.

"He's outside having a smoke. Just this way."

He led her to an exit and opened the door.

"I really hope it's yours," he said as she faltered. "Wouldn't it be amazing to get it back?"

She stepped out the door into the cold night. The door clanged behind her.

"Where—" she said, but that was as far as she got before a hand clamped over her mouth.

Pen struggled. Pen fought. Pen cried and prayed and cursed and begged. She threatened. She wept. In the end, she just stared at the starry sky over the two men's shoulders and wished herself away.

If I were a bird, she thought, *I'd fly, fly, fly away home.*

After her body and soul were used up, Tom and his friend left. Pen sprawled in the alleyway, her feet bare, her dress, so carefully chosen not to show too much, ripped nearly from her body. Her toes were painted a delicate rose. Her necklace was broken on the beer-soaked ground.

She tried to gather herself, but it was too hard, and her body hurt too badly. She stared at the moon, a cold witness to her horror until it began to change. It swelled and grew brighter, shining, shining, shining, until it hurt her eyes to look at.

"Hey, lady. You okay?"

It was no longer a moon but a flashlight beaming directly in her face. She squinted against it.

"Mama?" She asked, and the man pulled out his radio and called for help. Somebody brought out a thin fleece blanket and wrapped it around her, covering her brokenness.

"This isn't right. It doesn't have any feathers," she said, and the ambulance doors shut behind her.

THE hospital visit was grim. The police report was grimmer.

"His name is Tom, and he is beautiful," she said, and turned her face into the pillow to cry.

Her friends dropped by, guilt dripping off their faces in the form of tears. Her ex-boyfriend sent a bouquet of carnations. She hated carnations because they were cheap, and he knew this. But he was also cheap, and so was their old love at this point.

Tia held her hand as a sister does. Her hand was cold and strong, but it trembled every now and then.

"I wish it had been my jacket instead," Tia said, and Pen hushed her.

There was internal damage. Liberties had been taken, things done, foreign objects used.

"It doesn't matter," Pen told her sister. "A kiss would have been too much. What does it matter? It doesn't anymore."

She was on the news. She was on the web.

"Did you see what she was wearing?" People asked. A picture of Pen and her girlfriends getting ready for the club flashed across the screen. "A good girl doesn't dress like that."

"It's just leg," somebody argued.

"It's advertising," somebody else said.

"Rape is never okay."

"It isn't rape if it's wanted."

"Consent is sexy."

"You can't rape the willing."

Strangers argued about her body, about her clothes, about her stupidity to go into the dark. Pen wasn't Pen anymore, but a face used for agendas. They lambasted her friends, accused her sister, and accused her ex-boyfriend of masterminding the whole thing.

"That's what you get when a slut gets pregnant to trap a man. They get revenge."

Pen thought it couldn't get any worse. She was wrong.

"Tom" and his buddy had filmed it. The whole thing. The camera was carefully kept away from their faces, but it was front and center on Pen's. It captured her body. It captured the shattering of her soul and psyche. It captured the precise moment when her spirit curled up and died, and her dark, perfect eyes stared far, far away.

It went viral. Of course, it did.

Friends saw it. The members of her church. Children shared it at school; it was uploaded online, it was shared on porn sites and through personal emails, and it was downloaded again and again and again.

"No," she had said.

"Please stop," she had said.

"God help me," she had said, but most of these things were uttered with a strong hand clapped over her mouth.

"It smelled like cigarettes and tasted unclean," she had told the police, but that wasn't enough to identify an assailant.

"Excuse me, sir, but do your hands smell like cigarettes, and do they taste unclean?" an officer had mocked outside of her hospital door when he thought she couldn't hear. But Pen had heard, and heard the responding laughter, and she thought of the sharp piece of gravel pushing into her back and sides and stomach while that sturdy hand kept her swan song silent.

Pen's body gradually healed, but her mind didn't. It couldn't. A mind is used to capture and retain, to relay information, to process and show things over and over and over. Pen relived that moment every night. Everyday. She covered herself in layers of clothing, cheap replacements for her jacket of resplendent beauty, and hid in her apartment.

"Do you want to go for coffee?" Her friends asked.

"Do you want to go shopping?"

"Do you want to go into public and have the fingers and eyes of strangers touch your soul again and again?"

Stress and terror made her languish. Her hair molted, and her skin pulled back from her face. She had become married to this new version of herself quite against her will.

"I just want to be me again," she told Tia, and they cried together.

"Come live with me," Tia urged her. "Stay with us. I'll take care of you until you're well enough to fly again. You can be free."

"I'll never be free," Pen answered, and she slept on the floor that night, curled up between the bed and the wall. It was a prison, safer than the prison her soul currently inhabited, and she slept restlessly, hoping that the dreams and the media wouldn't find her.

They always did.

"Do you think the attack had anything to do with race?" A reporter asked her.

"How do you feel that the attackers haven't been found?"

"Did you bring it upon yourself by taking your jacket off in the first place?"

"If you dance in front of men, what do you expect?"

She had been a maiden before this but became something else after. She was no longer Pen but became the girl who traded her virtue for a coat. It didn't matter what she said. It didn't matter what had really happened. She had walked into a club, all dolled up and slid her protective covering down so she could dance.

"Mama would be so ashamed," Pen cried to Tia. Tia was the only one who came over anymore. Everyone else had stepped away.

"Don't say that. You didn't do anything wrong."

"I did everything wrong. I'm a woman, aren't I?"

"You can't think that way."

Pen's face was tattooed with tears that her eyes would no longer shed.

"That's what the world would have me think. Who am I to deny it?"

Pen faded more day by day, her long neck hanging down, her breast turning toward the sky. Tia couldn't take it anymore. She gathered up her flock, and they donned their finest coats.

"We need to fly," she said, and they took wing. They went to the police, to the media, to the Internet.

"We need to find these men," they said. Their voices were bold. "We've waited long enough. One of us was attacked and stripped naked, first by filthy men and then by an even filthier society. One of us dies of a broken heart. Did you know that heathens used to mark a swan's beak to show ownership? What have you done to her? You scratch your name into her beak with claws, with your fingernails, with screwdrivers. It is enough. Bring these men to justice and let our sister come back to life."

Their words stung. The beating of their wings against injustice stirred them up. Suddenly, armchair reporters stopped ripping apart the feathers of

Pen's outfit that night and set upon Beautiful Tom. They analyzed the video and studied the features of the men, of the club, and compared it to other videos popping up online.

Beautiful, Disgusting Tom and his friends showed up over and over. So many women, so many Pens, left crying and broken, tattooed and scarred.

"They will be found," Tia told Pen. She stood strong, regal, and proud. She pulled Pen beside her and brushed her hair away from her face. "There will be justice."

Pen practiced standing upright, folding her arms about her like wings. This was how it was supposed to be. This was how she had been raised. Stand tall instead of hiding. Face the sun instead of hiding her head under her wing.

"I have something for you," Tia said. She opened her bag and pulled out a beautiful jacket decorated with feathers.

Pen gasped.

"Tia, I couldn't. That's the jacket Mama gave you before she died. I could never take it."

Tia draped it around Pen's shoulders and took her hands.

"She made it herself from her own jacket. It would always protect us. It's the most precious thing I own, but you are far more precious."

Pen's eyes filled with tears, and they were beautiful.

"Fly away," Tia whispered. She closed her eyes. "Fly, Pen."

There was a rustle, a handful of feathers, and Tia's hands were empty.

Love is a Crematorium

It was Saturday morning, and Kelly was mowing the lawn. The grass smelled good, and his shirt was stuck to his scrawny body in a sweaty, happy way. He was tired. Good-work tired.

A beat-up green car pulled up and parked in the middle of the dirt road to his house. Joy got out, her blonde hair more disheveled than usual. She wore a HEART band tee and was holding her arm in a disturbingly careful way. Her mascara ran down her face, and her eye was red and puffy. It was going to be a glorious shiner.

She moved toward him, and even her walk wasn't quite right.

"Joy," he said, and turned off the mower. He jogged over, and she threw herself into his arms.

"I'm sweaty," he said because it was the automatic thing to say. He meant to say, "Whatever happened, we can handle it." He meant to say, "I'll kill your father this time; I really will." He meant to say, "You're safe here. I'll never let something like this happen if you stay with me." But "I'm sweaty" is what came out of his mouth.

"I can't do it anymore, Kel. I can't." She pulled back, and her brown eyes were angry and wild, so un-Joylike, and Kelly nearly took a step back she looked so fierce.

"I'll kill him if he touches me again; I swear I will." She bared her teeth, and suddenly, she was all fireballs and fury and deep, poisoned seas. "I'll chop off his hands. Then I'll chop off his head. I'll stab him in his creepy staring eyes, so help me!"

Kelly pulled her close again, holding her while she sobbed and raged and wailed. He felt her soul grind to dust in his arms. Felt her lose the strength that anger and terror gave her.

"I love you," he whispered into her hair after she had become quiet. His shirt was doused with sweat and tears and probably tasted like a salt lick. He wanted to run his tongue down it to be sure, but instead merely dipped his head and sucked on his shirt collar.

"You're the only one who does, Kel. The only one in the whole world."

She raised her face to look at him, and he studied her cheekbones, her bruised eye, the way her lip had been busted open. *Again.* He looked at her injured arm, looked away, took a deep breath, and reached for it, but she cradled it closer.

"Remember going roller skating as kids?" He asked.

Joy blinked.

"What?"

"You were always Hell on Wheels. Busted your face up something awful. I'd see you like this all of the time."

She tried to smile, and Kel felt curiously close to crying.

"A portent of things to come, huh?" She asked.

"Maybe."

"If I remember right, you were always trying to put me together then, too."

Kelly smiled. It was a goofy smile, full of teeth and something dark he was trying to hold back.

"It's my job. Always was. Always will be."

He kept his tone light, but Something Serious ran underneath it, and it was this Something Serious that Joy latched onto.

She took his hand in hers and studied the length of his fingers, the squareness. These were hands that had never hit a woman, never hurt a child. Quite the opposite. These were hands that washed away dirt and picked out baseball bat slivers from her young fingers. Hands that staunched blood and applied bandages. These were healer's hands.

Joy held Kelly's hand up to her cheek, over her eye. He ran his fingers gently down the bruises and imagined blood vessels knitting themselves back together, swelling receding. He wished the pain to disappear, but when his fingers left her face, she winced, and her tight lips told him she was still hurting.

"I always expect you to have magic in you, Kel," she said, and he grinned that goofy grin again, but he felt that his eyes had gone primal and a little bit dangerous.

"What's goin' on, Joy? You have something real big on your mind."

She dropped his hands and stepped back as if she needed to give him some distance, some formality. It was almost like a business proposition. He somehow felt undressed, like he should be standing there in a church suit with a leather briefcase, his shoes polished nicely.

She squeezed her eyes shut.

"I'm leaving. I have to leave. He was going to kill me this time; I know it."

"Joy—"

"I *know* it," she said and opened her eyes. He saw everything then, and soon, he was nodding his head.

"Okay. Okay. So, what are you going to do?"

She looked over her shoulder at the car.

"I have a bag. I have a little bit of money. And I have his car. I thought I'd just drive until I couldn't drive anymore, then sell it. After that, I'll walk. I'll...I dunno. I'll sleep in ditches. Find a city, get a job. I don't know," she said again when he looked at her, "but I can't stay anymore, Kel."

"Did he break your arm?"

She shook her head.

"I don't think so. It's just awful sore. But I can't go back."

"You could stay with me and my parents."

She stood on her tiptoes and kissed his cheek.

"Sweet Kelly. You know I can't."

"They just don't know you like I know you. If you stayed, they'd get that chance. I could talk 'em around, you know I could."

Give them enough time, and they could see past the donated hand-me-downs and the dilapidated trailer, Kelly was sure of it. Joy was so much more than Buck's daughter, and his parents would realize it. But seeing how Joy babied that arm, he knew time wasn't theirs to spend. Her dad was mean at the best of times, but the fear in her eyes was stark. Kelly's stomach felt like he had eaten something sharp, something pointy with spines. The edge of a newly hewn axe or the points of one of Buck's knives.

"He'd come looking for me, and I don't want you to get hurt. You or your family."

"He doesn't scare me," Kelly said automatically, but they both knew it wasn't true.

"It's okay, baby," she said and kissed him. She tasted of blood and Orange Crush Chapstick.

They'd only kissed a few times, out where nobody could see. The kisses were deep, and they were funny, and sometimes they laughed, and a time or two Joy had cried. But the kiss this time was saying something deeper. It was a Last Kiss. That's what Kelly was afraid of.

"Got any money?" She asked him. Her lips were still so close to his that he felt them move. She didn't want to pull away, to have that distance between them. He didn't either. He blinked and felt his lashes flutter against her cheek.

"Some."

"Come with me," she said, and burrowed her face into his neck. She pushed her body as close to his as she could get it, and his arms went around her automatically.

This is how it's supposed to be, he thought, and the grasses and dust around him nodded yes, yes, this is exactly how it is supposed to be.

"Joy, I—"

"Please don't tell me no. I don't know if I can do this without you. I need you to be with me."

His heart hurt. In the best of ways. In the worst. Her hair smelled like sweat and lavender and something else that tugged at the very base of him. He put his hand to her scalp and pulled it away. His fingers were red and sticky.

"What did he do to you?"

He almost didn't recognize his voice. It was a dark thing, roiling and full of teeth. It hurt as it came out of his mouth, and he had to bite it back.

Joy's fingers fluttered to the wound in the back of her head, hovered, and then moved away. She tried to step back, but Kelly held her closer and rested his chin on her head, careful not to hurt her. Her body was fragile, made of spun sugar and spider webs. There was only so much pain the human body

182

and mind were meant to take, and then everything exploded into showers of shadows and powder.

"When are you going?" He asked. His voice was gentle this time. It was just right.

"Right now."

"Let me throw together a bag."

She pulled back and looked at him. Her eyes were huge and full of hope and pain and wariness and disbelief. Kelly remembered the first time they had held a rabbit from the fields. It was tiny and furry and dying, an accident from a lawn mower if he remembered right. Her eyes had looked that same way. There was magic in the world but also death and horror. He knew he was making the right decision, then. Knew it was what needed to be done. He couldn't send this broken little bunny out into the world to die alone. He needed to be there with her to soothe the wounds, to keep the monsters away. He needed her to do the same thing for him.

"I'll never leave you, bunny," he told her.

She blinked rapidly in the sun, her smile crooked and a little unsure.

"What's with the new name all of a sudden?"

He shrugged and kissed her forehead.

"It fits you."

He packed a duffle in only a few minutes. What does a teenage boy really need, after all? He took his wallet, thought about it, and took the envelope of grocery money from the kitchen cupboard.

Mom and Dad.

His handwriting was fast and hard. Gangly, like the rest of him. He wrote quickly, a born lefty, dragging his hand through the ink before it had a chance to dry.

Joy needs me. I promise to call.

He pondered whether to say it or not, but then he thought of his mother reading the letter.

Love you, he scrawled and stuck the note to the fridge with a magnet.

Joy was sitting cross-legged on the hood of the car. Her eyes were closed, and whether she was sleeping or praying, Kelly couldn't say. Seemed that both did the same amount of good, far as he could tell.

"Ready?" He asked her.

She opened her eyes and stared at him for a long time. He wondered what she saw. A boy in a sweaty shirt holding a duffle bag and a couple cans of Squirt. This was who she was going to depend on. He looked down at himself and frowned.

"Guess I should've taken a shower. I didn't even put the mower away. Sorry, Joy. I just thought, what if your dad is comin'? I was just thinking of being quick, not really of anything else. Maybe—"

Joy slid off the hood. She stood on tiptoe, bumped noses with Kelly almost playfully, and then she kissed him again.

Not a Last Kiss, he thought hazily. *A First Kiss. The First of their adventures together. This is the beginning of everything.*

"I love you, Kelly Stands," Joy said. "From the bottom of my heart, I do."

His stomach did flipflops, and he found it strangely hard to talk.

"I love you, too."

He did. And she did. The way she blushed and wrapped the fingers of her good hand into his shirt sleeve told him all he needed to know and more.

He tossed his duffle bag into the backseat of the car.

"Mind driving, Kel? My head hurts something fierce."

He opened the door to the passenger seat and helped her in.

"Here," he said, and pulled a bottle of aspirin out of his pocket. "Got something for your head."

"Thank you, baby."

She swallowed it dry while Kelly walked around, hopped in the driver's seat, and started the car.

"You're sure about this?" He asked her.

"Absolutely."

"Then let's go."

She leaned her head against the window. She slipped her hand into his.

A few hours later, they were outside the state line of Alabama.

THEY drove until the car ran out of gas. It was a good five hours of driving. They filled it up twice before deciding that was far enough.

"It's time to ditch it," Joy said. Her eyes were red, and her face was white from exhaustion, but she still looked happier than Kelly had ever seen her.

"All right."

Kelly had wondered how they'd sell the car, but it was easy. Joy took a deep breath and wandered up to a pair of long legs sticking up from under a truck in a driveway. She bent down, and the legs slid out and turned into a young man, who unfolded himself and stood up.

Kelly watched Joy put her hands in her pockets, tilting her face up to see the stranger. She squinted in the sun, and something in Kelly wanted to stand between them, to look the other man in the face and see what exactly his intentions were. Something else wanted to duck quietly into the background. Kelly felt himself actually bunch up in the passenger seat of the car, getting smaller and smaller before he forced himself to stop and stretch out.

Joy pointed at the car, and the man followed her gaze. Kelly waved awkwardly and put his hand down. Joy stood on tiptoe as if she was whispering in his ear, and Kelly didn't like the way his stomach tightened when the man bent close to listen.

The man straightened. Nodded. Reached into his back pocket for his wallet. He handed folded money to Joy and then laughed when she hugged him with her good arm. He put his hand on top of her head like it had always gone there, like he had been teasing her about being short all of her life. They looked like old friends.

She could have just as easily been born here, Kelly thought. *He could have been me.*

The thought of this man, this stranger, being her parallel world made Kelly get out of the car. He ambled over a bit too casually.

"Hey," he said, and didn't like the sound of his voice, the note of question and concern and danger and warning wrapped up inside of it. Uncertainty and chainsaws. High fives and electric fences.

The man nodded back, his grin wide and easy, and Kelly almost hated him more. All was right with his world. This was a man who knew where he was going to sleep that night, who didn't have to worry about Joy's fitful cries as she dreamed, who didn't have the responsibility of being the last one awake, watching to keep them safe.

"Joshua here will take it," Joy said simply, and that was that. It was over for her. Car discarded. Item checked off her list. Joshua swooped in to save the day.

"You'll want to paint it or…whatever pretty soon," she told Joshua, and he nodded again.

"Gotcha," he said, and Kelly looked down at his feet. They were large, and his sneakers were still stained from mowing the grass. How long would these shoes last? Suddenly, the weight of what they were doing hit him, crushed his chest in a way that nearly made him gasp.

Joshua studied him, seeming to really see him for the first time.

Joy slid her hand into Kelly's, almost timidly, and his fingers curled automatically around hers. She was shaking, and he noticed that her bright smile was tight around the corners, her eyes a little bit too wide.

"Right. Thanks, Joshua," he said, and then he was walking down the long dirt driveway with Joy at his side, their legs swishing through the grasses.

"We're going to be okay, bunny," he said, and as soon as he heard the words, he knew he believed them. He squeezed her hand, and she squeezed back. He made a face, and soon she was laughing up at him, her nose scrunched in the way that told him she was truly happy, not worried about passing her English test or hiding her shiner or wondering whether or not bones would break this time.

"I sort of dig you," he said, and laughed when she mock hit him in the chest.

"You're lucky that I sort of dig you right back," she said, and then she stopped and leaned against him.

"Thank you," she said. Her voice was thick and heavy with her sincerity. "Thank you, Kelly."

He hugged her, tucking her body protectively against his, and it felt right. This was how it was always supposed to be. He knew it, had known it since they were children, when she would flee through the trees to his house in the middle of the night, afraid of her mother and her father, of the screams and new holes in the wall. She didn't want to stay in his room, but she asked him to stay beside her next to the trees.

"Remember when I'd pull my blanket out through my window?" He asked her. "And we'd go back by the woodshed to sleep? We were safe there."

"How could I forget, Kelly? It was the only time I slept. You said you'd keep watch, that you'd be the last one awake, watching so my father wouldn't find us."

She was speaking into his shirt, burying her face into him like a newborn kitten.

"I loved you then, did you know that? Always, always. If my daddy found us, he would have killed us. But you still came."

"You were always there for me, too," he said. "You know it worked both ways. You were there whenever I needed you, and that was an awful lot."

She pulled away and looked at him. He saw himself reflected in her irises, realized that she saw him and through him, and it made him even more *him* than he actually was. She saw someone strong and safe and dependable, an eight-year-old boy who turned into an awkward almost-man, but he was enough for her. He was everything, and his heart felt strangely light and happily strangled at the same time.

"I'll always come for you," he said simply, and the flurry of kisses on his face made him smile, made him laugh with the purity of *being,* and then they were walking hand-in-hand by the side of the road again, and even when night came, and they were forced to sleep outside, without Kelly's blanket, it wasn't frightening. It was childhood, just like old times, and the scent of her hair and the cut grass was what heaven would smell like. He was sure of it.

JOY had nightmares during the night, but each time she would twist and cry out, Kelly would whisper, "I'm here," and "You're safe," and "I love you."

The *I Love Yous* didn't come as as he would have thought. They were still unsure and sounded a bit grandiose, but they were real and sincere, and it pleased him that each time he whispered this, she quieted and turned toward him.

That's what love was, he thought. Being the warm blanket for somebody else. Being the rain that brought their parched roots back to life. It was being their tether, so they didn't float off into space. It was growth and pain and responsibility. Love was a crematorium that lit you up and burned you out at the same time.

Joy woke up with sticks in her hair.

"I'm hungry. Are you?"

"Starved," he answered.

They walked until they came to a filthy old gas station. "Dilapidated" came to Kelly's mind, possibly for the first time in his life. They used the restrooms and washed up, then bought prepackaged sandwiches and drinks. They counted their folding money with an intensity that made the attendant behind the counter take notice.

"Where you headed?" The attendant asked.

"Nowhere in particular," Joy said. "What's around here?"

"Not a thing."

Joy was biting her lip a bit too hard. The attendant watched this, too.

"Where do you live?" Joy asked, and both Kelly and the attendant were taken aback by this.

"About two miles up the road."

"Where's the nearest city?"

"Probably Macon." He pointed.

"Goin' there anytime soon?"

Her voice was breathless. Hopeful. This is what hope sounded like. It sounded like a young girl asking a stranger for a ride to the city.

"Nah." The attendant's gaze narrowed. "Whatcha looking for in Macon?"

"Work. You're sure you're not going that way?"

"Nope."

Joy shrugged.

"Too bad. Later."

The bell dinged as she pushed her way out the door. Kelly was right behind her.

"What was that? That guy gives me the creeps. He'd rob us blind and leave our bodies in a field somewhere before he'd help us. What did you do that for?"

Joy kept walking fast.

"Because he scares me, Kel. I knew he wouldn't help us. But now, if he's looking for us or wants to tell my daddy where we went, if there's a reward, he'll be looking in Macon. And that's exactly where we won't be."

"Where will we be?"

"I don't know, and I don't care. But not anywhere close to here. We'll go somewhere wonderful. Somewhere just for us. Any place you've always wanted to see?"

Some people dreamed of Egypt and Turkey and Thailand and other exotic places. Kelly had never done that. He assumed he'd be working right in town, or pretty close to it, all his life. Just like his daddy and his daddy's daddy. There wasn't any shame in it.

"I don't know," he said. "Never thought of it. You?"

"Anywhere," Joy said, and that was it.

Anywhere. He was pretty sure they'd make it.

She smiled up at him, blonde hair blowing in her eyes.

"Keep your expectations simple, and you almost always get what you want," she said, and squeezed his hand. "Then everything else that happens, well it's just a gift."

He wanted to tell her that she was his gift, but it was too hokey to say. Maybe if he thought it hard enough, she'd hear it.

"I never thought I'd get you," she said simply. The honesty cut through his teenage bone and sinew. He flushed, and she laughed when she saw it.

"You're my wish," she said, and jumped up to ruffle his hair. "I'll always take care of you. Always."

THE heat and the humidity and the walking and the car exhaust and the long Southern grasses crowded in on Kelly's lungs, making them smaller and fuller and unable to work. The air was all dust and dirt and pollen, and he sucked it in, shrieking for oxygen, but each breath had less air than the last. He collapsed on the ground, gasping, pulling in dirt and bits of weeds into his body, into his throat, and he felt them lodging there, making a home, taking root.

"I have you, baby. I have you," Joy said, but words alone couldn't make him well, and they both knew it.

Joy left him lying there, sprawled on the ground with his duffle bag as a pillow, and she ran to the road.

"Help!" she screamed, waving her arms, and a pretty young thing radiating hope and desperation in the Southern sunlight would make anybody stop. A car slowed down immediately, and she leaned in the passenger window.

"I think my friend's having a terrible asthma attack. Could you help us? Please?"

The driver seemed doubtful, but Joy's eyes sparkled with tears, *real* tears, honest-to-goodness tears, and the driver realized he had a chance to be a hero. The time for heroics seemed long past, left someplace back in the war, but here was a woman who needed help to save a person she cared for, and this driver was just the one to help them.

He hopped out, grabbed a backpack from his trunk, and followed the girl through the weeds until she stopped at the side of a tall, lanky boy, just this side of manhood. He'd curled up into the fetal position and was breathing in dirt with every gasping breath.

"This won't do," the driver said, and he pulled the boy up, cradling him.

"You need to sit up," he told Kelly. "And you need to take deep breaths. Deep ones, son. Darlin', open that bag and hand me the inhaler, would you? My stepson uses one. We keep one in every vehicle."

Joy's hands shook, but she unzipped the bag and did what he asked.

Kelly was gasping, taking in half a breath, less than that. Joy watched his face, reaching out to briefly touch his blue lips.

"This boy needs a hospital," the driver said. He started to pull Kelly to his feet. Joy helped him.

"We can't go to one," she said. Kelly was draped over her, and she kissed his cheek over and over as she and the driver pulled him to the car. "We don't have any money. And they'll take him away from me, that's what they'll do. They'll bring him back home. We can't go back."

The man looked at both Kelly and Joy, and then sighed.

"Okay. Fine. Let's do what we can."

Joy hopped in the back seat and pulled Kelly in beside her. The driver leaned in and checked Kelly's eyes.

"Good, you're back with us. Keep breathing, boy. In and out. Good air filling your lungs. Hold on to that pretty girl next to you, and I'll get you someplace safe."

Kelly rested his head on Joy's shoulder and closed his eyes. He felt her hands run across his face. He remembered those hands holding cotton candy at the state fair last summer, beautiful and graceful even though two of her fingers had been broken and bandaged.

"Are you okay, baby?" She asked him. Her voice was as sweet as honey. "Are you okay?"

"Okay," he managed, but any more words were too hard to say. He breathed in and out, in and out, for what seemed like a very long time.

The car stopped.

"Just a second," the man said, and stepped out.

Kelly struggled to open his eyes, but they were too heavy. "Is he…?"

"He brought us to a motel. I don't think he'll tell anybody."

They didn't say another word until the driver opened the back door.

"Come on, kids," he said. "I'll help you."

"I can walk, sir," Kelly said politely, but unfolding himself from the backseat took more energy than he expected.

"I know you can," the man said, "but let an old man feel useful."

They made their way up the metal steps, and the man opened the door with a keycard. The room was small and dingy but clean enough. It had a bed, and that was all that mattered to Kelly.

"I'll just lie down for a second," he said and was asleep immediately.

The driver filled a plastic cup up with water and handed it to Joy. She pulled Kelly's shoes off his feet and then took it.

"What are you going to do now?" The driver asked.

Joy drained the cup in two gulps. The driver refilled it and handed it back.

"Guess we'll rest up for a day and then head out again. Thank you so much, sir."

The driver sighed.

"I don't like it. You know I don't. Asthma is scary at best, fatal at worst."

Joy paled, but the man continued.

"But I can see how stubborn you are about not going back to wherever you came from, and from the looks of you, you actually might be better off. So stay. And take this. He should keep it on him. Just in case."

He dropped the inhaler onto the cheap motel table. Then he also slid a couple of soft, worn bills beside it.

Joy's lip trembled.

"We won't be able to pay you back."

The man smiled.

"You don't have to. I get the sense you've had a bad time of it. Not everyone is out to get you. Get yourself into the city and away from all of this dust. You seem like good kids."

He nodded his head, stepped out of the room, and quietly pulled the door shut behind him.

Joy looked at the money on the table. She looked at Kelly asleep on the bed. She kicked off her own shoes and curled up next to him. She watched him breathe in and out for a very long time, clean breath after clean breath, careful not to fall asleep until she was certain he was safe.

KELLY woke up with sunshine in his eyes and an ache deep in his lungs. He groaned and stretched out. His stocking feet were hanging off the short bed. He could see his big toe sticking out of his right sock.

"Baby?" Joy was right there, her eyes wide. Her hands were baby birds, fluttering here and plucking there. She tested his arms and chest and neck and collarbone as if she was afraid he had shattered apart during the night.

The way his body and head felt, perhaps he had.

"Hey," he said, and that was all he got out. A simple "hey," and then he was breathing in her hair as she flung herself at him. He was choking again, going under once more, but this time it was a glorious thing.

"I'm okay," he assured her, and he very nearly thought of sitting oh yes, he did, but it felt so good to lie there, rest his weary body, and simply take a second to bask in the experience that was a happy, relieved Joy.

"Never again, never again," she told him. "We're not walking in those weeds anymore. Look, the man from yesterday gave us some money, and we're not too far from a bus station. That's what we should do, Kel. Buy two tickets and go as far as the money will let us. But maybe breakfast first. Are you hungry?"

Was he hungry? His stomach had more teeth than a barracuda. He could eat everything ever cooked in the world. Yesterday, he swore that if he walked past one more cow chewing its cud, he'd leap over the fence and bite the animal right on its haunches, he was so hungry.

"I could eat," he said politely.

Joy looked at him. She looked at his face and his body that housed his traitorous lungs. She looked at his one pale toe poking out of his stupid sock. She looked hard, and then she covered her face and laughed. She laughed so much that tears slid out from under her fingers. She laughed, and then she was sobbing, and then she was laughing again.

Kelly didn't know what to say. He laid his hand on her knee and waited until her breathing had righted itself.

"I'm sorry," she said, wiping her eyes. The bruise was starting to heal up some. That made Kelly happy. "I don't know why that was so funny. I just...I need you, Kel. You're my North Star and the thing that always sets me to rights. You're something special. What would I do without you?"

He struggled to sit up.

"Feed me, and you'll never have to know, bunny. But if I don't eat soon, I'll waste away to clear nothing, and that will be the end of me. Then you'll be alone."

"Don't say it."

He grinned.

"Alone and forgotten."

"Don't you say that!"

He tickled her, and her pale hair in the sunshine was the prettiest thing he'd ever seen.

"Alone forever and ever and ever unless you feed me right now!"

She laughed, and this time he laughed with her. They tickled and fought and kissed, and then they kissed some more, this time with more intensity. Joy pulled the curtains, and the sun prowled around outside, wondering why it wasn't allowed in. Years from now, when he thinks back on his last truly happy moment, this was the one that would come to mind.

THE money was carefully tallied, and bus tickets were purchased. After walking through the weeds, the bus felt like a grand thing, a chariot of the finest paint and steel. Kelly sat in the window seat with a freshly showered Joy asleep on his shoulder. This was how it was always supposed to be.

The woman in front of Kelly turned around in her seat.

"Where ya from?" She asked.

Kel's mind stopped, a rabbit frozen at the sight of danger. This danger was wearing a kerchief and had sparkling eyes, but danger all the same.

"Um. Utah."

She raised one eyebrow. "You're going the wrong way for Utah."

Kelly shrugged. "I want to see everywhere."

"And your girlfriend. She from Utah, too?"

Kelly felt his face change. It went dark, pulled itself into an expression he didn't know his face muscles could make. He briefly imagined that he looked at the woman through slitted pupils like a cat or a venomous snake. He tightened his arm around his sleeping Joy.

"You have something against Utah?" he asked, and the woman turned herself around.

Kelly leaned his head against the window. His limbs still felt heavy from yesterday, the brush with fragility, and the way that his body took in new flora and fauna and rejected it. At home, he mowed the lawn and ran outside without issue, but this was somewhere different. All of this was…different.

Kelly wondered about his mother, who would be beyond hysterical by now. He bet she lit up the phone tree at home, calling all the neighbors. He wondered if Joy's dad was one of them.

He shuddered, and Joy made a small sound in her sleep.

"It's okay, it's okay," he whispered into her hair. "It's me. I'm awake. I'm watching over you."

They rolled closer into the city, and Kelly tried to keep his soul from crumbling in despair.

"We can do this," he whispered to Joy. "We can."

The city was gray sky over gray cement over gray pavement. Rain shimmered down and pasted the wet garbage to the street.

"Joy," Kelly said and nudged her. "We're here."

They grabbed their bags. They grabbed each other's hands.

"We made it," Joy breathed, and Kelly bit back his desolation.

She turned to him. Her eyes shone with tears that had nothing to do with broken bones or terrified humiliation. "He'll never touch me again," she said, and Kelly could hear Joy's heart sing. It was a cheerful melody in C Major.

"Never," he agreed. "We won't let him. He'll never find you."

He had always read about happy tears but hadn't ever heard them until now. They sounded sweet. They sounded like horror. Kelly and Joy strode away from the bus station like two people who had purpose, but this was a lie.

They never had such little purpose in their lives. After the bus tickets, they had only enough money to grab a fast-food hamburger two times.

Twice.

At home, Kelly would be downing burgers and spaghetti and milkshakes and whatever his mom would place in front of him. She understood lank teenage boys with hollow legs and grumbling stomachs. But here, food was harder to come by. After five days and two hamburgers, things felt dire.

"I'm hungry, Kelly," Joy said. She wrinkled her nose in frustration. "I thought it would be easier than this."

"It will get better," he said, and he hoped with all of his might that this was true. It had to be the case, didn't it? Isn't that what the old saying said? *When you are going through Hell, keep going.*

"I know it will," she said, and her hand wrapped in Kelly's was still what mattered most. It was safe and cool and unbroken. He thought of her fragile little bird bones and held on a little tighter.

"How long do you think you'll stay?" She asked him. She was looking at the ground far too carefully, and he knew she didn't want to see what was in his eyes. "I mean before it becomes too much, and you'll go back?"

He thought. He thought slowly and carefully. They had barely slept in days but had walked around the city holding hands and pointing at buildings. He'd never seen anything so tall and imposing in his life.

"We're going to live up there," Joy had said, gesturing at the tallest apartment building she could find. Its windows shone like stars. "We'll wake up every morning and look down on this city and all of the people and know that we own it, Kel. It's going to be something real special."

It was a different place when you were up high. They'd rode in elevators and climbed stairs, and being at the tippy top of the world changed the

195

bleakness of the city. It opened beneath them like a cavity, a void. It showed the gentlemanly hollows beneath its concrete cheeks.

But down here from the street, they were face-to-face with the trash and refuse that this tall utopia excreted. Sewage rats, that's all they were. Kelly bared his teeth briefly.

"That depends, Joy. When are you going to be ready to go back home?"

She was shaking her head adamantly before the words were fully out of his mouth.

"Never," she said. She pulled her hand from his and crossed her arms across her chest protectively. "I'll stay here for a hundred years before I ever set foot back in that town again."

Kelly shrugged. "Then you just answered your own question. I'll stay here for a hundred years. Wherever you are, that's where I'll be, too. You'd just better get used to it."

She searched his eyes then, looking for the anger or deceit that she was half-afraid would be there. Kelly gazed back, his face as wholesome and open as fresh ears of corn at the supper table or a new bottle of milk.

"How did I get to be so lucky?" Joy asked, and Kelly laughed. His stomach growled at the same time.

"Guess it depends on your definition of luck, bunny," he said, and Joy's bright smile told him that she was the luckiest girl in the entire world, and wouldn't change a thing as long as it meant they were together. They could have a room in the penthouse or a little cottage by the sea or sit side-by-side, chained in the gulag, and it wouldn't matter as long as she had her Kelly.

That night was the first night it happened.

Kelly squirreled food out of a public dumpster. He used his long orang-utan arms to reach in and pull out a fast-food bag full of trash. Amid the plastic forks and dirty napkins was a container containing a half-eaten salad and most of a chocolate chip cookie.

"Dinner is served," he said, and although he and Joy winced as they first touched the old food, the spiked mace in his stomach insisted he eat it.

"Put the pride away, you fool, and feed me," his stomach demanded, and Kelly, being a very good Southern youth, did as he was told. A quarter of a salad and a bite of cookie wasn't enough to satiate him, but it was enough to convince his ravenous body that he was, at least, trying.

Within two weeks, all pride was completely gone. They became more furtive. Their movements became darting. They went after garbage cans and dumpsters, pulling out half-eaten meals in Styrofoam and dining on rewrapped cheeseburgers with gusto. They scavenged deftly like the street mice they had become.

"Chinese, lover?" Joy would ask, and they'd eat quickly, using their hands and wiping them on the cold concrete later.

Their bodies stank, and Joy's blonde hair turned into straw after washing it in gas station bathrooms with hand soap. Nobody wanted to hire two high school dropouts who wore the same clothes day after day.

"Please, sir," Joy begged. It was her third job interview that morning, and the look on the man's horsey face said everything. "I'm smart, and I learn really quickly. I type well. I just need a job. I'll do anything."

He eyed her too closely. "Anything?"

She stood up, her hands fisted at her side.

"Not anything." Her voice was quiet with rage, and she stomped out the door. Kelly met her outside, saw the way her mouth bitterly twisted, and wisely said nothing.

More weeks passed. She was shrinking away. The skin was pulling too tight over her face, and her ribs showed even more than normal. But Kelly, skinny to begin with, looked like a corpse. One evening, Joy looked at him and studied the way the gray light of the city washed the color from his face.

"I love you," she said, and he broke out into his goofy grin.

"I love you, too," he answered, and his glowing face bobbling over his scrawny body broke something in Joy. She kissed him, long and deep, like she was stealing his taste away. He was a treasure to save for later. Something to think of during the bad times.

"I'll be right back," she said, and touched her forehead to his. "Save my spot, okay?"

"Sure," he said, and watched her walk down the alley, disappearing in the warm steam from the manhole covers. Save her spot, she said, as if people were scrambling to steal their particular section of gritty horror town. But

Kelly was dependable, and Kelly was truthful, and if Joy asked him to save her spot, then he would guard it with his life.

She returned nearly an hour later with a bag of fast food in her hand.

"Here," she said, and sat down. "This is all for you. I already ate."

His stomach roared and ached as he opened the bag. The smell was teenage heaven.

"Fresh?" He asked hopefully. It was more than he dared.

Joy smiled, but something was lost there. "Fresh. Eat up, Kelly."

He wanted to enjoy it. He wanted to take his time and savor it, but the burgers called his name too loudly. They were decimated, the burgers swallowed, and the fries pushed into his mouth six at a time. When he finished, he licked his fingers, each one, starting at the thumb and working his way down.

"That was good, Joy. Thanks," he said and leaned his head against the wall. "Where did you get the money for it?"

She shrugged. "I had something to sell."

"What?" He asked, but she didn't answer. She slid close to him and pulled his arm around her.

"I'm not feeling so well, Kel. Mind if I take a quick nap?"

"I'll stay awake," he promised, and kissed her bird-nest hair. She settled into a fitful sleep, squirming in a way that reminded Kelly of frightened kittens, and he whispered over and over that she was all right, that he was here, that she shouldn't have to sell herself to feed him, that she could deny it all she wanted but he wasn't an idiot. And he loved her anyway, always, no matter what, he murmured, and that's when she finally quieted.

He held her all night long and hated this horrible bone-gnaw city.

IT began little by little, bit by bit, like leaving a cobalt blue bottle hanging on a tree on hot summer nights and watching the rain fill it up. Joy's spirit began leaking out of her eyes and her mouth while she slept, and something else began to take its place. What was left of her began to be distilled, perfect and pure, precious little drops of Joy. He could let each taste of true Joy rest on his tongue for hours, to be delighted over, and it was a glorious thing when he could get it.

It became harder and harder to obtain.

Joy traded her time and her body for things. Food mostly, at first. Sometimes for something that seemed precious at the time.

"Hey, pretty girl," a man said to her one night. She was standing with other kids in an alleyway. They pretended to talk about movies they liked and boys they had dated, but it was an open ruse. They were really standing there in order to be seen, to show how their skinny legs would wrap around a person's waist if they could pay. Their thin, bony fingers became deft at undoing zippers, buttons, and clasps. They picked at food in the trash heaps and shoved them into chapped lips like tiny raccoons. Kelly stayed in the area, too, but far enough away that he didn't intimidate the customers with his tall frame. He crinkled himself into the smallest ball of bones and rags that he could, trying to look as harmless as a newborn puppy without milk teeth.

"Hey back," Joy said, and Kelly turned his face away so he wouldn't have to see the way she arched against the man, the tiny buds of her breasts attempting brazenly to be those of a fully-grown woman.

"I don't have much money on me," the man began, and Joy immediately turned away.

"Then I don't have much time."

"But I have something shiny and I have some beers back in my car."

Joy pretended to study her manicure. Her nails were bitten so far that they showed blood, the tender skin around her finger shredded and torn.

"I don't work for beer," she said.

"That's just a bonus," the man said, and held something up. It was a necklace, a cheap chain and some kind of pendant that glittered and reflected the sad streetlights. "How about this? Something pretty for the pretty lady."

Kelly would think back to this moment often. It would come to him in dreams, completely unbidden. He'd be running down a grassy hill with a herd of wild horses, their hooves pounding around him. He'd have his arms out like an airplane, feeling the wind and freedom and the exhilaration of being in wide, open spaces with these beating hearts of feral muscle, and then he would stop. He'd pull up short, trapped in this piss-scented alley, and the horses would thunder on without him. He'd stand, and see his Joy staring at this cheap trinket like it was the most beautiful thing on God's green earth.

He'd try to reach out to her in this dream, to raise his hand or shout her name, but the most he could do was watch helplessly as she reached out to touch the pendant, pull her hand back tenderly, and turn to walk away with the man.

She didn't come back that night. Not at all. Kelly waited, his hands shoved deep into the pockets of his hoodie, his head against the rough brick wall. He stood straight and stretched, not caring if he looked like a long shadow unboxing itself from its dybbuk prison. He paced back and forth, his feet scraping against the broken bottles and used syringes that littered the area.

"Knock it off," a short girl with ratty black hair said. "Your creeping is going to scare guys away, and I'm sick as hell and need something to fix with."

"I'm waiting for Joy," Kelly said, and glowered at her.

The girl was unmoved. She looked at him with eyes that seemed cloudy. She had to have been born like this, hopeless and bored. She couldn't have ever been a tiny little girl with a favorite stuffed animal who loved riding on her father's shoulders. That couldn't be true.

"I don't care who you're waiting for. Do it somewhere else."

She turned away, her small back blocking him as firmly as any bolted metal door. He wanted to throttle her, to pick her up by her slim throat and shake, shake, shake her while her legs bicycled in the air. He wanted to see her face purple and her mouth open, see her tongue starting to protrude as she tried to scream, as she tried to breathe, as she—

Kelly reared back, gasping. He realized that his hands were reaching for her. He tucked them up under his armpits and hurried away.

It started to rain, a cold, cheerless rain. It wouldn't make the flowers bloom. It wouldn't clean the streets or wash heavy makeup away, leaving rounded cheeks fresh and cool. It just plastered wet hair to faces and made the night feel even crueler. It made every hope and dream sodden. It did, however, run down Kelly's face and drop from his nose and chin better than any tears ever could.

He walked all through the night.

During the day, he caught a few hours of sleep next to the vent by an old laundry. It smelled like mold and dryer sheets. He thought of his mother and curled up around himself. After feeling good and sorry for himself, he painfully got to his feet and looked for Joy.

He looked all day.

And then all night.

The next day, he ate a crushed-up taco shell and drank as much water from a public water fountain as he could hold. He thought his stomach would burst. He sloshed away. No Joy.

No Joy that night. Or the next day.

The sun made noises like it was time to retire.

"Whoops, time for bed," the sun said, and the city widened its sleepy eyes in horror. "Time for me to rest and for the things of the night to come alive and take hold. It is the hour for things to hiss and creep and take the tender hearts of the young in their teeth. Fare thee well."

Shadows swept long and deep, turning the daytime parks and playthings into that which was dark and sinister. Kelly himself felt his arms stretch and elongate, felt fangs protrude and his walk turn into something prowling like a wild animal. He was no longer the good-natured, corn-fed boy who bagged groceries and helped little old ladies out to their car. He was here. He was Joyless. Anger built a fire in his chest and fed it with logs of resentment and shards of glass.

He scuttled with the other wild things away from the edges of the light, preferring to teeter outside where the darkness was deep and horrific and hungry.

He bypassed his usual route and walked around the back of a boarded-up store. He smelled filth and something sharp that reminded him briefly of gasoline. If he had a match, he'd burn the entire city to the ground with all of them inside. There was so much trash and refuse around that the area would catch immediately. He'd make a wall of fire so high that astronauts could see the fire from space. A burning, roaring inferno on a hill should never be hidden under a bushel, so the Bible said. He'd burn the evil out.

He nearly stepped on a bag of soggy rags covered in fallen leaves. He adjusted his footing and then stopped suddenly. He saw something move.

"Ugh, a rat," he thought, and his first thought was disgust. His second thought was whether or not he could catch it. Could he grab it in his shaking hands and bash its head against the concrete ground before it had time to bite him? How much meat would a rat have on it? How would Joy feel if she came strolling by and saw her Kelly with actual meat cooking over a fire? Would that be enough for her to forgive him for not protecting her?

He blinked rapidly and wiped his nose on his sleeve. He crouched down, looking for something to hit the rat with, if that's what, indeed, it was.

It wasn't. The leaves moved again, and he saw fingers poke out. Just a flash of dark skin. He fell back onto his butt, scrabbling away in surprise. Then, his mind cleared. This was a hand. A moving hand.

Somebody was buried under the trash and leaves.

He sprang forward, grabbed the hand, and pulled. What he thought was a pile of garbage was instead a man who looked a few years older than him. His face was slack, and his eyes refused to open. Kelly pulled the leaves from the man's face and tried to get him to speak.

"Hey. Hey! Are you okay? Sir?"

The man wouldn't sit up, and Kelly couldn't make him. He kept falling limply back to the ground, moaning. He slurred something out, but Kelly couldn't understand him.

It was there, on his knees behind the garbage bins, that he heard the most beautiful sound of his life.

"Kel?"

His name, spoken whisper-soft, and suddenly his ears pricked like those of a dog.

"Joy? Joy, where are you?"

He crawled on hands and knees, completely ignoring the man who was again unconscious beside him. Back in the farthest corner, tucked away from the streetlights and police sirens, was Joy.

"Oh, bunny!" Kel exclaimed, and he clasped her to his body. Her head lolled, her eyes rolling back until he could see the whites. "Bunny, bunny, you're alive. You're alive. I'm here. I found you. It's me, your Kelly. I have you. Everything is okay. You're safe."

He was lying. He knew he was lying, but he didn't care. He would promise her everything if she just stayed with him, and he did. He promised her heaven and hell and a home with a hundred milk cows and flashy cars and everything she ever wanted. She'd bathe in champagne and dress in new clothes, a different gown for every single day.

"You'd wear it once and then throw it away," he said, and his voice sounded different to him. It was high, like a child's. "Or we could donate them to people who live on the street. We'll box them up and wrap them like birthday presents, and we'll bring them to this very city with all the food we could carry, and we'll give them out. Right here. It will be like Christmas every single day. People will be walking back here wearing nothing but fine things. And it will never rain. Can you imagine what that will be like, Joy?"

She didn't answer. Kelly could feel that her body was warm, and she was still breathing. Her tee shirt was torn and bunched up, exposing her filthy bra. The rest of her clothes were missing. She was completely naked from the waist down, and Kelly's mouth trembled at that. He wrapped his arms around her, pulled her onto his lap, and cradled her.

She had needle marks in her arms, fresh and raw, and they nearly made him sob. They were ugly against her white, white skin.

His traitorous brain filled in the blanks and showed him how Joy had spent her last seven days. Human monsters poked sharp needles through her soft flesh, into her fresh veins, injecting evil into her blood, telling her lies, and filling her with poison love and a sinister high. If he had protected Joy, she would not have needed to feel that high. He would have given her that high.

"No, Joy," he said, and buried his face in her hair. Something foul had been rubbed into it, but he didn't care. "We escaped your father. We're here together. Come back to me. Don't go away again and leave me alone. You're all I have."

He tried to pick her up, but he wasn't strong enough. She was dead-weight against his twiggy arms, now starved of all their muscle. He covered as much of her body as he could with his hands, giving her as much privacy and body warmth as possible.

"I'll sing to you. Would you like that? How about a little Whitesnake?"

He sang every old song he knew. He went through all the classics, and the old rock that he and Joy had listened to through the years. After he sang those, he did some country and even some R&B, although he didn't know much. After that, he made up words to tunes he vaguely knew. Hymns and old tunes that his grandfather used to play on the phonograph when he was just a kid. The sun was just peeking over the city to assess the night's damage when Joy finally stirred.

"Kel...ly?" She asked and peered at him through slitted lids.

"I'm here," he said quickly. He tried to smile, but his mouth wouldn't work. It opened and attempted valiantly to turn up at the corners, but he knew it was just a big, blank maw of darkness. He could swallow Joy and the stars and the world and the universe with the huge void inside of him. He closed his mouth and swallowed instead.

"Joy. I'm glad you're awake. I've been watching over you."

"Shin—y," she said, and her hand moved toward her breast. It was clumsy and heavy. Kelly grasped her fingers. She pulled away weakly and gestured to her chest.

Around her neck and under her shirt was the necklace. The pendant was a star made out of something that looked like glass. It shimmered dimly in the light of the rising sun. It was beautiful and horrible, and Kelly wished he could worship it and break it between his back teeth. He'd grind it up and spit the bloody shards onto the sticky sidewalk; hallelujah, all praise be to its name.

"Yes, it's here," he said and wrapped Joy's nearly lifeless fingers around it. That despicable, coveted thing. "It's beautiful. I hope you keep it always."

She turned her head toward Kelly's chest and fell asleep. It seemed much more natural this time, a healing sleep instead of near death. Her chest rose and fell, and her heart stretched and beat. Blood rushed back and forth, to and fro, hurriedly spreading disease and who-knows-what to every part of her body.

"What did I miss?" The sun asked, shining over the city. "Today is a brand new day, full of beauty and promise."

Kelly traced his fingers down the needle marks on Joy's arms, terrified of the holes in her skin, that an infection had been injected inside her, and the infection was about to spread and replace her soul.

He let his tears fall.

THEY had been gone for several months. Kelly had hoped things would get better, but that was his usual, optimistic nature. Sweet boy. Poor boy. Boys like him had their souls ripped away and their hearts cubed and put through the meat grinder. That was just the way of it.

Joy had turned into a bundle of sticks. Her eyes peered out from dark circles, and her lips were perpetually cracked. Half of the people she solicited roughly turned her away.

"You don't know what you're missing!" Joy screamed back at them. She was usually so drunk that she barely managed to stand. This particular time was no different. "Think some other girl is going to give you such a good blow?"

"Joy," Kel said, putting his hand on her shoulder. She jerked away from him.

"What, you gonna preach at me now, you goody two-shoes? Tell me how I'm not taking care of my holy temple?" She gestured at her body with both hands, and her eyes were burning in the hollows of her sockets. Kelly knew she was spoiling for a fight, but he wasn't going to be the one to give it to her.

"I got a couple of hours of work today. I have some food."

He handed her a small package wrapped in tinfoil. She grabbed it greedily.

"Ah, thanks, Kelly. You're so sweet. Always thinking of me."

"Always," he said. "Come sit and eat with me."

He took her hand and led her to a spot near the wall. She sat down unsteadily.

"I want to see you happy, Joy," Kelly said. He kept his voice quiet, even, the same way he used to when talking with a scared cat or wounded pup.

"I'm happy," she said, her mouth full. "Food makes me happy. Hey, you didn't bring me anything else, something else I'm hungry for, did you?"

He shook his head.

"Just that."

She finished and wiped her face carefully with her fingers. For a second, he saw the Old Joy, the True Joy. She used to fastidiously wipe the blood from her face so nobody would know what happened at home. He knew. The entire school knew. Everyone in town knew, but that didn't help her much, did it? It was all a façade. Joy pretended that everything was perfectly normal, and so did the town. Whatever kept the status quo, right?

He had never hated his hometown as much as he did at that very moment.

"What?" She asked, looking at him. "Why are you staring at me?"

Kelly smiled, and it was real.

"Just admiring your beautiful face," he said truthfully.

She laughed.

"Stop it. I know what I look like."

"Like sunshine," he told her. He ruffled her hair with his hand. "Like Joy."

"Like Hell itself came here walkin', and I know it, baby. You think I don't, but I do." She leaned back and looked at where the stars would be without the city's light pollution. "I used to be pretty."

Kelly slid closer to her and put his arm around her.

"Don't say that, bunny. You're still pretty."

Her laughter sounded more angry than mirthful. The sharpness of it startled both of them. Kelly felt like it was a sharpened shiv that found its way beneath his skin and into the tender part beneath his ribs. She continued twisting it.

"I see myself, Kelly. I know what I look like and how I act. Sometimes I'm so horrible to you, and it's like I'm inside of myself, watching. I know I'm hurting you. I want someone to hurt the way I do, but nobody cares except for you. So I hurt you, and that hurts the rest of the world. But it isn't right." She took his hand in hers and looked at him intensely. "I do love you, Kelly Stands. Sometimes I almost forget it, but it's true."

He cupped her dirty face in his thin hands.

"I love you right back," he said simply. "You're my Joy."

"That's correct, sir," she said, and leaned in to kiss him.

His lips touched hers, and he remembered their sweet, awkward kisses behind the woodshed, or in the barn, or once in the supply closet at school. She was in there looking for board erasers. He had been sent in for paper towels.

"Oh, sorry," he had said, and shuffled his too-big feet in his too-small shoes. "I didn't know you were in here."

She had whirled around, her eyes wide, her blond hair spinning around her like a halo or firefly glow. He had never seen anything so startled or wild or pure. She slid past him to the door, and her hip bumped into his. His hand came to the small of her back to steady her, and he wasn't sure how it happened after that, but suddenly, his mouth was on hers, and her arms were wrapped around him so tightly that he thought she was going to squeeze his heart until it popped like a balloon. Even if it did, it would erupt with sweet, Joy-colored confetti.

He kissed her now, leaning his body into hers the slightest bit. She responded, pushing her breasts against him and sliding her tongue into his mouth aggressively.

He pulled back just a little, but she mashed her lips against his and moaned. It sounded like theatrics, not like his Joy. He felt her fumble against the button of his jeans. The fingers of her other hand slid searchingly into his back pocket.

He ripped himself away, breathing hard.

"What are you looking for, Joy?" He growled like a beast. Naïve Kelly had disappeared along with the memory of that day in the supply closet, of the sweetest kiss he had ever experienced. He felt his face furrow as he grimaced.

Joy pressed herself into him again. "I'm not looking for a thing, baby," she said, her mouth against his neck. She moved to his earlobe and bit gently. Kelly hissed in his breath, and Joy took that moment to surge into the corners and hollows of his body. She was a liquid, and he was a container that needed to be filled.

He was drowning. He was drowning in Joy. Her hot mouth and clutching fingers made him want to sprint down the alley away from her and also hold her so tightly that she melted into his skin. They could share one body, become one person. She could run through his veins like the heroin she wept for in the middle of the night, and they could both get high together.

This thought splashed over him like filthy water from the gutter. His senses cleared. The heady vapor of Joy and her scorching kisses lifted enough that he realized her hand was in his pocket again.

She was going for his wallet.

"Joy," he groaned painfully. "Stop."

She mistook his disappointment for passion.

"Never, baby," she said, and deepened the kiss. Kelly slowly slid his hand down her arm.

"Yes, baby," she whispered and moved against him.

He circled his fingers around her wrist and then grabbed it roughly. Joy squeaked, and the wallet fell from her hand.

"What is this, huh?" He asked her. His voice was hoarse from want and pain. "You're stealing from me? From *me,* Joy?"

"Baby," she began, but Kelly pushed her away and shot to his feet.

"Joy," he rasped, and there were a thousand emotions as he said her name. His eyes threatened to spill tears. He was going to be just another teenager crying on the sidewalk, another little boy bawling because of some girl. "Do you think I'd honestly keep anything from you?"

She peered up at him from the ground. Her mouth moved like she was trying to say the words "I'm sorry" or whisper his name. Perhaps she was simply telling him to go to hell. He dashed his sleeve against his traitorous eyes. They threatened to expose him for the absolute child that he really was inside.

"I've given you everything I have," he said and winced when his voice broke on the last word. "I don't have anything left. I walked away from everything for you."

"Kelly," she said, and sorrow and something shinier flashed across the surface of her eyes for just a second. Then the moment was gone, and her gaze drifted to the wallet on the ground.

Kelly's stomach went cold. He could imagine what they looked like to someone standing far away. They didn't look like lovers at all. They looked like two destitute people who just couldn't find it in themselves to care anymore.

Kelly's chin trembled slightly.

"Do you remember," he asked slowly, "the day of my asthma attack?"

She didn't move, but her body language told him she was listening.

"You saved me that day, Joy. You ran out into the road and got help. If it hadn't been for you, I would have died."

Her voice was low.

"If it hadn't been for me, you wouldn't have been out there. You would have been at home where you belonged." She climbed unsteadily to her feet. Kelly almost reached out to help her, but what was the use? How could you hold a ghost? You can't. You have to let her whoosh right through you on her way out the door.

"You would have been home," she continued, and her voice was rising, "with your *mother* who loves you and your *father* who thinks you hung the moon." She hit him with each emphasized word. He took the blows stalwartly. Her frail hands were too weak to do any damage to his body, but each time her tiny fists struck out, his heart shattered in half. The pieces of it became smaller and smaller until he thought his blood would cease flowing through his body without anything there to pump it.

"You'd be home going to *school* and dating other *girls* and finally being happy, Kel. You'd be happier without me, I know it. Now don't deny it," she said as he tried to interrupt, "because I know what you want to say. But you would honestly be better." Her hands fell to her side. They stood bathed in the sick glow of a neon sign.

"I have to see you every day, knowing that you're here because of me. Starving because of me. Because I'm too selfish to make you go home. I can't deal with it. I can't look at you because it hurts too much."

He tried to say something. He was a beaten dog, and she was holding a stick made of words. He cringed and shuddered at what she was going to say next, but he couldn't leave. He just couldn't. That wasn't what a loyal dog did.

"I'm a cancer, Kelly," she said, and her voice was crystal clear. The slurring was gone. She was clear and wholly present for the first time in months. It terrified him. The sheer force that was Joy was almost more than he could bear.

"Joy," he said. At her name, her eyes flicked to his. They held each other's gaze for a very long time.

"A cancer," she repeated. "Sure, it will hurt at first when you cut me out. You'll have to heal. But then everything will be better." She put her hand on his chest, curling her fingers into his shirt like she used to. Back when Battered Joy and Terrified Joy and Desperately in Love Joy were the same person, and she had been Her Kelly.

He put his hand on top of hers.

"I don't want to cut you out. I want you with me, always. Even like this."

But the moment was gone. It had flown by as the best things always flew by, and she was gone. The heartbreak and craving were back, her body trembling in want of the next fix, her brain eaten alive by the insects swarming inside of it. The insects would keep swarming, desperate, and hungry until they were fed the one thing they wanted. Needed.

Her eyes fell back to the wallet, which was still lying on the ground.

Kelly teetered as though the world had dropped out from underneath him. That's what it felt like. There was stability and his steadfast love for this beautiful, broken, bizarre girl, and then suddenly there was...nothing.

"I don't have any money in there, Joy. I used it all on food."

Her tongue darted across her lips, too fast, like a lizard's. Kelly was afraid that if she met his eyes again, he'd discover she had yellow, slitted reptile eyes.

"On food, Joy," he emphasized. He could see the cogs turning in her head as she studied him and the wallet, gauging how long it would take for her to swoop it up and pelt down the alleyway.

"Take a look inside if you don't believe me," he said. His voice sounded like an echo of itself. He sounded utterly defeated.

She cocked her head and looked at him. The craftiness on her face destroyed anything that resembled the old Joy. This wasn't the woman he loved. This was just some desperate stranger looking for an easy mark.

He slowly turned out his pockets, one by one. She watched carefully.

"Look," he said, turning around so she could see him from all angles. "No money. No other food. No score, nothing to trade or sell. I've given you everything I have. All of it."

Her lips twitched as if in disappointment. Her skin was clammy and sweaty, her flesh in constant motion from a million muscle cramps inside. She slowly slid down to the ground by his wallet.

He held his hand out to her and held his breath. His hands were cracked and dry, the fingernails bitten. They weren't the hands of a boy who could save her. They weren't the hands of a boy who knew how to be saved.

She picked up the wallet. She opened it. She looked at the picture shoved inside. It was the two of them, two years ago, smiling into a camera that some random friend had held. Kelly was grinning his easy, ridiculous smile, and his arm clumsily draped around Joy. Her eyes were screwed up against the sun, her head thrown back in laughter.

She looked for a long time. She traced her finger over their faces and clothes as if she had never seen them before, as if these were new beloved people with amazing adventures and lives that she wanted to commit to memory. She'd sit at their feet and ask how they met and what their favorite flowers were. The boy looked like somebody she could marry and have babies with and trust to raise their children with love. The girl looked like someone she wanted to share her secrets with. They could sit in her bedroom at night, braiding each other's hair and gossiping about the things that happened at school.

"Do you remember?" Kelly asked. He hardly dared to breathe, lest this skittish animal bolted and broke away. "We used to be so happy. We can be happy again."

Joy finished opening the rest of the wallet and ran her fingers through the billfold and tiny pockets. She came up empty. She looked disappointed before regarding Kelly with a fake smile and blank eyes.

"Hey, baby, maybe you could go out and score me something good. I need to get away from all of this for a while."

She slapped the wallet into his outstretched hand and walked away, disappearing into the cold darkness of the alley.

THIS time, Joy had kept her distance for nearly a week, and each morning, Kelly woke up alone instead of with Joy—Morning Joy—who was the most desperate, the most foreign and infected and sick and irritated. It was like a thousand mosquitoes were nipping her skin, and she would do anything, sell anything, or take anything to make them stop. Kelly stood in front of a store that sold glass sculptures and studied them through the window. Maybe if Joy was with him, she'd look into the glass and be cured from the inside out. The glimmer of glass made the stars shine beauty into his veins, and there was no room for anything else.

"Pretty, aren't they?"

A voice to his left, down by his elbow. He turned and saw a tiny woman with a crinkled face.

"Yes, ma'am," he answered.

She grinned, and her face crinkled even more.

"Oh, a polite one. I like that. Where you from, boy?"

Kel paused awkwardly. The old woman nodded.

"One of those," she said knowingly. "Hope whatever you were running from, or for, was worth it."

Kelly thought of Joy and how she used to burrow into his side while sleeping. She wasn't as hard, then. She was simply herself, Joy with her Kel, and that was the only moment when either of them was truly happy.

"It's worth it, ma'am," he answered.

The woman peered inside the glass store. "Ever go inside?"

Kelly cleared his throat. "They've asked me to leave. Twice. Pretty sure they think I'm going to steal something or knock it over."

She looked at him innocently. "Would you?"

He shook his head vigorously. "Never, ma'am. I just would like to look, that's all."

She was quiet for a while. Then she said, "You seem like a nice boy. Does your family know where you are?"

He shook his head, suddenly unable to speak.

"They cruel to you?"

He shook his head again.

"Think they're worried sick?"

Kelly nodded and dashed at his eyes with his filthy sleeve. The woman patted his arm.

"You're a good boy, and I like to trust good boys. Here's what I'm going to do. Take my phone and make a phone call home. Go on, take it. I'll be browsing in this store for a few minutes while you do. When you're done, you can return the phone. Sounds to me like that would work right well for everyone."

She reached into her purse and handed him the phone. He couldn't meet her eyes.

"Good boy," she said again and patted his hands. She wandered into the store.

Kelly stared at the phone as if it couldn't possibly be real. It was more likely that he had caught a fairy or a magical talisman in his hands. His finger shook as he punched in the numbers and held the phone to his ear.

One ring. Two.

Maybe this wasn't such a good idea.

Three rings. Four.

Nobody was home to answer.

Five.

What would he leave on the answering machine? Should he say anything at all? Hang up? He didn't know what to do, he didn't know what to do, he didn't know...

"Hello?"

Her voice was weary. His mother had grown tired while he was away. Kelly's breath caught.

"Mama?"

He hadn't called her "mama" in years, not since he was a little boy, terrified of the monsters in his closet. Joy had real monsters in her house, but Kelly's could be chased away with his parents' love and a little bit of Monster Spray.

"Kelly? Kelly, is that you?"

"M-mama?"

His mama screamed, then made a sound so happy and loud and forceful that Kelly didn't know whether to laugh or cry, so he did both.

"Kelly, I've been so worried, you have no idea! Are you okay? Are you safe? Is that girl with you? Are you coming home?"

Kel wept into the sleeve of his hoodie and assured his mother that yes, he was all right, and yes, they were alive, and yes, he still said his prayers and tried to be a good man, and he loved his mama, yes, he did, and he always would, and tell his dad he loved him, too, because he did, it was true, he loved them so much that his soul hurt.

"Kelly," his mother said, and her voice had that Very Serious Tone that made his body chill. "I have to tell you something about your daddy. His heart hasn't been so good, and he's been real sick. I think you need to come home, son. Come home and...tell your daddy goodbye."

"It's...that bad?"

Her voice was somber. "It's that bad. But God told you to call today so you could come home before it's too late. Will she come, too?"

"I don't know, Ma. I don't think so. She never wants to come back."

"I don't blame her. Her daddy is right awful. I think he'll kill her if he sees her. You keep her safe as much as you can, but you get on back here, even if it's just for a little while. Okay?"

"I love you, Ma."

He hung up the phone and stared at the cold cement under his feet.

The old woman came outside and took her phone.

"Well?" She asked. Her face was alight. It was aglow. Kel wanted to sweep her into her arms and thank her a million times, but his head was full of marbles and thoughts and fears.

He simply looked at her.

"Everything's changed," he said.

JOY didn't want to hear it at first.

"You're just trying to get me to go back, you son of a–" She took a swing and missed. She staggered and glared at Kelly as though he had pushed her.

"My dad is dying, Joy," Kelly said. His hands hung limply at his sides. He couldn't have defended himself if he wanted to. He stared at something behind Joy's shoulder, some spot in the distance with nothing to offer except a place to rest his eyes.

"You'll say anything, won't you?" She spat. "I'm tired of this dance. I'm not going home, and nothing you can say will make me." She looked like she was going to say more, but Kelly's strong skeleton betrayed him, and he slid down to the ground, seemingly boneless. He wrapped his arms around his skinny legs, his embarrassed face held low and sobbed.

Joy watched him for just a second, and something seemed to move inside her heart. Street Joy disappeared, and Real Joy came creeping back.

"Kel," she whispered and squatted down next to him. She pressed her forehead to his and kissed his salty face. "Kelly, I'm so sorry. You're telling the truth. I know you are. I'm sorry I've been so awful. I know how you feel about your daddy."

The tears felt so good, so strong and cleansing, and they had brought Joy back to him. *There might be worth in human tears,* Kelly thought vaguely. *Maybe one day we'll collect them and trade them like diamonds. Tears will be our new currency. Wouldn't that make us appreciate everything we had if we had to earn each and every item with our tears?*

"I'm losing my mind," he said aloud, and Joy was right by his side.

"You're not. You're a good, strong man and a good, strong son. We need to get you home."

He looked at her, puzzled, not sure if he heard her correctly.

"Home?" He asked. The word tasted...sweet.

"We'll need to get you cleaned up first," she said, looking him up and down. "It's been a while, and your hair is awful long. Your mom might pass out when she sees it."

He turned his head and watched her flit around, making plans. He had to say it again, say the words slowly, and make sure they were absolutely real and that he wasn't stuck in this strange half-shadows/half-light dream world that might be his undoing.

"We're going home?"

He hated the hopeful note in his voice. He was disgusted with his weakness. He saw Joy's shoulders slump. She turned to him, brown eyes full of pain.

"No," he said, and shook his head. She took both of his hands in hers.

"Baby," she said and kissed his fingertips. He shut his eyes like a child. If he didn't open them, perhaps he'd be safe from the monsters that swarmed underneath his bed and in the dark streets. Maybe he'd be safe from the horrific disappointment he knew was coming.

"Baby. I know you need to go home, but I can't. Do you understand? I can't go with you."

"We won't see your father," Kelly insisted. "You'll stay at my house. I won't let him touch you, I swear. I'll—"

"It's more than that," she said, and she spoke so solemnly and low that he could barely hear her. "There's nothing to go back to. I have nothing left. I can't go like this," she gestured at the bruises and tracks in her arms, "and I don't want to. But you, my love. You need to go home. You know you do."

They huddled together that night, her thin fingers tucked into the hole in the knee of his jeans. A couple of Joy's friends approached them, but she shook her head and mouthed "No." Kelly fell asleep, and Joy ran her fingers through his hair. She rubbed her cheek against the filthy sleeve of his hoodie.

He stirred.

"Joy?"

"Shhh," she soothed and kissed his shoulder. "Go to sleep, love. I'm the last one awake. I'll watch over you."

He faded back into oblivion, and Joy pressed her back into the stone wall, staring at the smoggy sky far into the night. There were no stars there. Sometime before daylight, she slipped away. She returned with a torn shirt, cauliflower ear, and a single, solitary bus ticket.

They cleaned up the best they could at the bus station. Kelly washed his face and tried to comb his hair back with his hands. He smiled awkwardly at Joy.

"Is this a face only a mother could love?" He asked, and waggled his brows.

Joy laughed, and it almost sounded normal. "A mother and me. I love that face more than life."

Kelly's smile faded.

"I love you more than life."

Joy handed him his backpack, staring at the ground. Kel reached out and tipped her chin up so she'd meet his gaze.

"I'll stay if you need me to. You know that, Joy. I'll do anything for you."

Her brown eyes washed over with so many emotions that Kelly was nearly dazzled.

"I know. You've proven it over and over and over again." She took her necklace off, the one with the shiny glass star, and tied it around his neck. "It suits you," she said. She hugged him, and it was the old days. He was just a young man worried about school and a job and making sure the lawn was mowed in the right pattern so it looked nice and neat for his mother. He closed his eyes and rested his chin on her hair.

"I'll come right back," he promised. "I'll bring money and more stuff for us. Clean up good and get a job this time. I'll make someone hire me, anyone, doing anything. Things will be different." He pulled back and looked into her eyes again. "Promise me you'll be here. Promise I'll be able to find you."

She reddened at his intensity. "I'll be here, Kel, waiting for you. I can't wait to get into some clean clothes. Will you bring a band for my hair? If I don't tie it back soon, I'll go crazy and chop the whole thing clean off."

"So many bands," he swore. "A hairband for every day of the month." He pulled his hoodie over his head and handed it to her.

She looked confused.

"It's your favorite one. You'll need this."

He shook his head. "No, you're my favorite one. It will keep you warm until I get back. Just…don't forget me while I'm gone, okay?"

"In a week?" She teased. She leaned her forehead against his chest. "I could never forget you, Kel. Never ever, not even if you never come back."

"But I will," he promised. His eyes were fierce, fiercer than he had ever felt them. "Don't you doubt, Joy. Just be where I can find you."

He kissed her again and climbed onto the bus. He slouched down in his seat and squeezed his eyes shut as it began to move. He hoped his hoodie would somehow turn into a magical shield, covering Joy from the top of her head down to her knees, keeping her soul inside instead of letting it seep out through the pinpricks in her arms.

He slept. There was no one awake.

HIS mother met him two days later at the station. He wrapped his long arms around her, and she cried into his shirt. "You're filthy," she sobbed. "You're so skinny. I've missed you so much. I've never seen a boy who needs a shower more than you."

"I love you, too, Ma," he said, and slung his arm over her shoulder as they walked to the car. She couldn't stop touching him the entire drive, picking at the lint on his arm or poking at his hand with a shaking finger. Finally, he took her hand and held it.

"I'm here, Ma. You aren't imagining it. I'm real."

She drove the rest of the way home with his hand clenched tightly in hers, occasionally pulling it up close to her heart.

It was late when they got in.

"Take a shower while I put something together for dinner," his mother said.

The hot water was a sin, hitting his face and back as brutally as Joy's father had ever hit her. He scrubbed the city out of his hair and the grime from his body. The horrors of the past months sluiced down the drain along with the dirty water. He climbed out and wrapped a towel around his hips. He studied his face in the mirror, all eyes and too-long hair and still no beard. He wasn't sure he would ever grow one.

What would Joy do for a shower?

The thought turned his stomach because he knew Joy would do just about anything for anyone. But not after he came back. He'd take her, and they'd run to another city, a better one where she didn't have regular johns and her sickness and her strung-out friends. They'd start fresh, and she'd have sunshine on her hair every day.

He ate dinner with guilty gusto.

He climbed into his bed. It was plenty warm and soft, topped with a quilt his mother had made. After two hours of sleeplessness, he folded the quilt and set it aside as something to bring back for Joy. A blanket for both of them, just like old times. He huddled on his side all night, thinking of Joy shivering in the cold without him.

You aren't alone, he mentally told her. *It's safe to fall asleep. I'm awake and watching.*

He held the star pendant in his hand and counted the seconds until the sun rose.

The morning was full of breakfast, a haircut, and a visit to his father in the hospital.

"Kelly," his father said, and his meaty hands, sans meat, clasped around Kelly's fingers. "You're home."

"I didn't mean to worry you, Dad," Kelly answered. He knew the words sounded weak, but they bloomed with truth.

"I know, son. And I feel so much better now that you're home to take care of your mother."

"Don't talk like that, Dad. You're going to be fine. We can take care of her together."

His dad clapped Kelly's hands again and met his eyes.

"I wish you could be a child again, Kel, and not have to worry like a man worries. But you are a man now, and we have to face up to things. I'm not getting out of here. This is where I end. It's up to you to care for your mom now that I can't."

"But Dad…"

His father smiled at him, and it was rife with sadness. It was the type of smile a boy should never have to see.

"Make me proud, son."

Kelly tried. Every day he woke up, and his first thought was "Joy." Then he thought, "My parents," and he set to work. He painted the house and fixed all the things his father had meant to get to. He let his mother make him his favorite meals. He sat by his father's bedside and cooled his fevered face with a cool cloth. Days passed. Soon, it was weeks. Then the season changed, and his father was gone.

Nobody was ready.

Kelly wore a new suit with enough fabric to cover his daddy-long legs, and he carried his father's casket on his shoulder. The physical weight was also born by other men, but Kelly carried the emotional weight alone. His mother had long stopped sobbing and simply stood there at the gravesite, her eyes sightless as she stared at the love of her life being lowered into a hole in the dirt. Kelly stood beside her, scowling at the brazen sun that dared to show its face on this day. Shouldn't it be raining at funerals? Shouldn't the atmosphere itself drip with sorrow like the rest of them? He thought of his father. He thought of Joy.

"I don't know what to do," Kelly's mother murmured. Her fingers picked at her new funeral hat. "What am I supposed to do?"

Kel took her hand to stop the birdlike tremor. "We go home. We serve food and nod our heads. And then we go to sleep. Tomorrow is a new day."

"How do I live without your father? Who do I make breakfast for? How do I sleep in that big bed without him? It's so very big. I...I can't do this alone."

Kelly hugged his mother close.

"You're not alone, Ma. I'm here."

Kelly left his father in the cold, hard ground. The ride home was long and silent. Neither he nor his mother said a word. The car seemed far too empty with just the two of them. No, it wasn't just the two of them. Joy and Kelly's father rode along with them.

The car was full of ghosts.

When they returned, Kelly sat for a second before getting out and opening his mother's car door. He took her elbow and guided her into the house. They walked into a room of hushed conversation and ambrosia salads. Grief is overwhelming, but a casserole seems to help. Neighbors pressed pies into their hands. Baskets of warm rolls. Fragrant breads wrapped in tinfoil.

Kelly's mother stood there, robotically holding the food, until a kind woman guided her to the kitchen and helped her find a place to set it down.

The door blew open, and the air changed. It became hard, jagged. It pulsed like something with far too many tentacles and a spiny beak.

Joy's father, Buck, stood in the doorway, emanating an energy that made Kelly look up from his untouched plate. The man saw him and strode over.

"Where is my daughter?" He demanded. His eyes were brown like Joy's, but that's all they had in common. "Why didn't she come home with you?"

"Buck, this isn't the place," an older man said, and touched Buck's arm. Buck shook him off.

"Where is she? She needs to be home where she belongs."

Kelly set his plate of food down and drew himself upright. He was taller than Joy's dad now. When had that happened? How could such a small man do so much damage?

"She needs to be wherever you aren't," he said. "Home is anywhere far away from you."

The nervous chatter stopped. The house of mourning was silent. Kelly looked Joy's father squarely in the face, but his mind was far away. Joy cradling her wounded arm. Joy, with both eyes swelled shut. Joy damaged in the most private and secret of ways that she couldn't tell even Kelly about. Kelly's brain was full of electric wires. His attention sharpened.

"You little..." Buck's words were lost in the deep roar that was ripped from him while he swung. The sound startled Kelly. It was barbaric, something primal and not altogether human. The beefy fist caught him in the face, and his nose spouted blood. His teeth clacked together, and he felt a tooth chip. Buck knew just where to hit. He had plenty of practice.

Something in Kelly burst, then. He roared back and started windmilling his arms, connecting with flesh more often than not.

"Kelly!" His mother's voice.

Joy crying over him in the fields when he had his asthma attack. Joy sifting through garbage cans, looking for something to eat, the bone of her spine pressing too hard against her skin.

"Kelly!"

Hands pulled at him, but he was all rage and wiry young man muscle.

Joy counting out change so carefully. Disappearing into the night with a man while Kelly squeezed his eyes shut and pretended to be asleep because it was easier for both of them that way. Returning with dead eyes and a heroin habit and scabbing needle marks and that cheap star pendant that she found so beautiful.

"You did this," he screamed. His voice was the only sound in the room, encompassed all. "You did this to her! You broke her, you ruined her, you destroyed your little girl, and how could you? That isn't what a father does!"

Worn out, he finally stopped panting, held back by hands dressed in mourning black. Blood ran from his face onto his new, tattered suit. Buck crouched on the floor, shielding his face with his hands. Kelly's eyes roamed the room until they found his mother. Her face was white. Her hands shook.

"Ma," he said and had to clear his throat. He spit blood onto the carpet. "Ma, I'm sorry. I don't know what came over—"

"Find her, Kelly," his mother said. She dug into her purse, came over, and pressed her wallet and car keys into his hand. "Don't leave that little girl out there for one more second. You bring her home to us, do you understand?"

Kelly nodded and pulled her into a quick hug. He ran upstairs, his long legs eating the steps, and grabbed the bundle of things he had squirreled away for Joy.

"We won't let him touch her," his mother shouted after him. Kelly slammed the car into reverse and screamed out of the dirt driveway.

He flew. He flew. He drove through the night, as fast as he dared, stopping only to gas up the car.

"Ahem." An attendant cleared his throat politely and nodded toward Kelly's aching face. "Do you want some ice?"

"Oh. No, thanks." Kelly headed toward the bathroom and cleaned up the dried blood. He dabbed at his suit with paper towels and washed his hands carefully. He ran his wet hands through his hair, trying to look presentable for his Joy.

His nose was swollen, and his face scuffed and cut from Buck's rings, but his eyes burned with something dark and deep and full of resolve. This wasn't the lost Kelly who usually looked back at him from gas station bathroom mirrors. His face had changed, the bones somehow shifting beneath his skin until he looked wolfish and whole. His thin shoulders had straightened themselves under the suit he had bought to honor his dead father. This Kelly didn't need his Joy to watch over him while he slept. He would do the watching for both of them.

"I'm coming," he said aloud, and his chipped teeth looked sharp. He felt that he could dip his head down and pierce somebody's jugular if it came to it.

He almost hoped it came to it.

He bought drinks and snacks with his mother's credit card. He bought so many things that the clerk gave him four bags. He was going to shower Joy with treats, cheap gas station chocolates and caramel popcorn and all the soda she could possibly handle. They were going to be ten years old again, stealing away in the dark to hide in the trees and eat SweeTARTS and penny candies because they could buy a whole ten with a dime. They were going to stuff themselves with chips until they were sick until Joy's shriveled stomach nearly burst from the goodness, and she would curl up in the passenger side of the car under his mother's quilt and sleep while he drove. He would drive and drive, under the sun and the stars, while she was safe and warm and protected, and every bad memory would leak out the syringe holes in her arms. He would keep watch. He'd be the last one awake.

"Think this will be enough for you?" The cashier asked wryly, eying the bags of snacks.

Kelly's face broke into a smile, and it felt deep. Genuine and natural. It spread and warmed his body from the face down.

"Enough for a bit. I'll be back soon. My girl and I will buy out the entire store."

He winked as he left. He held the door open for a striking brunette who was speaking to an Asian man with white sneakers. The man was gassing up an 18-wheeler.

"Sure thing, Lu," the woman called over her shoulder. She smiled her thanks at Kelly, and the world was full of stars. It was going to be a day of magic. He could just feel it. He nodded at her companion by the gas pumps, and the man nodded back.

See? Magic.

He jumped into the driver's seat and started on again. He sang with the radio. He sang his beating heart out.

The city was as gray as it had ever been, but this time his heart leapt a little in his chest. Somewhere huddled on that cracked concrete was his Joy. He was so much later coming for her than he intended to be. He hoped she forgave him. He hoped she jumped into his arms and showered his face with kisses like she did when she was happy. He knew she would be happy.

"I beat your dad up," he would say, standing there in his scruffy, ruined-suit glory. "I beat him up in front of everybody after my father's funeral. He'll never touch you again. We won't let him. Mom says to bring you home to live with us now. We can help take care of her. She needs us, Joy. And we need you."

"Oh, Kel!" she'd exclaim, and her brown eyes would be the warmest things he had ever seen. "We're all rescuing each other. We're all keeping watch. It's perfect. It couldn't be better."

This is what love is. Spark and ashes and light. Ignition and desecration.

He threw his backpack over his shoulder and hurried to their usual squatting spot, but she wasn't there. No matter. He'd look elsewhere.

She wasn't behind the Chinese place, or the gas station, or window shopping at any of the fine stores. His Adam's apple seemed bigger than usual, and it was hard for him to swallow.

He'd keep looking. He'd never stop looking.

She wasn't buried in the leaves or strung out in the park. He searched all of her favorite places and a few areas she swore she'd never go again. She wasn't anywhere to be seen.

The sun yawned and cooed about it being a busy day. It slid cozily behind the horizon.

No, no, no. It was so much harder to search in the dark. Kelly walked until he was snowed under by sheer despair. His footsteps were slow and heavy as he made his way to their usual spot.

He huddled against the wall, waiting. The cement seemed harder than it had before, the night more chilled. Without Joy's body warmth, he shivered and shook. Had she been this cold without him, without her Kel-Bear to keep her warm? He felt even more guilty and he wasn't sure that was even possible.

Morning came, but no Joy. It was an utterly Joyless day.

He didn't find her the next day, either.

Kelly's heart didn't fit in his chest quite right. It wasn't made of muscle, after all, but uncomfortable gears and springs. His lungs were too small, tucked incorrectly into his rib cage somewhere. He couldn't breathe, couldn't focus, couldn't think of anything except that he couldn't find his Joy, couldn't find his love. Had she left the city? Started staying in a different spot? Why didn't she wait for him?

Because he hadn't come for her, that was why. Because life and death and everything in between stopped him. No, because he *let* it stop him. It was his watch, and he blew it.

He saw some shapes through the steam from the manholes. Heard voices. Voices he didn't particularly like, but voices he recognized.

He stood and approached them.

"Hey," he said. His voice sounded weedy, so he tried again. "Hey. It's Kelly. Have you guys seen Joy?"

Moon faces swung in his direction. Vacant eyes didn't blink.

"Joy," he said impatiently. "Tiny. Blonde. She shoots up that junk with you sometimes."

One of the figures spoke. "Kelly, man. Where have you been? Thought you got out of the city."

"My dad died. I'm back for Joy. Where is she?"

His eyes roamed over them until he saw a girl in the back. She was filthy, her hair matted, and her skin covered in sores. She was wearing his favorite hoodie. It fell down halfway to her shins.

His arms snaked to her, grabbing her by the collar.

"Where did you get this?" He demanded. "It isn't yours!"

"Screw off," she shouted and clawed at his face. Kelly winced and grabbed at his smarting skin.

"That...that's Joy's. I gave it to her before I left," he said, trying to keep his voice calm. "How did you get it?"

They didn't speak. Behind them, the city raged and churned and vomited out sirens and whistles and cellphone chatter. But here in this alley, the human silence was so great that it was crushing. It spoke without words. It relayed agony to his great, big, broken, mechanical heart.

"No," Kelly said and leaned heavily against the wall. "Don't say it."

"Hate to tell you," a boy said, "but she met up with a guy with kinks. Not anyone we'd seen around."

Kelly thought he was going to throw up. He doubled over, staring at the cement, his breathing coming faster and faster.

"What happened?" He asked.

"I don't think—"

"Tell me," Kelly screamed.

The boy was silent as he debated. Finally, he spoke.

"He stabbed her, man. He left her out back. The city cleaned her up."

Cleaned her up. Disposed of his Joy. Just another nameless runaway who didn't matter to anybody. Another junkie out prostituting herself on the street.

"Maybe she was high and didn't feel much," the boy offered. Kelly squeezed his eyes closed. The thought of Joy bleeding out while her soul was so very far away... this almost made it hurt worse.

Didn't they know who she was? How special? Didn't they know how her eyes shone with secrets and how her hair glittered in the sun? That her mother had been inspired by heaven itself when she decided to name her "Joy?"

"When?" The word was a gut punch, a breath forced from his body.

The girl in his hoodie shrugged, already disinterested and drifting away. "Two weeks ago? Maybe. Got anything to eat?"

Kellyshook his head automatically and watched them as they wandered through the mist. They disappeared.

He dropped his backpack to the ground and slumped beside it.

He stared at the sky.

There were no stars.

MERCEDES M. YARDLEY

Epilogue

Kelly's hair was carefully combed, but still refused to lie flat. It stuck up in wonder, curious, wanting to see everything around it. While Kelly bent over textbooks, his hair waved like plants in the sea. It was an antenna when he mopped the university buildings at night. It peered over his shoulder as he presented in class, and chicken-feathered behind him when he threw his clothes into the car and drove home to visit his mother every few months.

"How's it going, Ma?" He said, dropping his bag on the ground so he could hug his mother. "I've missed you."

"Oh, Kelly, it's so good to have you home," she exclaimed. "Look at you, all grown up and so handsome. You look more and more like your father every day."

He blushed. "You say that every time you see me."

"Because it's true, sweetie. Do you have any clothes for me to wash?"

"I'll do it, Ma. Tell me what's been going on since I was here last."

She would talk, and he would listen. He'd measure detergent and start the washer while she told him about the small parade they had, or the pumpkins growing in the patch, or how the library had just purchased two new stuffed chairs in a beautiful blue. He hung shelves and replaced lightbulbs while he told her about college and how his roommate called him "Hayseed" and only came up to his chest, but they were still inseparable.

"Bring him home next time," his mother said, and Kelly agreed. He knew his roommate would bloom under the love his mother would lavish on them. It would be a house of healing and goodness.

Later, after his mother was sleeping, Kelly sat on his bed for a long time. He listened to the house settle and creak. He could name every sound. The pipes knocked softly, and the air conditioner hummed. He realized he was listening for his father's footsteps as he walked around, putting the house to sleep.

Closing windows and locking doors. Flipping off lights and unplugging electronics. Kelly had done these things earlier in the evening, but it just wasn't the same. He hadn't realized his mother had heard his quiet footsteps and wept.

He stood up and went downstairs. He slipped outside and closed the door carefully behind him.

It was a warm Southern night, so different from his school back East. He'd grown to love the history and the biting cold, but knew that, deep down, he was a simple thing who wanted bare feet and magnolias.

His footfalls were soft on the grass. He was careful not to disturb anything that ran or slithered. He was simply a shadow ghosting toward the trees.

He'd driven by Joy's house on the way home. Buck was in jail for some petty crime or another and had a bit more time until release. The house had taken on that forlorn, waiting look of recently abandoned homes. Kelly's chest had squeezed tight, but he drove on. That place had never really belonged to Joy anyway; she had simply slept there sometimes. It was nothing but a building held together with secrets and old nails.

The woodshed looked the same as it always had. It was a place of safety in the dark, beautiful in its familiarity. He thought of two small children curled up in the fragrant grass behind it, their heads close together as they shared crackers and terrors and nightmares.

If Joy was anywhere, she was here. A girl that good inside had to get to heaven somehow and deserved that rest, but he knew she wouldn't go without her Kelly. She would be the last one awake and stand watch over him until his old bones were tucked safely away into the dirt.

He stood for a long time, the sounds of the night piercing him through with their melancholy remembrances. He remembered Joy's quiet tears threading through the frog song. His young, helpless anger at some school injustice evaporating as she held his hand. The night sounds were the soundtrack to his entire life. The honking horns and heavy bass of the city wasn't music at all; it was simply noise.

"Joy," he said, and fireflies floated lazily away from him, riding his breath to the stars.

He didn't know what to say next. He couldn't put anything that he felt into words.

He wanted to tell her how he thought of her every day. That there was an enormous hole inside of him that he didn't know how to fill. He wanted to tell her that he studied with an intensity that was almost frightening, driven by a demon he couldn't name. He was doing college for both of them. He was going to make something of himself.

He wanted to tell her that he'd stare every time he saw a woman with blond hair, and even after all this time, his stomach would be a sinkhole when she would turn around.

It was never Joy.

He removed the necklace that he wore beneath his shirt. The clear points on the star had rubbed smooth with years of use, but it still shone. He held it in his hand for a long time.

"I'll make you proud of me," he said, and hung the necklace on the thin branches of a tree. It rotated slowly, glimmering in the moonlight. The fireflies surrounded it, fading softly in and out.

She was one more thing of beauty in his life. One more star.

The universe was awash with them.

Notes From the Crematorium

"Loving You Darkly" This is a dystopian tale that takes place in dirt and mud. Humankind is forced to live in burrows, and a lonely girl has a lover made from old bones. It's a story about hope and revenge, and I wanted to show that scraps and refuse, the pieces of ourselves that we slough off and throw away, are useful. Memories are important. We should never forget who we were at different times in our lives.

I was pleased that this story was a Bram Stoker Final Ballot Nominee in 2017.

"The Making of Asylum Ophelia" One night, I said to my husband, "Do you remember that strange man who said he was attracted to my sadness?" Yes, he remembered this strange man. Yes, he remembered that conversation. What a horrific thing to find a woman's unwanted melancholy enticing. Why this interest in the tragic Ophelias of the world? I wondered what it would be like to be groomed for despair from a young age by someone who is supposed to love you most.

"Clocks" Ah, Clocks. This is one of my very favorite stories. "Clocks" is based on the old Grimm Brothers' tale "The Story of a Boy Who Went Forth to Learn Fear." It's about a boy who doesn't understand the emotion but wants to. It made me think of my son, who has Williams Syndrome and autism, and how he is so fundamentally beautiful and different. He is the inspiration for the incredibly rigid Henry. This story is about my fear of what will happen to my own personal Henry when I'm no longer here to care for him. I feel the tick-tick-ticking of the clock running out.

"Night's Ivy" I was invited to write a story about a vampire. Oh, I dearly love vampires! Instead of the usual blood-sucking sort, I wanted to explore those who drain us of our time, our energy, and our resources. There are far too many people who grow fat on what they unrightly steal from us.

"A Love Not Meant to Outlast the Butterflies" Once upon a time in New Orleans (I just love stories that start like this) my friend and I were at Faulkner House Books in Pirate Alley. My hair is a daring, bold thing and the humidity had it wrapping around absolutely everything. "I am going to write a story about a woman with sentient hair," I said, and that is exactly what I did. I named her after a childhood friend. She met a love who burned from the inside out, like so many people do.

"A Threadbare Shirt" I am slowly (because it is painful and beautiful and because I want to get it right) working on a memoir about my son and his unique genetic syndrome. This is a chapter from that memoir. It's very simple but says exactly what I want it to say.

"Just Beyond Her Dreaming" This story is loosely based on Robert Chambers' *The King in Yellow.* But now it has taken on new life! My musician friend J. Francis Ball asked me to name a piece of music for him, and I chose a similar title to this story. He rewrote the music based on its new title and asked me to add spoken word poetry to it. We're having a speakeasy listening party next week to hear the result. Do you see the beauty of it? How art follows art? There is a spoken word piece based on the music based on the story based on the collection of Robert Chambers' 1895 short-story collection *The King in Yellow.* All of it is exquisite.

"Mean Girls" This short story takes place in the *Nameless: The Darkness Comes* world. *Nameless* was my first novel, and in all honesty, I've written two sequels to it, but I don't like them enough to publish them. This story, I like. It talks about cruelty, demons, and bullying in schools, which is a public issue near and dear to my heart. This piece mimics a school shooting in devastation and meaning. It's brutal, but it's meant to be.

"Heart of Fire, Body of Stone" This story is a scene from the novel I just finished. Meet Italia, the witch-of-the-wood, if you will, who lives in the fictional town of Paradise, Ohio. It rains indoors, babies are made of stone, and the moon is a carnivorous beast. Italia bears the town's ire for being different and knowing more than perhaps she should. "Heart of Fire, Body of Stone" is a story about what a woman gives up for motherhood, and how that sacrifice is sometimes rewarded with loss.

"The Bone-Shaker's Daughter" This is a high fantasy piece, and it was such a fun experience. It takes place in the city of Redoubt, a post-apocalyptic city that towers high above a desolate land full of the undead. It was written for an anthology that pairs with the RPG game titled The Last Citadel. It's very much a story about a girl who is told to remember her place, but sometimes she chooses to forget.

"This Broken Love Story" Ever have an unhealthy, toxic love that eats you from the inside out? Me, neither.

"Water Thy Bones" I wanted to write something wild and wonderful, dark and fanciful. I wanted to write about true love, where one person adores the other from the inside out. I ended up with "Water Thy Bones." This story received quite a bit of praise, but it was also controversial because it had to do with self-harm. It's an extreme take on beauty standards and the way they affect us. I thought, "What if you could just peel away the physical and truly be seen for what you are?" This is a tale of love, as most of my tales are.

"Unpretty Monster" Sometimes you just want to rewrite the past, and I think the Titanic is one of those times. There was such senseless tragedy there. It's rumored that I had family aboard the Unsinkable Ship, which is why I gave the male character my maiden name, Murdock. But what if Murdock's last minutes were full of magic and sea lights and everything the unprettiest monster could give? You can't change what you are, but you can change *who* you are.

"Salt" I realize as I write these notes that I am processing many fears about being the parent of a child with special needs. "Salt" seemed to resonate with others and was a Mother's Day contest winner.

"Stanley Tutelage's Two-Year-Shiny-Life Plan" Oh, I love this story. No publisher would touch it with a ten-foot pole because it's about suicide, you see, and that's such a Very Sensitive Subject. This is where I share the uncomfortable truth and say I understand suicidal ideation; I fight the teeth of the Black Dog and require medication to put my mind to rights when it concerns intrusive thoughts and mental health. If you feel this way, you are not alone. There are many of us out there who understand and love you even more fiercely for it. If you are in danger, please call 988 in the USA. This will connect you to the Suicide and Crisis Hotline.

"Urban Moon" In the old fairytale of The Swan Maiden, a man sees a pen (a female swan) land in the lake, take off her feathers, and turn into a beautiful woman. He steals her feathers and forces her to become his wife until she finds her feathers locked in an old trunk. She puts them on and flies back home to her sisters.

Well. What a horrible tale. It's often cited as a romance. A romance for who?

"Urban Moon" uses The Swan Maiden to talk about not only rape culture, but how it plays out in social media. I tried to be sensitive to the act itself and the aftermath. I didn't want to provide a blow-by-blow of Pen's sexual assault. I wrote it simply as "...her body and soul were used up." And that is enough. But the horror of it presses into you, even after using such delicate words. The act itself was only the beginning of Pen's nightmare. I hope you, as a reader, feel absolute dismay at how victims are treated in our society. I hope you shake with anger as I shake with anger. But also take note of the healing care given by her sister.

"Love is a Crematorium" What to say about this one? Maybe a lot of things. Maybe nothing. This story made me weep because Kelly and Joy felt so very real to me. They deserved better. I can't say anything more without cheapening it.

NOTES FROM THE CREMATORIUM

As a fun aside, there's a point in the story where Kelly leaves a gas station, holds the door for a beautiful woman, and nods to a Chinese-American man outside. This is Lu and Montessa from *Apocalyptic Montessa and Nuclear Lulu: A Tale of Atomic Love.* This is right before the gas station fireworks. I do love my little Easter eggs.

Thank you for reading, my friends. I am truly humbled.

With love,
Mercedes

Previous Published

"Loving You Darkly" 2017 F(r)iction Magazine Issue 8

"The Making of Asylum Ophelia" 2020 Miscreations: Gods, Monstrosities & Other Horrors

"Night's Ivy" 2016 Dark Discoveries Issue 34

"A Love Not Meant to Outlast the Butterflies" 2014 Lamplight Volume 3 Issue 2

"Just Beyond Her Dreaming" 2015 Cassilda's Song

"The Bone-Shaker's Daughter" 2019 Tales of the Lost Citadel Anthology

"This Broken Love Story" 2020 Pen of the Damned

"Water Thy Bones" 2016 Gutted: Beautiful Horror

"Unpretty Monster" 2018 Fantastic Tales of Terror: Histories Darkest Secrets

"Salt" 2016 A Mother's Love: An Anthology of Murder and Mayhem

"Urban Moon" 2019 Other Voices, Other Tombs

"Love is a Crematorium" 2020 Lullabies for Suffering

Artwork Accreditation

Loving You Darkly – Brian Demers

A Love Not Meant to Outlast the Butterflies – Luke Spooner

The Bone-Shaker's Daughter – Mercedes M Yardley

Water Thy Bones – Luke Spooner

Stanley Tutelage's Two Year Shiny Life Plan – Mercedes M Yardley

Made in the USA
Middletown, DE
27 January 2025

69983788R00133